Philippa Blake was born in Kenya and educated in Britain. She lives in London and combines her life as a writer with a career in the City. *Heat of the Moment* is her fourth novel.

HEAT OF THE MOMENT

The only son of a retired stockbroker, Michael's life has been mapped out — Eton, Cambridge, a promising career in the City. All that's missing is a suitable wife — a girl with breeding and good sense. Then he meets Olivia. Breathtakingly frank, headstrong and utterly unconventional, she turns Michael's life upside down. When Olivia disappears in a remote African desert, Michael abandons his City life to go and search for her — but nothing has prepared him for the journey that lies ahead. Following a trail of torment and personal tragedy, he unravels a terrible family secret . . .

Books by Philippa Blake
Published by The House of Ulverscroft:

WAITING FOR THE SEA TO BE BLUE

PHILIPPA BLAKE

HEAT OF THE MOMENT

Complete and Unabridged

ULVERSCROFT
Leicester

First published in Great Britain in 1997 by
Orion
London

First Large Print Edition
published 1999
by arrangement with
Orion Books Limited
London

British Library CIP Data

Blake, Philippa
    Heat of the moment.—Large print ed.—
Ulverscroft large print series: mystery
1. Love stories
2. Large type books
I. Title
823.9′14 [F]

ISBN 0–7089–4094–3

Published by
F. A. Thorpe (Publishing) Ltd.
Anstey, Leicestershire
Set by Words & Graphics Ltd.
Anstey, Leicestershire
Printed and bound in Great Britain by
T. J. International Ltd., Padstow, Cornwall

This book is printed on acid-free paper

1

The lane led into a valley of birch wood, bark more grey than silver, past a cluster of houses with matching front doors.

'Those houses are for the staff,' said Olivia.

'The ss . . . staff live so close?'

'Oh yes . . . it's more than just nursing. For these people it's a vocation.'

Half a mile further on they came upon the perimeter of the hospital. Milk white, walls that were not walls, but a fence rising almost to the level of the trees. Wire, finely meshed, one layer and then another; opaque from a distance, close up a haze, with figures moving behind.

Michael turned into a small car-park and stopped the car. 'I'll wait for you here.'

'I thought you were going to come in?'

'I don't want to intrude.' He tried to sound gentle, considerate, to shut out the flat distaste that had taken hold of him.

'I'm sure they'll let you in.'

'Go and ask. I don't wa . . . want to have the door shut in my face.'

He waited by the car while she went through a narrow gate, and held out a card to a man wearing a blue uniform. The car-park was empty, shaded by sweeping, restless birch trees. On the far side was a bus shelter — for visitors, he presumed — and beside it, a dustbin with a funny face painted on

1

its lid. The funny face should be reassuring, part of a happy childish code, but against the white fence it only fuelled alarm, as if the craziness had leaked out, a vapour seeping through the mesh.

He took the ash-tray from the car and emptied sweet wrappers and car-park tickets into the dustbin. The yellow Porsche looked vivid and misplaced. He should not have come. The asylum, even from the outside, was more real than he had allowed for, hard evidence of the great spaces in Olivia's life of which he knew nothing, of which until now he had been almost content to know nothing.

He should not have come. He should, at that moment, have been working, chasing a new deal, talking to a potential client, using the combination of sharp intellect and easy charm that had made him a director of corporate finance in a respected merchant bank before he was thirty-five.

The only son of a retired stockbroker, Michael's life had been mapped out before he left his cradle. Prior to joining the bank, he had trained as a solicitor with a prestigious City law firm, whence he had come from Cambridge, and before that, Eton. His career had disappointed no-one. Even the lower second from Cambridge was acceptable, evidence of the vigour with which he had enjoyed his time at university. If there was a failing to discuss, for his two older sisters to contemplate in his absence, it was his tendency to attach himself to unsuitable women, his failure, even as his thirty-ninth birthday approached, to choose a girl who would make a suitable wife for a merchant banker.

Their mother having died very young, it was

Michael's sisters who inspected the girlfriends who appeared from time to time at Highhurst, the family home in Hampshire; who saw to it that unsuitable candidates, while catered for without a murmur, were, in the private language of the family, gently condemned.

These rejections caused little difficulty. Beside his success in the City, his substantial salary, the yellow Porsche and the flat in Notting Hill, Michael knew what was required of him.

He worked hard, was available at all hours to his clients. His free time was divided between shooting on the private estates of his clients and fishing with his 'muckers', old friends from Eton and Cambridge and his brief spell in the Honourable Artillery Company — the gentleman's regiment of the territorial army. Over the years, as all his friends had gradually succumbed to matrimony, found their wives turning into mothers, Michael had enjoyed his bachelorhood, rejoiced in his Porsche and the lovely girls who came so willingly into his life, who cooked for his dinner parties in Notting Hill and allowed him unlimited sex — with condoms but without consequences.

Before Olivia.

Before Olivia he was content. Before Olivia, it was only a matter of time, in his own calendar and that of his sisters, before the flirtations, affairs with the lovely unsuitable girls would cease and he would produce a wife of whom the world would approve, a girl from the Home Counties, one of the many who bided their time in the offices of estate agents in Belgravia and Chelsea, or assisted

3

interior decorators operating around Kensington Church Street. A girl with breeding; brains were unimportant. A girl whom he could marry in the traditional manner, a service in a flower-filled church, his elderly father telling the jokes that everyone would understand and his sisters taking the place of their mother, proud and tearful and particular about etiquette. A girl who would bear children who would continue the Ballantyne name, with whom he would one day live in Highhurst, taking the train up to the City each day, a girl who would drive the station wagon and be a fine hostess and talk vaguely and grandly of school fees and Michael's share options, cushions for the future.

Before Olivia.

Olivia had never been to Highhurst. Olivia was unimpressed by his car, had looked with question rather than reverence at the photographs and smart invitations that cluttered the mantelpiece of his flat in one of the restored squares in the area just north of the Bayswater Road. The flat, as Michael was inclined to say, had a very fine drawing room. The fireplace was original, an ornate marble affair on which he kept a large photograph of Highhurst, and, as well as the smart invitations, a fine carriage clock that had belonged to his grandmother. His grandmother was in evidence elsewhere, in the good 'pieces' he had inherited from her, a lacquered cabinet in the hall, a mahogany tallboy in his bedroom, inlaid tables that stood on either side of a large, slightly shabby sofa in the drawing room, a pair of substantial lamps, the bases of which were gilded porcelain.

Olivia hadn't admired the flat. She was indifferent to the furniture and mildly critical of the portrait of his grandmother that hung in the dining room. 'Too much yellow, and the proportions are wrong.' Olivia preferred whisky or cold beer to the impressive wines that he kept in the cellar. Olivia was not interested in his big deals for the bank, the bonuses that doubled his salary.

Olivia unsettled his world.

'I've never met anyone like you,' she said. 'I didn't believe your kind had survived.'

Michael had no answer. There was no reply in his repertoire, nothing that could express or disguise his feelings, the bewilderment of wanting a woman who did not appear to admire him. Was it not enough? All he had to offer? Could all his breeding and background and money mean nothing to her?

He had wondered, more than once, what his sisters would have to say about Olivia. In some ways they might not entirely disapprove. She had the right hallmarks, the voice of the colonial child, height, carriage. Even her age, a year or two past her thirtieth birthday, would probably have passed muster. What had kept him from bringing her to a Hampshire Sunday lunch was her fearlessness. The commotion her frankness would cause.

'My mother is in an asylum.'

'My sister prostitutes herself for a Greek artist of small renown.'

She would say it all if they asked her. He could see their faces, even the housekeeper, looking on. He could see how they would spot the difference. They would see that this one was far too complicated, too beautiful not to be important. They would see, for they knew their little brother: this one he loved.

Loved. Nothing had prepared him for it. Nothing in his easy, predictable world had forewarned him. Dozens of girls had made his heart beat faster, drawn his lust, instincts of protectiveness, the particular pride of a beautiful woman hanging on his arm. But since Olivia it was as if he had lived his life in a play-pen, a happy cage where sex and affection had been as transitory as Marmite sandwiches in the afternoon: tea for a toddler, enjoyed and forgotten. Until Olivia.

She had been an impulse. A girl who took his name at the reception desk of his dentist's surgery. Something in her manner suggested that the job was temporary. Beside the small switchboard on her desk was a bulky paperback, not of romantic fiction, but the biography of a third world statesman. On a sudden whim, not even because she looked especially pretty, but because she wore no rings and there was nothing in his diary for the evening, he suggested she should meet him for a drink.

'Why?'

Michael paused. 'B . . . because . . . '

There wasn't time to finish — he was led into the surgery for his check-up. Looking back, before the door closed, he saw her pick up her book, smiling.

She smiled again as he was leaving, came out from behind her desk to hand him his raincoat. He didn't repeat his invitation, her 'Why?' had unnerved him. She's too tall, he told himself. He liked his women to be shorter, softer, sweeter even, than this rather angular girl.

She waited while he put on the raincoat. Outside, through the squared glass of the window pane the black railings were glossy with rain. She handed him his umbrella.

'Yes.'

'S . . . Sorry?' Michael picked up his briefcase.

He blinked. She had said it as if he had just asked, as if there had been no interruption.

F . . . fine,' he stammered, catching in her eyes a flicker of amusement.

'You sound dismayed.'

'N . . . no. N . . . not at all. It was just . . . I just — '

'We needn't. There's still time to change your mind.'

He shook his head, felt himself flushing, wished he could control the damned stammer.

'Wh . . . where w . . . would you like to go?'

For a moment it seemed she would take control. She looked at her watch, spoke of something she had to do after the surgery closed. His briefcase hung heavy in his hand. He felt awkward, weak, incapable of escaping and yet knowing that it was not escape he sought but to settle the scuffling uncertainty she stirred, a failure of confidence such as had not beset him since adolescence, and an absolute wish to see her smile again. At last he thought of somewhere, the bar of a smart hotel, a place where he at least would feel at ease, bolstered by the expanse of carpet, the soft swallow of upholstery and nibbles served in silver dishes.

She arrived late, a parcel under her arm and carrier bags in both hands, as if their date was nothing but a postscript to another, more important errand.

'What have you b . . . been buying?'

Without answering his question she gestured to the waiter who had scurried forward with a bottle of champagne. 'Is that what you're going to drink? I'd really prefer a whisky and soda.'

The champagne was taken away. When her whisky arrived she stirred the ice as if it were sugar and reached for a pretzel. 'Thank you. I didn't mean to be rude. I just find champagne a bit sickly.' And then she smiled again, and the slight irritation he had felt, impatience that they would never progress beyond these small dislocations, evaporated.

He raised his glass. 'It doesn't matter at all.'

She resettled the carrier bags beside her chair. 'I'm sorry about these. The shops open late tonight and I just had to get some hot weather gear — if I don't grab it now they'll be filling the shelves with clothes for the autumn.'

'Are you going on holiday?'

'No — home, actually. Well, where home used to be.'

'Where is that?'

'Kenya — in a week or two.'

'How l . . . long are you going for?'

'I don't know. There's something I have to do, it could take some time.'

She's just a date, Michael thought. It doesn't matter if she's just about to leave the country. He wasn't even sure it would go further than the drink.

Their glasses were empty. Instead of summoning a waiter he went up to the bar and watched her in the mirror while the barman poured. Her hair, which had been tied back at the surgery, hung loose round her shoulders, dark and straight. Sitting back in the plush hotel chair, her legs stretched out, she seemed utterly at ease, relaxed, unposed. Desirable.

He suggested dinner in a quiet restaurant but she led him to a noisy pizza place off Kensington High Street. Live music meant sitting very close in order to talk. Her hair smelt warm and sweet.

The waiter who came to take their order had to bend down to hear over the noise. She wanted extra anchovies and a green salad. Michael asked for the wine list but she touched his hand. 'I'd rather have a beer.'

When the waiter had gone he said, 'Are you always so sh . . . sure of what you want?'

'Only when it doesn't matter.'

There were grissini in a tall jar. Michael fiddled one out of its cellophane wrapper, wondering if this was a mistake. He preferred laughter, women who would flirt and banter with him, not these silences, these eyes that watched him so steadily through the heat and noise.

Feeling the need to talk, he started to tell her about his job, about a deal that had just been concluded where the bank had orchestrated the sale of a chain of prestigious hotels.

'You don't stammer so much when you talk about yourself.'

Michael sat back. People rarely mentioned the

stammer. His small disability, the slight hesitancy over certain words, a source of misery when he was a child, had become one of his tools, a point of access, a gentling factor that in a difficult negotiation made his opponent more inclined to listen, to believe, to give him an extra atom of attention, an extra moment to work his charm.

As if on cue, drawn by her bold observation, the stammer returned, he felt the familiar grimace and the small explosion of consonants. 'Do . . . does it b . . . bother you?'

'It was why I said yes. I wanted to see if it was a pose.'

'Do . . . do you think it is?'

'Some of the time. I don't mean you can help it, but I think you use it to your advantage.'

Her bowl of salad arrived. Ignoring the cutlery, she ate it with her hands, watching him as she licked vinaigrette from her fingers. 'Surely other women have said the same?'

Michael opened a second grissini. He changed the subject. 'So tell me, wh . . . a . . . when did you come to live in England?'

'When I was ten.'

'Are your f . . . family still in Africa?'

'My mother is in an asylum.'

'W . . . wh . . . '

'A secure hospital for the criminally insane. I also have a sister in Hammersmith, a brother in Africa whom I am going to see and another brother who is dead.' She drank two long gulps of beer and put down her glass. 'You know, it would be much easier to talk in bed.'

The grissini snapped in his hand.

'That's the plan, isn't it? When we've had enough to drink we go back to your place and you take off my clothes?'

He took a breath. She was running ahead, like his sister's small child when he played uncle, tugging him further and faster than he wanted to go. 'I hadn't planned that far.'

The music thundered around them. Olivia put her lips against his ears. 'I just can't bear all this hedging.'

'What d . . . do you mean, hedging?'

'This ritual we have to go through. Slipping each other scraps of information, pecking to see if we like what we learn. And all the time sex is looming, and if that isn't any good then the rest is irrelevant. So why don't we do the sex first? Then if it's no good we can say goodbye with our secrets intact.'

She didn't want to take a taxi. They walked up Kensington Church Street, sharing the carrier bags between them.

'Does a woman live here with you?' she asked as they entered his flat.

'N . . . no.'

'All these soft cushions and ornaments — it looks as if a decorator has been here.' She walked over to the mantelpiece, examined the candlesticks and the invitation cards. 'Is all this important to you?'

Michael had been watching her movements, the way her sweater clung to her small, neat breasts. 'I thought we weren't going to explain ourselves.'

She chuckled. 'Clever.'

Nonetheless her confidence had ebbed a little.

When he covered her lips with his mouth he felt her pulling back.

'Are you changing your mind?'

'No.'

But there was a tremor as she placed her hand on his chest.

His own desire was uncertain. He wished they had drunk more, talked more. He wished he could believe that this was what she always did, that she was just a natural whore, to be fucked and forgotten.

2

'Can I help you?'

A uniform behind the gate, white-meshed blue, a boy's face peeping through. Marks of authority on his sleeves, in the keys chained to his belt.

Michael shook his head. He wanted to say, 'No, I am just a chauffeur. I have no connection with this place.' But Olivia was coming back. She smiled. 'It's all right. Eugenie is in the open ward today. You can come in and see her.'

The youth in uniform unlocked the gate to let him through and locked it again behind him. Michael paused on the threshold. 'Olivia, you have to tell me.'

'What?'

'You have to tell me why she is here.'

'She killed someone,' said Olivia. 'She killed someone with a panga. Severed the head.'

Michael had no time to react. A woman in a blue trouser suit, plump and brisk, a set of keys dangling from her belt, rubber shoes soundless on the polished floor, led them to a room with tall, barred windows, a television set on a trolley in the corner.

There was a smell of bleach and stale food. 'Look Eugenie,' said Olivia, 'I've brought someone to see you.'

The woman she addressed remained seated, dwarfed by the high-backed upholstered chair in

13

which she sat, gloved hands folded neatly in her lap. Her hair was loose, the colour of Olivia's but streaked with grey.

Olivia kissed her cheek. 'Mama, this is Michael Ballantyne. Michael, this is my mother, Eugenie.'

Eugenie's face had a pixie quality, wizened, pale eyes that were wide and over-bright. She held out her gloved hand, winced as Michael shook it. 'Careful now. I've broken my fingers.'

He let go. 'S . . . Sorry.'

'Mama, you know very well that your fingers aren't broken,' said Olivia.

The patient's shoes were smeared with mud. She followed Michael's glance. 'You have to put paraffin on sweet peas, did you know that? Otherwise the mice eat the seeds.'

He tried to think of something to say. 'Have you been gardening?'

'I've been putting in bulbs. Daffodils for Regina.'

Olivia moved in front of him. 'Has she been here? Mama, has Regina been here?'

The little woman seemed not to hear. 'She fell down the stairs, dear. We all fell down the stairs.'

Olivia was silent.

'Shall we sit down?' Michael pulled up a chair for Olivia.

Eugenie's eyes were unfocussed. 'Regina had a bruise like an egg. And a mark on her elbow, like black ink.'

Olivia sat in the chair he placed for her but Michael remained standing, fighting his urge to leave.

Outside, between the thick, white-painted window bars he could see the asylum garden, trees and grass, delicately coloured by hazy sunshine. Eugenie continued to chatter, as if someone had asked a question.

'Gareth looked dreadful, poor lamb. He hadn't shaved. The children weren't being fed. I had to come out of hospital. Though I could only sit on a rubber ring. The taxi man told me his wife was the same. They'd cut her with a pair of shears. He said, 'Your husband'll have to be a patient man'. That's what he said. Gareth had no patience. Regina came home early from school. She'd written Rubber Johnnies on the cloakroom wall — '

Michael started. 'What?'

'Mama, please,' said Olivia.

'That's what Regina had written on the wall. 'My Dad needs a Rubber Johnny.' '

Michael reached for Olivia's hand but she pulled away. He felt another shiver of distaste.

Eugenie continued as if there had been no interruption. 'I always knew my Gareth wouldn't be there. I knew it all the way out on the boat. I could not think what to do and then Harry came back for his guns. Dennis carried the gun bag. I saw Harry's look. No mistaking that look. When a man wants a son. Would you like some tea, dear? Would you like a biscuit?'

Michael turned, caught by the change in Eugenie's voice; sane and ordinary, as if another woman had entered the room.

★ ★ ★

15

They sat in the car-park for a long time. The guard had been sitting in his little office as they came out through the gate, listening to the radio. Sheffield Wednesday winning at half time.

'I . . . I couldn't keep t . . . track of what she said.'

'There is no track to keep to,' said Olivia in a weary voice. 'She recites things at random.'

Not really wanting to know, wanting only to start the car, roar away, put space between himself and this unhappy institution for the mad, Michael found himself asking a question. 'Who . . . who are all those people she talked about? Regina is your sister and David is your b . . . brother but who are Gareth and Dennis and Harry?'

Olivia took a piece of black ribbon from her handbag and used it to tie back her hair.

'Gareth is my father. Was. Maybe still is — I have not seen him since I was a child. Dennis was my older brother.'

'So there were f . . . four of you?'

Olivia nodded. 'Eugenie had four children — Dennis and Regina and me, and then David.'

' — Who was Ha . . . Harry?'

'Harry Crane.' Olivia's look was distant. Her thoughts had left him, the world she could see was far away from the car-park and the trees and the looming fence of the asylum. 'Harry was our saviour and our doom. He was the best and worst thing that ever happened.'

'Your mother didn't . . . ah . . . mention David at all. I thought that was why you wanted to c . . . come, to hear her talk about him.'

16

'She did last time,' said Olivia. 'Last time I came she talked about him non-stop. About his childhood, when he was in hospital with dysentery. She was a nurse — did I tell you that? She did night duty — so she could slip in and hold his hand while he slept.' Olivia turned her head. There were tears in her eyes. 'She was really much better last time I came. Something has driven her back.'

'D . . . does Regina come to see her?'

'I've no idea.' Olivia waved her hand.

They drove away, past the birch trees and the staff houses. Half way back to London he stopped at a motorway restaurant, a place of fast food, 'Kiddies' menus' and large plastic animals in a garden at the side. He carried their tray to a corner table and Olivia sat with her back to the glass wall. Traffic streaked soundlessly behind her. The coffee was too hot to drink.

Michael could feel the expression on his face, the look she would see, his falling heart, his want — in spite of all that he had seen that day — his absolute want of Olivia.

She leaned back in her chair. 'I guess it shocked you.'

He wanted to lean across the table, grasp her hands. Do you know? Do you know how much I want you? Did you take me there to bring me to my senses? Instead he shrugged. 'I've never been to an asylum before. I had no idea what to expect.'

'And I've never taken anyone with me before. Perhaps it wasn't a good idea.'

'Tell me again how long she has been there.'

'Years. For a while she was in custody at home.

There was an appeal against her sentence. When that failed they brought her back to England.'

'Is she still serving her sentence?'

'No. Now she is there because — because it seems that she wants to be. Whenever they think she is well enough to move she has a relapse.'

'Do you mean it's deliberate?'

Her face changed. He had seen it before, the flash of impatience, the placid blue eyes turning hard. 'Mental illness is not a game.'

'Sorry, I just m . . . meant . . . '

'To do what she does deliberately — to behave as she does sometimes — is remote from what we call sanity.'

'Does she — ' Michael leaned forward. 'Olivia, I have to ask this question.' He took her hands as he had wanted to earlier but now the gesture was clean, he wanted no more than her attention, no more than that she would answer his questions, without hiding her hurt in a feigned disdain for his ignorance. 'This is all so new to me, I n . . . need to understand. When you talk about her b . . . behaviour, do you mean she gets worse than we saw this afternoon? Does she — '

'Get violent?' Olivia pulled her hands away. The movement was abrupt but Michael saw that what she sought was freedom, for her fingers to play upon the table, fluttering, pressing a little as she searched for words.

'Yes. Last year she attacked another patient. It was another woman, a depressive. God knows why they quarrelled, the other one hardly speaks, but my mother was pushing furniture around, flinging chairs at the walls.'

'It . . . it's hard to imagine. She's so small.'

'I know.' For a second Olivia grinned. 'But then we're all slightly stronger than men like to think.'

'So, what happened?'

'She got what she wanted. They will keep her there for a bit longer. No-one is prepared to authorise her release while she is still behaving violently.'

Michael swallowed his coffee. On the other side of the restaurant a child was screaming, long unreasoning shrieks. He could hear its mother, loud and equally inarticulate, too overwrought, too embarrassed to exert her authority. There was a smash as the child swept its plate and cutlery onto the floor. Olivia caught his eye. Her smile was wry.

'There is only one thing I can do for Eugenie, and that is to try and get David to see her.'

'And will it make her well again, if he does?'

'The doctors think it might help.'

Michael finished his pastry and without a word she pushed hers across to him. 'It would be good,' he said, with his mouth full, 'if we could get her discharged.'

'Good for whom?'

He looked up, surprised by the bitterness of her tone. 'For us all. For her.'

'For you Michael, especially. I'm sure you'd rather not have to tell your sisters that my mother is mad.'

'Olivia!' He couldn't, didn't want to disguise the

hurt in his voice. 'I just w . . . want her to be better for your sake.'

'And because it would be more convenient.'

'Is th . . . that so wrong? Isn't that why all of us want people to be w . . . well — so that we won't have to bear their illness?'

She said no more. Michael knew that there was truth in what he said. Not the whole truth, but an angle of it, like the truth of a neon sign shining in a dark street. One truth of the sign is its light, the glow of bright colours. The other truth is hidden, the day-time truth of ugly wires and scorch marks on the glass.

★ ★ ★

He followed her across the cafeteria. The collar of her coat was turned up against the chill. The part of him that still wanted to escape, not to be dragged into her world, tried to be critical, to be irritated at the way she strode ahead, as if his following her was a matter of indifference. But the irritation wasn't real, only his wish to catch up, to pull in the reins and make her safe.

As she reached the Porsche she turned. 'Do you mind if I drive?'

'Wh . . . what?'

'I do have a licence, you know.' She laughed. 'You should see your face!'

He touched his mouth, as if to smooth away his expression. 'It's j . . . just — '

'I promise I'll be careful.'

She drove fast, hogging the outside lane, flashing

20

the headlamps at anything that got in her way, weaving around cars who would not move aside.

When they reached the end of the motorway and she was forced to slow down, she said, 'How does it feel?'

'How does what feel?'

They had stopped in a queue of traffic. She turned to face him. 'To have me driving your car?'

Michael thought of telling her how his sex had risen at the sight of her behind the wheel, commanding, manipulating his car. Instead he asked, 'D . . . d'you always go at s . . . such a pace?'

'Were you scared?' Her cheeks were flushed pink.

'N . . . no.'

She smiled. 'If we were to live together this would be part of it. Me, driving your car.'

'You could have a car of your own.' It was the easiest answer, a way of leaving aside the suggestion that they might live together, a thought suddenly so sweet he could hardly bear to acknowledge it.

'And that would be the solution?'

Michael put out his hand and covered hers as it rested on the steering wheel. 'If it would make you ha . . . happy I'd b . . . buy you a car.'

Olivia laughed.

3

Back in the flat he lit a log fire. It was too late in the spring for heating but the night was cool and the fire would banish the slight musty dampness that lurked in the flat even when the weather was warm.

'Will this be too warm for you?'

She smiled. 'I'm fine.'

'I have some crumpets in the freezer. We could toast them.'

She smiled again. 'And honey?'

'I have honey too.'

She continued to smile. One side of her face was glowing in the warmth from the fire. 'You think of everything, Michael.'

He almost answered, almost said, 'I try to.' Almost babbled out, for the umpteenth time, how it pleased him to please her, the pleasure it gave him when she asked for something he had thought of in advance.

Toasted on the fire, the crumpets soaked up butter and honey like warm sponges. She laughed and licked the dribbles from his chin. He put his hands inside her sweater. Her skin was very smooth and warm. As she turned he could feel the small sturdiness of her ribs and then her breasts, spreading as she lay back on the hearth-rug, the remaining shape of them fitting exactly into the palms of his hands.

When the crumpets were finished he pulled an atlas from the bookcase. 'Show me where you're going.'

The index listed 'Turkana L. (Rudolph)'. The lake, like a fat blue sausage, occupied the upper quarters of two adjoining pages. At the top was a river delta, a scribble of islands and waterways bisected by the broken line of the border with Ethiopia. The area around the lake appeared empty of detail, an uninhabited region of desert and spot heights; only when he had taken the atlas into the kitchen and spread the pages out under the sharp white light that illuminated the counter could he see, in fine print, the name of a town, Loyangalani; the merest dot of a place on the lake shore. He stared at the surrounds. There were no other dots to be seen, nothing but meandering contours and a pair of parallel lines that the key listed as an unmade road.

'David's postbox is in Loyangalani but the mission is way up here.' She turned the pages of the atlas, to find the area east of the lake. The space was empty, not even a track was marked, just clusters of lines indicating extinct volcanoes. 'It won't be hard to find him, there can't be many white men up there now.'

Michael felt his stammer building, watched his finger stabbing at the map. 'This place is a d . . . desert. You c . . . can't . . . g . . . go . . . You can't go . . . You can't go there on your own.'

She didn't answer straight away. Her eyes came up, blue and wide, carrying her scorn for his fear, and with it, a kind of gratitude. 'Would it matter so much to you if I didn't come back?'

'It's n . . . not necessary for you to go. S . . . someone else could go for you. We could send a courier, a fax — '

'Don't be silly,' she laughed. 'There are no land-lines up there, Michael. No telephones, let alone fax machines!'

He persisted. 'I still don't see why you have to go all the way out there.'

Olivia covered her face with her hands. After a moment she said, 'You don't realise what it means, Michael. For twenty years she hasn't so much as spoken David's name; she blotted him out, as surely as if he had never existed. And then suddenly, a few months ago, she said, 'Olivia, where is David?' ' Just like that. ' 'Where is David? When is David coming to see me?' '

'But why does it ha . . . have to be you?'

'Who else will go?'

'What about Regina?'

Olivia's eyes hardened. 'Regina has chosen how she wants to live. We have no contact.'

'But you could write to David.'

She shook her head. 'That wouldn't bring him here. I've never written to him before. He's probably forgotten I exist.'

'Isn't there s . . . someone else? Couldn't we hire s . . . someone?'

'But I want to go, Michael. It is time. David is my brother, it's time one of us made contact. What happened back then is history now. For the first time in my life there is something I can do for my mother. If I can persuade him to come over — just

24

to see her — it might make a difference. It might make a difference for us all.'

★ ★ ★

Later he took her to bed, watched her undress in the half-light from the street. She climbed onto him, utterly naked, spread her legs across his hips and sucked the skin of his neck. His blood surged and like an over-excited teenager, he spent himself in seconds. 'Oh God . . . s . . . sorry.'

She rolled off him immediately but her smile was gentle. 'It isn't a contest, we're not one of your big deals. Can I have a bath?'

He switched on the bedside light. 'Of course you can have a bath. And then will you stay?'

He wanted the morning, the erection that would make amends, but when she came back she began to dress. Her bra exposed the shallow space between her breasts, freckled from her childhood in the sun.

He tried to imagine it all. A world full of black men and dust. Friends and colleagues had talked about the beaches, the hotels, a tame land of game parks and sunshine. Not this wild remote desert, dots and lines on an empty map.

She tossed a towel on a chair. 'It isn't the Dark Continent any more, Michael. I won't be eaten.'

25

4

David's home was a barren field; a grey ash-land of rocks, fractured by the searing sun, blown smooth by sand-bearing winds; a sky that was a vast, comfortless bowl of bleached blue, that began and ended each day in purple and scarlet.

Scattered on the plain were circular huts, upturned pots, walls of dung and roofs of stick and thatch carried, piece by piece, from the mountains.

Thirty people lived on the mission; David himself, twenty-two children, four old men, a girl who helped him in the school, and two ancient bibis whose job it was to prepare meals for them all, cooking on the charcoal stoves that made of the cook-house an inferno.

The children were taught to read and write, learned something of geology, poetry, strands of oblique, fatalistic philosophy. They learned to sing, to chant their tables, to play football on the hard ground between the school rooms and the chapel.

David counted only the mission land as his home. Beyond its boundary the plain was busy with the comings and goings of goats and camels, a donkey or two, when times were good. And the herders, and the families of the herders, who might settle for a season, bringing with them the precious stick and thatch from the mountain.

Parked beside the chapel was the old Landrover

that years before had brought David to the mission. Like David himself, it had become a part of the place, mission property, something that in the wind-blasted impermanence of the ash-land, endured. Barrels of diesel arrived intermittently from the coast; the supply was unreliable, deliveries made according to a schedule based on whimsy and fear of ngoroco and promises from David of alcohol and extra money and presents for the drivers. The fuel was essential, sacred, guarded night and day in a rotating vigil of old men who squatted beside the tanks with their rifles and their spears and their deadly rungu.

Twice, three times a year, David drove out to the distant settlements to the manyattas scattered across the ash-land. He spoke to the elders and counted the children. Packed in the rear of the Landrover were basic medicines, second-hand clothes and shoes. He promised rice for the children who would come to his school. Sometimes he was welcome and sometimes not and always with him in the cab was one of the old askaris with his rifle and his spear and his rungu tucked under the seat.

In David's kingdom, the coming of the priest was an event. News of it rippled like water, bringing in the flocks from the plain. The priest would say Mass in the chapel, baptise the children, there would be a barbecue on the sand, singing and dancing into the night. On these occasions David sat apart, a white man looking on. When the celebration was over, the visitors gone, fading away into the dark, the priest came to sit in David's room, to drink his whisky and smoke his cigarettes.

The priest's name too, was David, but the white man called him Leiguchu, the name the tribesmen used, which meant 'little tortoise'. David would give Leiguchu roasted goat-meat and the priest would pat the well-fed places of his soutane and ask the question that was always between them: 'If you will not pray, if you do not fear God, if you have no wish for a place in paradise, then why are you here on this mission?'

For others David had answered this question. Anthropologists, geologists, searchers after oil; each year brought another crop, digging for gold, for data to tabulate, statistics to bulk out theses and hypotheses. To these David was never rude and never helpful. Sometimes their question was, 'Are you one of them?'

'Who is them?'

'Well . . . '

'Do you mean am I human?'

'Are you a citizen of this country? Do you belong?'

His answer was another question. 'What else could I be?'

And, but for his skin, sun-browned and wind-burned, he was one of them. In the clothes he wore, the food he ate, he was entirely of the place.

The answer to the priest's question was at the same time simple and more difficult. David would say: 'I have known no other,' but his speech denied it, as his solitary life denied it. It was known that he did not draw the teacher's pay to which he was entitled, and yet there was money. Money downcountry, in the capital. Money for fuel and medicines, for the meat and maize that he gave away when the droughts came. Money for the things he brought back from the little town by the lake — a day's drive from the mission and the tyres stripped to ribbons. When he said 'I have known no other' it was plainly not the truth. His life had begun in another world; a white man's school, a place downcountry where he had learned the things for which the children crowded into his classroom: arithmetic and English — and geography, the 'why' of the desert around them.

There was another question. One that was asked less often, usually by women, researchers, aid workers with clip-on sun-glasses, dimpled thighs below the hems of their sensible, khaki shorts.

'Are you lonely?'

From time to time, when the eyes behind the sun-glasses were gentle, he took them to his room and gave them whisky. He made them laugh and talk about themselves and take off their sensible clothes. He smelled the sun-block on their skin, the metallic tang of deodorant in their armpits. He watched their surprise at the hardness of his bed, at the photograph on the wall beside it. A white man and a white woman, a small boy and a labrador dog. The visitors were always curious, greedy for his secrets.

'Is this your family?'

'No. But the dog was mine.'

5

Sixteen weeks since the grissini had snapped in his hand, sixteen weeks since that first evening when she had been so bold, and in the end so hesitantly willing. Her preparations for the trip had taken longer than she planned. He suspected — hoped — wished — that she had lingered because of him, let slip her timetable a little to allow their jerky, dislocated affair to flower into affection.

Her home had been a surprise, a treat for him that he should like it. She had written the address on the back of his business card. SW11.

'You mean Wandsworth?'

'It's actually Battersea, but what's the difference?'

Michael's recollection of Battersea was of bleak concrete towers, owned by the local authority, with views of a dirty river and arcades of derelict shops.

'Don't you find it inconvenient, to live the other side of the river?'

'I can see the Harbour, and Chelsea Bridge.'

'Yes, but — ' from the wrong side, was what he managed not to say.

'Who has the better view?'

This, as she led him through the front door of a forbidding 70s' block, red brick, festooned with creepers, gardens massed with flowers. They mounted stairs covered in strong carpet, walls of institutional beige.

Her flat was on the fourth floor. Several locks had to be turned at the panelled, varnished door with a stainless steel number plate.

'If you knew who else lived in this block, you'd feel more at home.'

'Like who?'

'The correct word is whom, isn't it?'

Michael wasn't sure, and was pondering the point when the door was finally sprung. A flood of late evening sun on a white painted wall.

He started to ask how long she had lived there but the question evaporated as she led him through an arch.

'God, what a view!'

Aware of her smile he stepped into the sitting room. Spacious and white, a mixture of traditional and modern furniture that he did not pause to examine. There, laid before him, with the lights just coming on, was the north embankment, a whirr of colour and strings of headlights from the traffic swinging towards Albert Bridge. A police car was among them, a flash of white-blue reflected in the great spread of the river.

He followed her round, mesmerised by the water, small waves rippling in the view from every window.

The banker wanted to know, hesitated to ask, do you own this place? Could there be money here, of which he was so far unaware?

'Since you're too polite to ask, the answer is that the flat belongs to a friend of mine, a South African who lives in South Carolina.'

'Who?' The question tumbled out, more important

than the matter of ownership. A rival?

'Someone I've known for a hundred years. I love him dearly.'

Michael sat on a chair, folds of bright cushions swimming around his back. 'Does he come over?'

'Sometimes. But never for long.'

Michael dreaded what she would say next. Hopeless then, his wish for her? A suntanned lover, to whom she owed the allegiance he wanted for his own?

She left him for a moment with the view, her voice, like her shoes, echoing on the hardwood floor of the red and black kitchen.

'Whisky and soda, yes?'

He didn't answer. Picked at one of the cushions and listened to the chink of glass, the thunk of the fridge door. The drinks appeared on a tray of stainless steel, tall green glasses.

'Welcome to my home.'

It was more domestic than he expected. On the tray beside the glasses was a bowl of curried peas, deep fried, hard and crunchy.

'Do you entertain often?'

She laughed, sat on a wide sofa, kicked off her heels. 'Is this entertaining?'

Unable to answer he sipped his drink, reached for a handful of the peas. Questions piled on his tongue. Did you buy these specially? Do you keep them just in case? Are you doing this deliberately? Is there smoked salmon in your fridge that you're keeping back? Is there — dare I ask it? — a message for me in deep fried curried peas?

She drank a large swallow of whisky. 'So you like the pictures?'

Michael looked at the walls. Huge, framed tapestries, prints with modern, dark surrounds.

'I'm not s . . . sure.'

'Does it matter if they're mine?'

'Are they?'

'Mine for now. It is all mine for now.'

'You mean they're part of what you rent?'

'Yes of course, they belong to Matti.'

'The South African?'

'Yes, though he is Scandinavian by birth.'

Michael added to his despair. A blond god had her heart.

'Don't look so miserable.'

'You love him, then.'

'I love him to death. I keep curried peas in the cupboard for his visits.' She leaned forward. 'Would it help if I told you he is gay?'

It was Michael's turn to laugh.

'Just a little, or does he turn when he is here?'

The question shocked her. 'You really do mean it, don't you? You really do mind?'

He sighed, stared at the tall green glass in his hand. 'Yes, I really do mind.'

Sixteen weeks, intermittent nights in his flat, in the comfort of his bed, but always, no matter the warmth of her body, the soft wetness of the sheets, the learned intimacy of their bodies, always behaving like a well-bred guest, her washbag discreet behind the bathroom door, nothing left behind, no jeans in the wardrobe or jumpers left in a drawer. On Sunday mornings he spread the papers across the carpet of his drawing room, creating a comfortable confusion with which he felt at ease; she tended to tidy them, smoothed the creases, threw the loose adverts in the bin — as if she feared this comfort, feared their ease.

He tried to plan their time together, filled their evenings with the plays most talked of, the must-see films. At weekends they ate in restaurants, took walks around the Serpentine. Though he feared she was bored he would talk about his job at the bank — believing, notwithstanding her indifference, that she should know what his prospects were; the security he could offer.

'I can't imagine you in that environment, Michael,' she said one afternoon. They had reached a corner of the park where grass gave way to gravel and a children's playground. 'I can't imagine you among all those ghastly people.'

'They're not s . . . so ghastly as all that.'

'But they eat each other for breakfast.'

'Maybe I eat them for breakfast.'

'Never!'

'You think I'm not clever enough?'

'Of course you're clever but you're just too nice to be a cut-throat.'

He smiled. 'And too boring?'

She tapped the end of his nose with her finger. 'Not boring. But nice and clever and careful. What more could a girl want?'

He wanted then, to gather her up, to tell her that he had nothing but love for her, to tell her all the plans he harboured; but the irony in her voice, the gentle mockery in her eyes held him at bay.

To the astonishment of his sisters, he took Olivia to Highhurst to meet his father. Their consternation was caused not by the fact of the visit — heavens, enough girls had been brought to Highhurst over the years — but its timing. He took Olivia to Highhurst on the evening of a Wednesday in July, breaching the family tradition that strangers were introduced at weekends, their father shielded by numbers, by one or both of Gillian and Margaret, their husbands and children; weekends when the men, including Michael, could go for a round of golf on a Sunday morning and leave the sisters to inspect the newcomer at leisure.

Olivia's visit to Highhurst was everything he could have wished for. Whether by oversight or because, even at eighty-five, John Ballantyne was cannier than his son imagined, neither Gillian nor Margaret heard of the visit in advance. The housekeeper left platters of sliced ham and salad, and soft home-made rolls. They set up a table on the terrace and his father opened a bottle of Chablis.

'Well, Olivia, welcome to Highhurst.'

Olivia smiled as they raised their glasses. 'Thank you, Mr Ballantyne.'

'You must call me John,' said the old man. Michael felt himself grinning.

'You look like the cat with the cream,' his father barked out, 'it is only my first name I have given her — not Highhurst.'

'Pops, please — '

John turned to Olivia. 'He may give you Highhurst, when they have finally got rid of me,

35

but that is for him to judge.'

'Pops! Father, you mustn't embarrass her.'

'Are you embarrassed?'

Olivia shook her head, on her face was an expression that Michael knew well, of amusement and irony, mixed with warm affection.

'You won't be embarrassed,' said John. 'You are the most intelligent woman my son has seen fit to present. It will not have escaped you that Highhurst is very large and very beautiful and in imminent danger of crumbling into the ground.'

'Hardly that bad, Pops — '

John Ballantyne interrupted, turning again to Olivia. 'What did you see when you arrived, my dear? The roses on the south wall, the way the setting sun plays on the leaded lights? Did you see those wonderful portraits in the hall, all that marvellous furniture? Or did you notice the mould on the kitchen wall and the cobwebs on the cornice?'

Olivia met his eyes. 'I missed the cobwebs.'

'Ah!' The old man slapped the table with satisfaction. 'Good answer, my dear. There is certainly mould on the kitchen wall, God knows the house reeks of it, but there are no cobwebs. If you had seen cobwebs I would have told Michael that he'd got it wrong again. For you see,' he leaned forward, eyes twinkling, 'cobwebs are forbidden. My daughter Gillian has let it be known to the spidery world that they are not welcome at Highhurst. A vast amount of money is paid to an army of Filipinos whose task it is to eradicate all forms of untidiness and natural life.

36

Only the mould is permitted. There Gillian is at a loss, for the remedy would require such a degree of upheaval, workmen and dust, that she would have no defence against mayhem. Spiders would get in, and, God help us, the odd fieldmouse might breach the fortress.'

John subsided in his chair, his face had grown pink.

'You make Gillian sound like a tyrant, Pops.'

'Hmm. Only for fun. She's a great girl, so is Margaret. Where would I be without them?'

They sat on until the last of the light had faded behind the trees. Michael realised, towards the end, that apart from occasional admonitions when his father's sense of humour got the better of him, he had hardly spoken a word. The dialogue was entirely between John and Olivia — dominated by the old man, but Olivia making him laugh from time to time, the two of them finding little ironies in common. When it was time to leave she helped to bring in the plates and load the dishwasher as naturally as one of the family. His father saw them out to the car.

'I like this one, Michael. You must bring her for lunch at the weekend.'

As they drove back to London she put her hand on his knee. 'Your father is a sweetie, Michael.'

'I haven't seen him on such good form for years.'

'But Sunday lunch — '

'No?'

She bit her lip. 'Not yet. I don't want to be measured.'

'They aren't as bad as that. Gillian's a softie at heart. Keeping everyone in order is her way of loving them. Her children are delightful.'

'Even so.'

'Perhaps when you come back?'

She nodded across the darkness. 'Perhaps when I come back.'

* * *

Michael judged the visit a success. Highhurst had looked its enchanting best. If nothing else she must have seen what the future could hold, the life they could have, that their children could have, in that glorious house, repeating his own fortunate childhood, the traditions of marriage and parenthood, all that her sad history had denied her.

He began to dream of their lives together. Privately, in moments when his office was calm, on solitary walks around the lunchtime City, his eye no longer straying across the bodies of secretaries stretched out on corners of grass, he dreamed of Olivia, of the wife she would be. Not what his family expected; she was too independent, too bold and angular to be the traditional mistress of Highhurst; too frank, too honest for a banker's wife — but a girl whom they would all learn to love as he did, a heart that was as gentle as could be, see the softness in her eyes, the sad tears that she would weep into the dark.

Marriage to Olivia would be like a perfect cake: dense and rich, a profusion of textures. Protected by a shell of conventional icing would be a structure of plain sponge, soft and predictable, homely and comforting; and at the centre, hidden from view, entirely private, would be cherries, instances of perfect sweetness, liquid at the heart.

The thought was premature. She shrank away, teased him for what she called his Disneyland idea of love, went back to her flat in Battersea, to her wild, red kitchen, a fridge full of supermarket meals, hors d'oeuvres that were no more than a gesture of hope; self-sufficient, spiritless.

He feared her gone for good but a week later she came to his flat bearing a gift — a pair of ceramic candle-holders, shaped like half-open water lilies. She lit the candles and held his hand and seemed to want to mend her words with kisses. He led her to bed and slowly took off her clothes and as he entered her body and could feel the strong beating of her heart he thought, silently, that here, whatever she might say, here was what bound them to each other, here the biding sweetness, here the heart of the life they would share together.

She bought him other gifts, 'nothing' presents she called them, gifts with nothing attached, unwrapped, without bindings. One was a paperweight in the shape of a scarab beetle. 'The ancient Egyptians believed the scarab holds the secret of life.' Then came a tiny wooden abacus with brightly coloured beads. She laughed as he lifted it from its plain brown paper bag. 'It's for your office, Michael, so you can go on being clever even when there's a power cut.'

His gifts to her were less successful. Not for

want of generosity. His gifts failed because they were too much, too important. A fine print in an expensive frame; a silk kimono, and, on the day of her leaving, a pair of earrings, sapphire drops like small blue tears. She shook her head, her expression twisted. 'You can't buy me, Michael. With these or anything else.'

★ ★ ★

He sat on the stool in her bedroom, watching her pack. They had woken before the alarm, disturbed by the geese that fed in the shallows of the river below her window, an early October day that was still and bright, light glimmering on the water, reflected on the white walls of the flat, catching on the dark silk of her hair as she bent over her packing case.

'Tell me your movements again.'

She flicked back her hair. 'Michael, I've told you already. Here.' She lifted a wallet from the neat piles of clothes and papers on the bed. 'The flight lands in Mombasa at about six. I shall take a taxi to Jessie's.'

'How far is that?'

'About sixty miles up the coast.'

'And then?'

'Two nights with Jessie, then I shall either fly or catch the train up to Nairobi and organise the road trip from there.'

'Won't Jessie want you to stay longer — after all these years?'

'It depends. She's quite old. I don't suppose her

life is very active. Two days of me may be all she can stand. Anyway, I can judge it when I'm there.'

'Where will you stay in Nairobi?'

'Somewhere cheap, if there is such a thing. I don't plan to be there for more than a day or two. There are stacks of safari companies — it won't take very long to sort out one to take me up to Turkana.'

'So it will be just you and a driver?'

'Yes.'

'For how long?'

'It depends how easy it is to locate David's place. I shall ask around when we get to Loyangalani. There'll be someone who knows where to find him.'

Michael handed back the tickets and went to stand outside on the balcony. Across the river plumes of steam rose almost vertically from the chimneys of a power station, the calm of the water broken only by the geese and a solitary duck nibbling at the moss on the wall of the embankment below.

'I'm ready.'

She had come out behind him, dressed in cotton jeans and a navy sweatshirt.

'Will you be warm enough?'

'I should think so.'

'It'll be colder here when you come back.'

'But you'll meet me, won't you?'

'Of course.' He pulled her close, folded his arms around her, his face against her sweatshirt, breathing in the warm soft smell of soap and shampoo and the faint sweetness of her skin. 'I'll be counting the days.'

'I'll give you a ring when I get back from Turkana.' She smiled, suddenly elated. 'You know, even if it wasn't for Eugenie, I am glad to be going home. It's the best time of the year. The jacaranda will be out.'

'Jacaranda?'

'Trees that bloom all over the city. The flowers come down overnight, carpets of purply-violet — almost the colour of bluebells.'

He looked at his watch. 'It's time to go.'

She nodded and then moved back inside his arms. 'I will come back, Michael.'

He kissed her neck, her lips, hiding the expression on his face, the look that would betray how much her words meant, the blind ache he felt, the unquenchable desire to grasp and keep this strange, unconventional girl of whom his sisters would so disapprove.

6

Regina let a small sigh escape her lips. There was no feeling in it, no pleasure. The sigh was a habit, like the habit of smiling at Thanos in the mornings — no matter how dreadful he looked, how old his face or foul his breath. The sighs and the smiles comforted them both.

She closed her eyes. The squeak of the springs and the thump of the head board had settled to a steady rhythm. It would be over soon. If only he wouldn't screw up his face as if it hurt him, too. Never did Thanos look so old as in that final lap, lips sucked in, brow puckered like tripe on a butcher's slab. When he was finished, there would be the weight. Too tired to roll aside he would flop down upon her belly like a beached seal, panting.

She didn't mind the weight. Pressed beneath him in the bed she felt safe, squashed but safe. It was a bit like being hugged and he would move away soon enough when he got his breath back. Then he would put on his dressing gown and go to the kitchen, switch on the kettle and make two mugs of coffee. It was the only time he did anything for her. For the rest it was always 'Regina, bring me this! Regina, bring me that!'

She did not want the coffee. What she wanted, after the squashing and the panting, was to roll over and sleep. But Thanos sat beside her on the bed, like a visiting doctor, and they would drink

43

the coffee in the dim light of the bedside lamps. When the mugs were empty he would climb back into bed, pat her bottom and pick up his book. She could roll over then, turn off her own lamp and close her eyes. But not yet sleep, not until the rustle of pages had ceased and his little snore signalled that she could lean across, take the book from his hands and turn off the light at his side.

Thanos was sixty-four years old. The age her father would be.

Her father. Gareth Jones, a dim shadow in her memory, an unsteady recollection of blue eyes, of shouting, unexplained rage, of her own hopeless longing to sit on his knee.

Regina opened her eyes. Thanos was propped up on the pillows. His book, *The Wind in the Willows*, rested on his chest. Above the small beard that perched on his folds of chin, his lips moved with the words. She had borrowed the book for him from the public library. Thanos wanted to improve his English. Regina did not tell him that she had once been Toad. Toad in an old green curtain, webbed feet made of cardboard. How they had laughed at the sight of her, Dennis and Olivia bending over, clutching their tummies, giggling still when Eugenie came home, walking along the unmade road, a white woman on foot, like a bibi. How they clung to their giggling, wishing that she would not shout, shutting their ears to her hoarse voice swelling across the hot, dry garden. 'They've bought a dog, a black dog. They've bought a ferocious beast to keep me away.'

Thanos's nose whistled as he breathed, whispering

the words into the cold air of the bedroom.

Suddenly he stopped reading, leaned round on the pillow to face her. 'This is a crazy book, Regina. Rats and toads! It is for children.'

'I thought it would make you laugh.'

'I am not reading to laugh. I am reading to get more words of your English. I am reading so I will know when the dealers are telling me lies.'

It is not the dealers who cheat you, thought Regina. It is your brothers who cheat you, Thanos. They had been in the house that very day. All five had come, kissing as the Greeks did, full of their false, greedy affection.

She had prepared their lunch, served them at the table and gone to eat her own alone in the kitchen, like a servant. When it was time to clear their plates, Thanos was signing a paper. She saw a thick packet of money. Thanos drank a bottle of wine. And then another when the brothers had gone. She tried to comfort him. He held up his hands. 'There is no art left in me. My brothers have taken it all away.'

★ ★ ★

Eighteen years with Thanos. Twenty years since she had caught the boat to England. Twenty years since her father had appeared in the court room. A conjuror's trick. Jessie Bell crying out.

Regina had worked her passage to England. Swept vomit from the cabin floors, cleaned lavatories, paid for drinks with her body. Even then it had been the warmth she wanted, the kind of hug there was in

45

a coupling. One of the mates gave her the fare to Waterloo. She walked out of the station in the late afternoon, shocked by the chill, the smell of the fog, the weight of her bag. A man offered to help.

'Lonely in London, isn't it?'

He gave her a hot dinner, a warm bath. His name was Joe Izzard. Izzy. A good name for a man with skin like a lizard, dermatitis. Crumbs on the bed sheets. Within a week she was one of his girls; seventeen years old, standing on the corner with her coat open, chewing gum and smoking simultaneously. She couldn't work without the gum. Often she had the same wad of gum after three different tricks.

The night Izzy was arrested she was on the other side of the square, a freezing wind whipping her legs, watching. They took his place apart, boxes and boxes piled into vans. Izzy's other girls were nowhere to be seen. She thought the policemen were ignoring her but later one of them came back and put her up against a wall in the dark, hard and fast, for five pounds.

Child pornography. Five years in the Scrubs. She visited him once. The dermatitis had spread to Izzy's scalp, corn flakes in his thin dry hair.

'You're a good girl, Regina. You're the only one who bothers to come.'

The visiting room was full. It was hard to hear what he said.

'Izzy, I want to be a dancer.'

'You should get yourself an agent, love.'

She looked in Yellow Pages.

'What have you done?' The agent wore dark

lipstick, dark glasses, dark clothes; an old, raggedy crow. Her office was a dingy room above a launderette. Regina could hear the thud, thud of the machines below.

'I did ballet at school.'

'You went to ballet school?'

She named the little convent where she had danced on the stage, where Harry Crane had paid for her ballet lessons.

'In Africa?' The crow laughed. 'Did they teach you to wobble your belly?'

Regina looked at her feet. The floor was warm from the dryers.

The crow leaned forward. 'Do you have any real dancing experience, dear?'

'I've never danced for money.'

That was the end of it. The best she could get was a job in a pub.

And then another.

It was easy to strip. Regina felt she'd done it all her life. She rented a bedsit, cooked packet soup on a gas ring, mixing it double strength so that it swelled in her belly and felt like food.

She went back to the crow.

'Don't you have a family, dear? You're a bit young for this lark you know.'

'My family are no good to me.'

'You'd eat better if you modelled. Think of it as dancing with your feet on the ground.'

They didn't want her feet on the ground. Even the Photography Clubs — who paid less but gave her tips, and sometimes a drink when it was over — wanted 'artistic poses'. Regina spent her earnings on a new dress and a second-hand cooker. She ate baked potatoes and macaroni cheese with tomato sauce and iced doughnuts from the bakery.

The crow approved. 'A bit more meat on you, dear. That's what they like. I'm going to try you with Paros.'

An artist. Regina felt she had been promoted. Instead of the endless words of the amateurs, the clicking and sighing, fiddling with lights and umbrellas, Thanos Paros tapped his teeth with the end of a paintbrush. He did not tell her to raise her arm, turn her head or bend her knee, but came across the room himself, to place her limbs, arrange her body, as if she were inanimate, made of clay. When the modelling was over for the day, he lay beside her on the couch in his studio and stroked her skin. 'You are pure, Regina. The other girls she sends me have marks.' His short finger stabbed a line across her belly. 'They have brown skin here, white marks below, as if they still wear clothes. You have none. Your skin is pure as a good Greek girl's.'

The crow had a cackle in her voice. 'He wants you again, dear. He wants you for a commission.'

Three portraits in a row. Her body made beautiful. The fourth still hung above their bed. A simple pose, a shawl around bare shoulders, a strand of hair hanging loose across her breast. It was the best work he had done to that day.

'You are good luck, Regina Jones. You will stay with me and bring good luck.'

His house was warm. She cleaned his kitchen; took his sheets to the launderette. The paintings were everywhere, easels on the landing, charcoal on the dining table. He let her tidy things a little and patted her bottom. There were no questions about her past. He did not care where she had been before.

'Why do I pay money for you to stay in that bedsit?' he asked one day. 'I would save my money if you stayed here with me.' She brought her second-hand cooker and her fluffy bath rug; all her worldly goods. Good luck came with her. Success was a spur. The paintings began to make money; exhibitions were arranged. For a while in New York and in the galleries of Europe, the name of Thanos Paros became known.

She stayed with him. Long after the good luck was gone she was still living in his house, sleeping in his bed, stacking the canvasses that did not sell. Thanos changed. The man who had never complained, who had taken each day, each minute of his life, entirely for his own pleasure, began to complain. He was tired. He was too tired. Her cooking was poor, her body too fat. His studio was dark, too small. 'I must go somewhere else, Regina. I cannot paint all my life in a loft. It is time for me to paint where I can see!'

He talked of landscapes, seascapes; an island in the sun and the white sails of fishing boats.

The crow still sent him models, young girls whose legs were unblemished. With each one Thanos would start a sketch or two, fiddle with his colours. Regina could hear him in the studio. No longer the artist with the brush against his teeth. He talked more than he worked. Before long

49

there would be the creak of the couch and later, the rumpled look of a girl departing, unpainted, the shame and glee of the old man's money in her eyes.

Thanos started to drink in the morning. Wine, sherry, ouzo. Canvasses gathered dust along the walls. Hairs clustered in his nostrils. His beard grew ragged and grey. There were long discussions on the telephone, shouting in Greek. Letters and bills unopened on the little table in the hall.

'Would you like to go to the sun, Regina?'

'If you would like to go.'

'If you would like . . . ' he mimicked. 'But what would you like? You never smile for me these days, Regina. How can I paint a woman who will not smile? Would you not like to go to the sun? Would you not smile in the sun?'

'I prefer the cool. I had the sun when I was a child.'

He did not ask where or how. In all the years he had asked her nothing.

★ ★ ★

The Wind in the Willows hit the floor with a thud. Thanos was asleep. He grunted as she lay across his belly to switch off the light. The curtains were open. He liked to see the morning sky, to see how light the day would be — as if he were planning to paint. Regina lay back on the pillow and looked through the window. The night was cloudy and starless. Tomorrow would be overcast. Thanos would not paint. Tomorrow's excuse would be the clouds.

50

7

A small item, filling the space beside an advertisement on the front page of the *Daily Telegraph*. The words jumped out. Heart-stopping.

'A British woman, believed to be Olivia Jones, 31, is reported missing with her driver and vehicle. The driver was hired to take her to the Turkana district, a sparsely populated area, subject to tribal strife and border raids. An aerial search has yielded nothing. Enquiries are continuing.'

Michael put the paper down, willed himself to take a calm sip of coffee from the mug on his desk. In front of him, beside his dictaphone and the electronic organiser that served instead of a diary, was the miniature abacus, the 'nothing' present, to make him clever 'even in a power cut'.

Through the glass wall of his office he could see his secretary chatting on the phone. Another girl was sorting the mail, the ordinary morning bustle of corporate finance. He rubbed his face and jabbed a button on his telephone. The secretary looked up, her smile fading as she saw his face.

'I want you to b . . . book a flight to Nairobi.'

She came through the door. 'Is something wrong?'

'I want to go there today.'

'Today? But you've got appointments all day. You're due at — '

'Cancel all the appointments.'

'But how long for?' She was coming towards his desk, watching the shake of his hands.

'I don't know,' said Michael. 'I'm going t . . . to see David Elliot and I want the flight booked by the time I come back.'

'Will you need a visa?'

'I've no idea. Please find out.'

The secretary turned, 'What about a hotel?'

'Book whatever there is.'

He followed her out, pulling on his jacket. David Elliot's office was the other side of the open-plan. As Senior Director Elliot was inclined to keep the door of his office closed and blinds drawn across the glass walls, but today the door was open. Michael walked in without knocking. He closed the door behind him and sat down before he was asked.

★ ★ ★

'Is this trip for a client, Michael, or what?'

His secretary was waiting as he emerged from David Elliot's room. He heard the growl in his voice, loose rage covering his fear. 'It is for my p . . . personal account.'

'I've booked you in First. They didn't have an economy seat and I thought . . . '

'It doesn't matter a bit.'

'And the hotels are a bit full, it's the tourist season.'

Michael paused. 'Yes, I know, the jacaranda is in flower.'

Ignoring the 'What?' forming on the secretary's lips, he picked up the folder of mail that she had

52

placed on his desk. 'I am going out now. I want you to give this lot to David Elliot. Anything urgent he will delegate. The rest he will give to you. You're to write holding letters — tell them I'll respond in full when I get back.'

'The flight doesn't go until tonight — you'll be here in the office today, won't you?'

'No. I'm going now. There are dozens of things I have to do. Did you find out about the visa?'

'You don't need one. Michael — ' The secretary, used to him flying around the world at short notice, finally lost her cool. She clutched the sleeve of his shirt. 'You can't just go like this, Michael. How long will you be gone? How will I contact you?'

'Which hotel have you booked?'

She handed him a fax. 'There's the confirmation. Your plane ticket will be ready for you at the check-in.'

'There you are then. That's the contact.'

'I've booked three nights.'

'Fine.' He thrust the folder of mail into her hands, picked up his briefcase and marched towards the exit. He looked at no-one, conscious of the redness of his face, the pounding of his heart. As he ran down the stairs, preferring movement to the stillness of the lift, he tried to make a list, to turn his rising panic into action, to focus on the things that needed to be done, to keep at bay the images already crowding into his head.

I must go to her flat. She must have Jessie's address there somewhere. Thank God she left me the keys. As he swung the car up out of the bank's underground car-park, he remembered the feeling

53

as she had given them to him.

'Will you keep these for me?'

'Of course.'

She had grinned. 'Your face is a picture, Michael. They're just keys.'

'Do you want me to come over here, to check everything's OK?'

'I'd be grateful if you'd water the plants. Just once a week or so will be enough.'

It wasn't yet a week since she'd gone. He had planned to do the watering on Saturday, to spend time in her home, see to the tap that dripped in the kitchen. To do something, anything to keep the link with her.

He stuck his finger in the dry soil of the cheeseplant in the hall, found himself muttering an apology. 'There isn't time. My darling, I have to find your address book.'

In the end, when he had managed to calm himself, the address book was easy, lying in the top drawer of the table in the hall where the phone sat. He resisted the urge to read all the entries, names and places that were part of her, all the people in her life of whom he knew nothing.

'Bell — Aunt Jessie.' The ink was faint, written years before. He copied it into his diary and then decided to take the address book itself.

'What else?' He spoke aloud. In his rush to leave the bank, to start doing something, he had imagined a day full of activity, a bustle of things to be done. Actually there was very little he could do. His eye caught her biscuit tin. Chocolate digestives that she never ate, bought just for him, for the hunger pangs that always accompanied the coffee she brought him in the mornings. He switched on the filter machine, crunching biscuits, and then, as if the sugar had helped him to think, went in search of the phone book and dialled the Foreign Office.

After a considerable wait, by the end of which the coffee machine was making the hollow gargling noise that meant the whole jug had filtered, he spoke to a woman in the section that dealt with tourist enquiries.

'Yes, the High Commission has reported her absence.'

'Is anything being done?'

'The organisation that provided the driver has already organised an aerial search. Apparently the vehicle was located quite easily. It was on a road — if you can call it that — '

'What about the passenger?'

'The report refers to a second set of tyre marks. I'm afraid it doesn't look very good.'

'What do you mean?'

'Well, this is not a stable territory. Recently there has been a spate of kidnapping.'

Michael felt himself lurch, a sense of unreality enveloped him. Around him was the calm of her flat, the plants that she had wanted him to keep alive, the coffee now gently hissing. 'I'm going out there tonight.' His voice was unfamiliar. The stammer entirely absent. 'Can you advise me whom I should contact when I arrive?'

'Oh,' said the woman. 'You should get in touch with the police. They'll be on the case if only because of the driver.'

'Did they find him? Did they find the driver?'

For the first time there was a pause, and when the woman spoke again her voice lacked the brisk efficiency of all that she had said before. 'The body of the driver was found beside the vehicle. He had been shot dead. I'm sorry, as I said, it doesn't look very good.'

He spent the night flight awake, drinking brandy, staring at the movie screen without the sound and without interest.

'Farther Safaris'. The Foreign Office spokeswoman had given him the address, a Nairobi box number. 'Not a big organisation, not on our records I'm afraid.'

He would ask in the hotel.

Tiredness and alcohol bred nightmares, images of Olivia alone in some desolate place, lost, hurt. He imagined black men, filthy, ugly bodies abusing her, he thought with terror of the fight she would put up, the strength he had encountered in her slender body.

He should have stopped her; he should have insisted, done more to prevent this escapade, this mad search for a lost brother. The thought made him sigh, even smile a little.

As if I could.

★ ★ ★

The land around the airport was stubbled with trees and yellow grass. In the fresh morning distance, Nairobi looked like any other capital of the third world: a huddle of tall buildings, a wide hinterland

56

of flats, shacks and shanty towns.

The air in the terminal stank of fuel. Above a sign of welcome hung the national flag. Dwarfed by unadorned concrete the colourful shield and spears looked strangely mute, as if the stark modernity of the place had drained their spirit.

A battered Peugeot taxi conveyed him to the city. The driver asked him for a cigarette.

'I'm afraid I don't have any.'

The man shrugged. As they approached the centre of town he pointed to the trees that grew along the central highway. 'Jacaranda.'

Michael stared blindly at the carpets of violet, billows of delicate blooms still on the branches. There were flowers underfoot as he carried his suitcase up the steps into the hotel lobby. Two faxes awaited his arrival. A client wanted him to attend an urgent meeting in New York. His sister had called him at the office. 'MICHAEL, WHAT ARE YOU DOING?'

The receptionist had long nails, scarlet against black, wrinkly skin. Michael leaned forward, trying to raise an expression from her bland, bored face.

'I wonder if you can help me? I want to locate a travel company, Farther Safaris.'

'Where is this?'

'That's what I want to know. Apparently they are based here in Nairobi. I have their box number.' He handed the scrap of paper on which he had scribbled the details. The writing was like that of an old man, shaky and uncertain. The receptionist stared at it.

'Do you know where I can find their office?'

He had to wait while she answered the telephone, an interminable conversation in another language. When it was over she appeared to turn back to her desk, ignoring him. Michael leaned towards her again, waving the scrap of paper.

'You were going to find out about this company for me.'

For a moment she stared at her nails. 'What is it you want to know?'

Michael tried to change his tone. 'It would be a real help to me if you could tell me their address.'

'The address is here.'

'N . . . no!' He heard his voice rise again, the English banker in a foreign land. He took a breath. 'I w . . . want to know wh . . . where I can find their office.'

With a slow movement, once again looking at her nails, the receptionist slid off her chair and walked to an office behind where a number of people were sitting at desks, telephones wrapped against their faces.

Sweat prickled on his neck. He could see her sitting on the edge of a desk, swinging her legs as her colleagues turned idly from their chatter to gaze at his scrap of paper and then at him through the open door.

Eventually she returned. He ran his finger round his neck, released his tie and opened the collar.

'You will have to ask later on. There is no-one here who knows this company.'

'But surely . . . ?'

She settled back onto her chair.

'Later perhaps, someone in the next shift may help you.'

Defeated, conscious of his crumpled shirt, he picked up his bag. There was no sign of a bell-hop. He felt her eyes on his back as he headed for the lift.

The hotel room was bland, adequate. He stuffed the faxes into a drawer and unpacked his things. Through the window he could see the city. Drab concrete and purple blossom. He ran a bath. The water was viciously hot, tinged with brown. Someone had let the shower splash the lavatory paper on the roll beside the bath. It was ragged and dimpled, grey white like his skin. He lay back, trying to recover himself. You are not going to be fazed by this, Michael Ballantyne. You are used to travel, used to foreign places.

But never like this; never where what he had come for was so personal. And so obscure.

The brandy, the sleepless night, all the nightmares of the aeroplane gathered around him. He tried to picture Olivia in this place, or some hotel that was even worse, being happy to be back, bargaining for a cheap vehicle from some outfit of which no-one had heard, thinking herself at home here in this bleak, charmless city.

At last he climbed out of the bath, shivering in the over-chilled air, and lifted the telephone receiver.

'I want to speak to the police.'

8

The marmalade was finished. Harry put the jar in the pedal-bin. Then he gathered the toast crumbs from the table into his palm, opened the back door and scattered them on the bird-table outside.

Jessie's letter was propped against the toast rack.

I thought you should know . . .

A letter from Jessie Bell. The first for twenty years. A flimsy airmail envelope lying on the mat as he came down the stairs. He had stared at it in disbelief.

I thought you should know that Olivia is missing.

He looked through the window, searching his memory. The youngest girl, Olivia. The last child before David. There was no face — only the long plait, a dark strand down the child's back. It was the older girl, Regina, who made the plait. Harry had seen them up on deck, Regina pulling the little one's hair, an ugly scowl on her face. June said it was too tightly done, that the plait would make the child's hair recede. Olivia never seemed to complain.

Thinking of it, he remembered how skinny the little girl was and — how easily the memories returned! — an expression she used, 'I amn't going to eat any tea.' June had laughed and so had Eugenie, friends then, on the boat, before the beginning of it all. 'I amn't,' making them laugh.

She came to me out of the blue. A flying visit, she said. Wanting to know where she would find David. Such a surprise, after all these years.

I told her what little I know — that David has a box number at Turkana — Lake Rudolph, as it was in our day.

She says Eugenie is better. I don't know what that means. Still mad but less so? Still swinging her panga? I did not press the question. I cannot help Eugenie. There was a time when I might have done, when I did nothing, when she called and I did not come. I cannot mend that now. Nothing will change that now.

I told Olivia that she should have come to you, Harry Crane. That you would be the one to know. She said she had no time. She left London in such a hurry. I think the truth is that she did not want to ask you. She was afraid to seek you out.

Harry washed his breakfast plate, wiped the table and hung the dishcloth in its place on the hook by the draining board. His cup and saucer had their place in the cupboard, the tea towel on the rack behind the door. Harry's days were built out of small routines, his morning shave, breakfast, washing up, laundry on Sundays. A safe life, controlled, as a house fire is controlled, guarded against stray coals, against sparks in the night. Thus he had survived, behind a fireguard of routine, of meals and work and sleep.

★ ★ ★

He started Jessie's letter again. Turkana? Lake Rudolph? Surely there was nothing there, even now? The most inhospitable of places. Just the salt-water lake, a cluster of huts around a spring. The Mountains of the Moon, explorers had called the place — so desolate and barren it was.

Harry had been there once, maybe twice, shortly before Uhuru. A man from Dundee had tried to start a farm — cattle, and then camels; there was talk of it in Nairobi. The man had borrowed a lot of money. The cows died and the camels were stolen. Harry represented the Department of Agriculture; he found the farmer living with a Turkana woman. Harry remembered the dust, clouds of smoke on the desert wind, the stench of burning carcasses and totoes running after his car.

I offered Olivia a driver. I have a good boy living nearby. Jackson has worked for these safari people, he knows the country. We all need the Africans now. But no, Olivia was making her own arrangements — some outfit in Nairobi who would drive her for a song. She had maps. She was ready for the heat. Tablets against the malaria. I asked her if she knew the sort of desert it is up there, though I hardly know myself. I was born here, she said, I know this country. Rubbish! She has no idea of how changed it is. She remembers only when we were still in charge, when the streets were swept and you could drink the water from the tap. She is like her mother, foolish and wilful. They are all the same, Eugenie's children.

I heard it on the wireless. They just said a European woman travelling alone. A photographer, they said, and then perhaps an aid worker, though it was surely her. And then, yesterday, they published her name, Olivia Jones.

Harry, I am an old woman. My heart is bad. What should I do? What can I begin to do about a girl missing in that wilderness?

Harry went into his bedroom and took a battered suitcase from the cupboard. His maps were faded, brittle along the fold lines. East Africa appeared in squares, like a flattened paper quilt. He used a magnifying glass to follow the blue smudge of the lake, stretching its fingers across arbitrary national borders. Perhaps there would be roads there now; the relief agencies would be there, and the missions, God on rough ground.

He searched for Loyangalani. A box number, Jessie said, 'but you will know it already.'

Harry knew no box number. For years he had heard only from the solicitors, Karanja and Co (incorporating Dolland and Black). 'He is living in the north, the old N.F.D.' (this from Karanja himself). 'He sends letters, people sometimes, without an appointment, to collect the trust money.'

Once, during a drought, Karanja reported a request for a lorry load of maize. 'We sent him money,' wrote the solicitor, 'but not the maize. My firm cannot get involved in maize.'

The map slipped back into its folds, square falling neatly upon square. It belonged so, like the letters, the memories, out of reach of Harry's daily eye.

Recently he had been strong minded. The little collection of photographs that he had kept beside his bed was gone. The shrine packed away. Only the wedding portrait remained: Harry with all his hair, June looking young and happy.

The rest were in the suitcase with the maps. He paused. A blue velvet-covered box contained the centre-piece of the collection; a row of silver-framed miniatures, linked together like a heavy silver bracelet. He lifted them out, feeling the weight in his hands. The back of the first picture was engraved, two hands entwined and the date: March 31st 1966. The print was faded, a scene from David's christening, June as the proud mother, holding a bundle swaddled in lace from her wedding veil. The next was undated: David when he could just walk, his chubby hand clutching the trouser leg of an unseen Harry; then a family group, Harry and June and the boy on his fifth birthday. The last picture was of David alone, 'Christmas Day, 1971', a handsome child smiling out, sunlight gleaming on the dark, muscular shape of the dog at his feet.

The frames fitted together, each frame clicked into the next, to form a cylinder the size of a torch battery. In a world where everything had to be portable, capable of folding or dismantling, the bracelet was a prize. It would take no space, the merest corner of a crate when the day came, the glorious day for which June had so longed, when 'long leave' would mean more than twelve weeks off before the next tour, when the crates would be packed for good, for the final journey to England. Home.

The frames were imported. Harry ordered the set through a jeweller in the Bazaar, waited seven weeks — almost the time since they heard, by indirect means, that the oldest boy, Dennis Jones, was dead, had jumped ship; AWOL. A motorbike, a wet road. Seventeen years old.

Harry drove out to see Eugenie. Even from the road the neglect showed, the white washed walls of the bungalow splashed with mud, the garden a wilderness.

It was Jessie Bell who had answered the door.

'You'll do no good here, Harry Crane.'

'I came to see if there was anything — '

'Her eldest son is dead. She sold the other one to you — '

Harry interrupted. 'Not sold — '

'Wasn't that what it was — a trade? The baby for this house, for the school fees for the others. Isn't that what was agreed?'

'It was what she wanted.'

'It isn't what she wants now. She wants her children. Dennis is dead but it is the boy you have that she grieves for.'

This conversation had taken place on the doorstep, Jessie speaking to him through the flyscreen. Harry was turning to go when there was a noise from behind. Eugenie in the passage. She said nothing. Her appearance made him draw breath. If he had not known it was she, he would have thought her a stranger, so different was she from the pretty young mother he had known, the girl on the boat, the woman who had given birth to David, whose screams June and he had listened to, breathless, outside the delivery room.

'I came to say how sorry I am about Dennis.'

There was no response. Just Eugenie's eyes, huge and vacant, staring at him from the gloom of the passage. Harry drove home, dry-mouthed.

June was sitting on the verandah, a picture of contentment, stitching name-tapes on to David's new school uniform.

'I can't believe he'll be starting proper school next term.'

Harry bent down to kiss her. 'I've brought you a little present.'

'A present!' June put down her sewing and stood up, delighted as a child.

He put the blue velvet-covered box into her hand. 'What is it?' She felt the weight for a moment and then lifted the lid. 'Is it a bracelet?'

'Not exactly,' said Harry. 'Open it out.'

'Why, it's for photographs! How ingenious!' She kissed his cheek, softened herself against him. 'We can put in a series on David, starting with the christening. And it's easy to pack. It will take up no space at all when we pack up to go Home.'

Harry responded to her kiss, delighting in her delight.

'And we shall be going soon, shan't we?'

Warily, for the conversation had taken a familiar turn, he nodded.

'When? Have you heard? Have they given you a date?'

'No. Nothing definite. After the next tour, perhaps.'

'After the NEXT tour! But that's years away.' June's voice rose, loud and sharp. 'Why? All the better people went before Independence.'

'I will stay on until there is someone properly trained to do my job. June, darling, please be patient, it isn't such a bad life. We have the sunshine, this is a much bigger house than we would have in England.'

'I don't give a damn about the house. We can't stay here for another tour, Harry! Eugenie is getting worse. She'll destroy us. She's poisoning everything. She follows me around. I've seen her in the supermarket. She doesn't shop there, she just hangs around.'

'She's bound to be worse for a while,' said Harry. 'She's just lost her oldest child. You can't imagine what it means to lose a son.'

'Of course I can! Both of us can. We imagine it every day of our lives — that our son will be taken, that she'll come and take him back!'

Harry waved his hands. 'There is no question of that. David is legally ours.'

'That's not what she thinks!'

'Things will get better in time. We must be patient.'

June screamed at him, 'In time? How much time?'

It was at that moment, or if not then precisely, another like it, during one of their many bitter arguments about Eugenie, about his job, and their being where they were, that Harry began to believe it was all of a piece. That Eugenie, with her handsome children, little more than a child herself, whom they had befriended, who had been such a source of hope, had carried a kind of curse into their lives; that by taking (rescuing?) her youngest child, that soft, beloved bundle from her arms, they had carried into their lives a sickness, a mad affliction, a punishment that would ruin them all.

The ayah came in from the garden, with David holding her hand.

Instantly June's anger dissolved. She behaved as if the child had been returned to her from a great distance, as if their separation had been long and not the span of a morning, the width of the hall between the sitting room and his nursery, or the garden, or from the gate to the small park up on Lavington Green where the ayahs congregated on the grass, each one with a white child in her charge. Harry liked to see the ayahs there, giggling and chattering, he liked their patience, the way the children were encircled, restrained and retrieved safe in the circle of plump brown bodies on the grass.

'Who's Mummy's boy, then?' June crooned, sweeping David into her arms. 'Who's Mummy's favourite boy? Her own boy? All her very own?'

June's voice, with its faint hoarseness, its hint of fear and hysteria, was as clear in Harry's ear as if she stood there with him now, after all these years, tormented still. She had been right to fear

Eugenie, to fear the child-mother who had once been a friend. She was right, her instincts were right, but she could not have foreseen how it would end, neither of them could have imagined those screams in the garden, the blood on the verandah, Eugenie Jones behind bars.

And David gone, lost, irretrievably.

He put the suitcase back in the cupboard and returned to the kitchen. A sparrow was pecking on the bird-table. A breeze shook the leaves from the cherry tree. The window was open at the top. Jessie's airmail fluttered a little where it lay on the table.

He put on his raincoat, felt in his pocket for his keys. The stamps on Jessie's letter were large and bright. What did she want? Why bother him now with useless news?

He pushed the letter into his pocket and hurried for the bus. For once he had the seat he liked, in the front at the top. Harry preferred the bus to the tube, though it took twice as long. It comforted Harry to see the world through which he travelled.

As the bus dallied on Putney Bridge, Harry turned to Jessie's letter. On the third page the handwriting changed, a different coloured pen, the writing firmer, as if she had rested.

I never thanked you for the car.

He looked away again, feeling himself smile, in spite of it all.

The traffic in the outer lane crawled by, droplets of rain on bright paint.

A hired car for Jessie Bell. Day after day. Little enough — even with the driver demanding double rates for running the gauntlet of reporters and spectators, the ugly crowds in the street — it was little enough to pay, a small gesture to Jessie, old even then, turning out of that cramped bungalow to sit in court in her blue hat, like a woman in church, a lone supporter for Eugenie Jones.

The trial lasted six weeks. Jessie never missed a day. Harry admired her. Admired how she stood up to defend her niece, twisting the handles of her blue handbag. 'Eugenie couldn't hurt a fly. She is a good mother to her children. Eugenie is not to blame.'

Only once had she cracked. Only once had Jessie cried. Others shouted and cried a good deal. African women, bibis, shrieking from the witness stand, the servants of neighbours pointing their fingers. Every one of them had seen something. No matter how high the fence or how large the garden, all had seen something that afternoon, or heard the screaming of the white woman, the barking of the dog. A dozen stories to shout out in the hot court-room.

Jessie Bell had raised her voice just once. On a day towards the end of the trial. There had been a stir at the back of the court. A noise from outside interrupted the droning of the lawyers. Heads turned as the door swung open. A man they had not seen before, his shirt open at the neck, like a labourer's, stubble on his cheeks, shambling forward.

Reporters called out, shouting like street-traders.

'It's the father!'

'Gareth Jones!'

Who had summoned him? Was he a witness for the Prosecution? Or the Defence? It was hard to tell who gained. Shouts and catcalls. The judge banged his gavel and in the short hush that followed, came Jessie's cry.

Harry could see it still, the flash of white, her hand going up to her mouth as she rose to her feet. At last here was something not to be borne.

'No!'

One word, but it could have been a bark or a howl or any other sound that could convey such utter astonishment, utter loathing.

'No!'

The car had been a small enough thing. Little enough for Harry to acknowledge her suffering. And here, on a London bus, in the rush and push of crowds and rain and motorbikes, here, after twenty years, was his thanks for it. Harry smiled, pleased as he had first been irritated, at the way she snuffed out the years, offered her thanks as though it were yesterday. And maybe the intervening years were for her, as they were for him, no more than a handful of crumbs for the birds.

9

'I am M . . . Michael Ballantyne. I am here b . . . ah . . . because of . . . of the girl who is missing. Olivia Jones.'

'We know who you are, Mr Ballantyne. I will tell you again what my officers told you yesterday, and the day before, and the day before that. There is no news. When there is news, we will tell you — immediately.'

The Inspector's beige safari suit was stretched tight across his belly.

'There must be some trace of her — it's been seven days — '

'Longer than that. Nine days ago the safari people told us their driver had not called in. They don't call in every day, these drivers. The radio links are not good up there.'

'But are . . . are . . . you really looking?'

'Of course we are looking. You know very well how much time has been spent on this case. Ground searches, aerial searches. It is a huge area, Mr Ballantyne. We have covered the territory as well as possible; but understand me, we cannot look under every rock. It is desert up there. Hundreds of miles of stony, volcanic desert. One of the most inhospitable places on earth. We do not have the resources to look under every stone, in every gully.'

'But you found tracks — '

'Of course there are tracks. Already, as you know, we have found the body of the driver. There are footprints all around this place. My people have followed them all but they lead nowhere. It seems the vehicle moved on after the driver was killed. She may have still been aboard. They may have thought of kidnap. Unfortunately the tracks are not preserved beyond a certain point. There has been too much wind.' The Inspector closed a file that had lain open on his desk. 'I assure you, Mr Ballantyne, you would do no better if you went to look. You would simply add to the trouble. Believe me. I have worked up there. The area is vast. There are safe places around the lake for tourists and fishermen but your friend was not content to be a tourist. She travelled into unsafe territory. I cannot have you straying there too, Mr Ballantyne. I do not want another statistic.' He shook his head. 'People do not realise. They come from London, Hamburg, New York — even Nairobi. They are driven around in safe comfortable vehicles and they look out at the animals.' He shrugged. 'Maybe they get out and walk about a little, take some photographs. And then they return to their safe, comfortable lodge and drink cold beer. They forget, Mr Ballantyne, there is another Africa. This whole region was unmarked on any map until just over a century ago — not even Turkana, the largest salt water lake in the world!' He sighed. 'And every now and then, some fools go looking for adventure. They go in one vehicle and leave the road and get lost. Every now and then they are found again.' He looked at

Michael with a steady eye. 'And sometimes, they are still alive.'

'So what ha . . . a . . . happens now? Surely you won't close the f . . . file?'

'The file will never be closed, Mr Ballantyne. We will always be looking for her. But my officers have other things that need attention. We cannot have you pestering them all day.' The Inspector spread his hands. 'This is a poor country. Did you see the notice in your hotel room? About wandering around the city after dark?'

Michael nodded.

'Not to walk in the city, Mr Ballantyne. In the city — let alone go up to the frontier, unescorted.'

'She was not at the frontier — '

'But she went alone — with her expensive ear-rings and her English belongings. How much were the ear-rings worth, Mr Ballantyne?'

'I'm not here to talk about ear-rings! I'm talking about a kidnapping!'

'Possibly a kidnapping, but certainly a murder. Or have you forgotten about the driver?'

'Of course I ha . . . haven't forgotten. But he is . . . is dead and Olivia is still alive — or would be if s . . . someone made the effort to find her!'

The African rose from his desk. 'Quietly now, Mr Ballantyne. Nothing will be achieved by shouting.'

'W . . . what else c . . . can I do?' cried Michael. A lump had risen in his throat, the words exploded, hideously. 'I h . . . ha . . . have ask . . . asked, I have badgered. I have been out here for nearly a w . . . week and there has been no progress at all.

Must I st . . . starve myself on . . . on . . . the steps of your office to get you to do something?'

'There are people starving on the steps of my office already.'

Ojekwo walked round behind Michael and opened the door to the corridor. There was an exchange of murmurs and then the policeman returned to the leather-backed chair behind his desk.

Wiping the sweat from his face, Michael turned to the window. Red dust stirred in the courtyard outside. Beyond the wall he could see the buildings of the city, skyscrapers squatting on the African plain. He was wasting time. What good could he do if this was his best effort? If, after waiting all this time to see the officer in charge, after all the telephone calls, and letters, struggling with thick-tongued English that he could barely understand, procedures that baffled him, madmen and clowns, rejection and encouragement, contemptuous eyes on the pale, stammering Englishman — what good was it all, if he could only shout?

He turned back to the Inspector. The African was relaxed, his hands resting lightly on the dull cotton of his suit. His eyes expressed nothing.

A noise at his shoulder turned Michael's attention. A young policeman proffered a cup and saucer.

'Take the tea, Mr Ballantyne,' said Ojekwo. 'Tea is something we make well here.'

It was strong and milky, sickly sweet. Michael forced it over his tongue.

'Now.' The Inspector waited until he put down

the cup. 'Tell me again, what she was doing in Turkana.'

Michael took a deep breath, 'You know why she was there. I've explained this a . . . a hu . . . hundred times. You must have a file as thick as — '

'But you haven't told me, Mr Ballantyne.' The Inspector's voice was soft, persuading. 'Please, I should like to hear it from you.'

Michael closed his eyes. Would it ever make sense to anyone? Could he make sense of it himself?

'She went for Eugenie.'

The Inspector raised an eyebrow.

'Eugenie is her mother. She is mad. I m . . . mean she is insane. Olivia goes every month or two. L . . . last time she went — '

'Where is this?'

'Castleton. It's a s . . . secure institution for psychiatric patients.'

'What does the mother's insanity have to do with this case? Is Olivia insane also?'

'No! But it has everything to d . . . do with her being here.' Michael shrugged his shoulders. 'You asked me why she went up there. It was to find her brother, David.'

Ojekwo interrupted him, shouted through the door.

'We will have some more tea.'

'We're wasting time!'

The Inspector sat back in his chair. He raised his arms. For a moment Michael thought he was going to yawn. Instead he rested his hands on top of his

76

head. 'We are not wasting time, Mr Ballantyne. What you tell me is part of the story. Everything that can be done in physical terms, has been done. Done more than once. Planes have searched for her, we have sent vehicles out, men on foot. Nothing has been found. We cannot even be sure she was ever in that vehicle. There is no information. She may simply be lost.'

'But there would be s . . . some trace . . . '

'If there was, we would have found it.'

'W . . . w . . . would y . . . you?' Michael leaned forward. His mouth working soundlessly, he could feel his face puckering, all the training he had had, to breathe correctly, to try a different word if the first wouldn't come, was forgotten. The words whooped and clattered off his tongue. 'W . . . wouldn't you rather find n . . . nothing than find her . . . her . . . dead? Isn't that true? Isn't tourism too p . . . precious to allow such bad . . . bad . . . bad . . . publicity?'

Ojekwo's eyes glittered. 'This is not true, Mr Ballantyne. All crime is investigated. Even the possibility of a white man's crime.'

'A white man?' Michael blinked. 'You don't think — you can't mean what I think you mean. Da . . . David had nothing . . . '

'Nothing to gain.' The Inspector interrupted, nodding. 'But you must understand that we have to consider every angle.' He pointed to the manilla file on his desk. 'Have you seen this file?'

He held the file open, showed Michael the contents, typed reports, duplicates of letters sent, faxes, internal memos, letters from England. Notes of meetings. The grand insignia of the British High Commission.

Held together on a separate clip were notes of enquiries for relatives. A letter to Mrs Jessie Bell, a Mombasa box number. 'The Government of the Republic regrets . . .'

There was an answer. A shaky longhand on fine paper, slightly yellowed, thanking the Minister for his kind letter, for all the effort that had been made. The Minister should take no blame upon himself . . . However, there could be another line of enquiry; one that may have been overlooked. If there was time, if a man could be spared, it might prove fruitful to speak to a young European who lived in that area. A young man she believed to be serving on a mission to the east of the lake. The man is the girl's brother. She was trying to reach him. His name is David Crane, or Jones. He might call himself Jones. Beside this paragraph a note had been scrawled. 'Located. No outcome.'

Michael drew in his breath. 'Did they really see Da . . . David? Did they interview him?'

The Inspector sighed. 'Naturally.'

'Why didn't you tell me?'

'There was no outcome.'

'Where is the report? Surely there is a report about David?'

'A case like this breeds many files. I have not shown you them all.'

'But he was seen? S . . . s . . . someone did go and see him?'

Ojekwo held out his hand. 'Come with me. We shall find the officer's report in another file.'

Michael followed the Inspector through the corridors of the police station. Doors stood open against the heat, overcrowded rooms, empty Coke bottles on a window-ledge, tables overflowing with paper. Uniformed men sat at the desks, speaking into telephones, writing, chewing their pens. He tried to push away the thought in his mind, that they were all play-acting, that a police-station in Africa could not be a serious thing.

'Here.' Ojekwo pulled at the drawer of a battered filing cabinet. It opened with a squeal. From a row of slings, packed tight against themselves, he prized loose a manilla folder, similar to the one Michael had already seen.

'Here it is.' A licked finger ruffled the papers, located a tattered page torn from a notebook. 'You see?' The Inspector's finger moved to the end. 'The interviewee had no information about the case. He said he had not seen any European women for some time.'

The Inspector put his arm about Michael's shoulders. 'Be patient, my friend. Pray for her.'

'I must d . . . do something. I can't just wait around, praying.'

The Inspector squeezed Michael's arm. 'You will not go up there yourself.'

It was a statement, not a question. The Inspector leaned forwards. Michael could see the fine line of pink where the brown skin of his lip gave way to the pinkness of his gums and tongue.

He pulled away. 'I must do something. She is my . . . we were to be m . . . married!'

'There is nothing you can do, nothing. Everything

has been done. No stone is left unturned in our search.'

He started walking back along the corridor. Michael followed. At the door to his office, the Inspector paused and turned. 'Earlier, you suggested that we — I — might prefer to keep this matter quiet, that I might fear damage to our tourist industry.'

Michael said nothing.

'I chose to ignore the insult your suggestion contained.' Ojekwo's eyes narrowed. 'But let me tell you now, Mr Ballantyne, I'd rather have some bad publicity, I would rather frighten away a few tourists than have to deal with all the cases like this that come onto my desk each year.'

Michael leaned against the wall. 'You have ab . . . abandoned her, haven't you?'

'No-one is abandoned.'

'But you . . . you think she is dead.'

Again, Michael felt the Inspector's hand on his shoulder. 'You are tired, Mr Ballantyne. You should rest.'

Michael pushed him away. 'I can't p . . . possibly rest. I'll go and see this brother of hers. It was David she went for.'

'He will not help you.' Ojekwo pointed back along the corridor, to the filing cabinet. 'You will find he has nothing to say.'

'But I w . . . will have done what she came to do,' said Michael. 'I owe her th . . . that much at least.'

Ojekwo nodded. 'Perhaps, but it is better that you go to the aunt first. You should learn about

80

this brother before you seek him out.'

'Her aunt is at the c . . . coast. Three hundred m . . . miles away.'

Once more Ojekwo squeezed Michael's arm. 'In Africa, we do not think that a large distance. You can take the train overnight. You will pass through Tsavo — one of our famous game reserves. It is an experience in itself. There are first class sleepers.' The Inspector smiled, 'Every luxury one can imagine. And,' he paused, 'if she is still alive now, after this time, it will be because she is being sheltered. And if that is so, the chances are she will still be alive in two or three days more.'

'And if she's n . . . not?'

Ojekwo shrugged. 'Then the same rule applies. Either way you have nothing to lose.'

Michael went back to his hotel. For days he had paced his room, eating little, phoning the police and the High Commission as often as he dared. He learned nothing, was told nothing. The people he had pestered were bureaucrats, too bored or frightened or ignorant to help him, their sympathies as impenetrable as their skins were dark and their features alien.

From Inspector Ojekwo he had learned where Farther Safaris were located. The taxi driver had been uneasy.

'You don't want this place, sir?'

'I do. That is the correct address.'

'I could take you to a better place. This one is no good for our visitors.'

'That is the one I want to visit. I have enquiries to make.'

'You a reporter. You asking about that girl? You are too late. She is old news.'

Michael cleared his throat but said nothing. The driver eased his ancient Peugeot into the traffic. They proceeded at a crawl, with much use of the horn, and then after only half a mile the car shuddered to a halt, steam rising from the bonnet.

The driver got out, scratching his head. 'This car is sick.'

'What about my journey?'

In other circumstances Michael would have participated, peered at the engine and shared the driver's gloom as water dripped from the radiator onto the tarmac. Now he felt nothing but rage. It was more of the same, more of the lazy incompetence that had thwarted him every moment since he arrived. He was dragging his bag from the car, prepared simply to walk off, when another taxi pulled alongside. The drivers exchanged words and then Michael was directed into the back, but not before what seemed an inordinate number of tatty notes had changed hands.

The new driver was silent, conveying him without comment to a small office on the ground floor of a peeling low-rise block on the edge of the city. Thinking of Ojekwo's caution, Michael asked the driver to wait.

Farther Safaris comprised a single room with two desks and two telephones, both occupied. A fan droned in the corner, circulating a stingingly sharp smell of sweat.

'We have nothing to say,' was all he could

extract when at last the nearest man put down the telephone. At the mention of Olivia's name both sets of eyes flickered, became blank.

'We have nothing to say.'

'Look, I'm not a j . . . journalist. I . . . I . . . I'm family, sort of.'

The second man waved his hands. 'My brother is dead.'

'What?' The word barked out, an echo of the banker, confronted by the irrational.

'It was my brother who drove.'

Michael's irritation collapsed.

The first man chipped in. 'We did not want this business. It was not a proper safari. We are trying here to give a good service for tourists. We do not want such scandals.'

The man whose brother had driven Olivia followed him out. Great tears had appeared on his cheeks. 'My brother had many children. Now how will I feed them all?'

Michael hurried back into the waiting taxi. Incongruously he thought of his yellow Porsche, longed for its soft leather seats, the hardness of the wheel, taking him where he wanted to go.

Back in the hotel, he drew another hot brown bath and then went down to the bar.

There had been a woman there the night before, middle-aged, tall. He had found himself sitting by her, telling her of his troubles. He learned that she was a nurse, that she worked for an aid agency which supplied nurses to the developing world.

'I am waiting for an assignment,' she said. 'I

hope to be sent upcountry and not, as sometimes happens, sent to nurse those who are rich enough to pay.'

'Do you know this country? Do you know the Northern Frontier?'

'I have been up there. It is not a place for the faint hearted.'

'Do you think I should go up there myself?'

'I do not,' said the nurse. 'Your Inspector Ojekwo is right. The chances of you, a stranger here, finding her are so slight, and the chances of you suffering an accident or an attack are so great, it would be foolish to attempt it.'

'Is it always so dangerous?'

The nurse shrugged. 'She is not the first white girl to go missing. You are not the first to want to search. Every year there is one story or another, often very like yours.'

'And these others? Are they found?'

She sipped her orange juice. 'Sometimes.' Her features softened, her eyes filled with sympathy. 'There will be aeroplanes, the Air Force has been up — and those that regularly fly that way — the charter planes and the flying doctor service — they will detour a little from their route. They may see her.' She finished her drink. 'Go and visit this aunt of hers. You can do no more up here — and wherever you are, you can pray, Michael. You can pray to God for your girl.'

Michael watched the shake of his hands as he lifted his glass to his lips. He knew that he would do as he was told. His life had been too well-ordered, too safe and predictable for him to disobey the policeman, or disregard the warning of this knowledgeable European. He sheltered in her common sense, stifled the words that clattered in his head. Coward! Coward! Coward!

10

The scuttling sounds of the desert night grew louder. The smear of stars across the sky had begun to fade. She detected a paling of the darkness, black and silver turning to grey, lighting the little basin of disturbed sand that was her resting place.

The grey was short-lived. In minutes the ground under her was splashed with red and purple, the sky exploding with the orange and scarlet fire of a swiftly rising sun. Looking for a bearing she fixed her attention on a high ridge of rock to the west. 'I'll climb up there,' she said, speaking aloud, her voice small and ridiculous in the vast emptiness. 'I should be able to see the lake.' Carefully placing her bare feet, one step at a time, on shattered stones and ridged lava that scraped her soles and bruised her toes, she picked her way across the ground. Several times she stumbled, stubbing her feet on sharp protrusions and once, while crossing a patch of loose, shifting grit she lost her balance altogether and fell, slithering and rolling down the steep slope, bruising her knees and elbows, rasping raw the side of her face. Several minutes passed before she could drag herself up and start again. The rising sun was heating the stones. She tried turning one over, to expose the cooler underside, but a small scorpion emerged, its tail curled upwards like a yellow prawn.

The ridge was further than it seemed. She tore

off the bottoms of her jeans and wrapped the pieces about her feet. The material wore through like paper. By mid-day her soles were raw, weeping wounds caked with dust. There was no shelter, no hint of shade, nothing but searing sand littered with black shards, like shattered tiles. Finally, reaching what appeared to be the top of the ridge, she found it was just a foothill to another, higher still, a long run of lava across the plain. There was no sign of the lake, nothing in all directions but rocks and ridges and prairies of grey sands. Exhausted and desperately thirsty, she lay down and curled herself tight, pulling her jeans and vest over herself, covering as much as she could against the fierce white heat hammering out of the sky.

★ ★ ★

Harry lifted the baby's pram down from the platform of the bus onto the pavement. Pain pulled at his back but as he straightened up he offered his hand to the young mother who was following. She jumped down independently and hurried away with the pram, without a word or a smile, his kindness abandoned, like an unshaken hand.

Wind flapped at his coat. He put his hands in his pockets and strode along Whitehall. The doorman looked up as he came into the foyer.

'Brisk today, Mr Crane.'

'It is.'

'Taking the lift, sir?'

'I think I will, I've given my back a tweak.'

'You can't be too careful with a back, sir.'

Harry smiled. There weren't many people who called Harry 'sir' any more. The doorman was like himself, a relic of another time. The steel lift doors slid apart and Harry stepped into the cage.

'Have a good day, sir.' The doorman reached in and pushed the button for the fifth floor.

As the lift ascended, Harry studied his face in the tinted mirror that covered the rear wall. Lit from above, the pink skin of his scalp showed through thinning strands of hair. His mouth had gone, his lips retreated to a pinched line. A snake's mouth, he thought, humourless and cold. How long since he had laughed? Really laughed?

Behind him the lift doors opened. He spun around, not wishing to be seen examining himself. There was no-one outside. He stepped out onto the corridor carpet that was patterned with blue and purple and had an unpleasant artificial sheen. When it was first installed, the carpet had caused minor electric shocks. Harry preferred the old linoleum; lino had better reflected the character of the department, the dogged endurance of bureaucracy.

His office was empty, both desks clear, unoccupied. Darren would be late. He was always late — slithering through the door at twenty past nine in his silly suit and pointed shoes.

Harry hung up his coat and placed his sandwich box in the drawer of his desk. He had already dealt with three items from his in-tray when Darren appeared in the doorway.

'Wotcher, Harry!' The boy flung his raincoat on a chair and crossed the room to the window, separating the horizontal slats of the blind and peering down at the street.

'Did you see it?'

'See what?'

'The amazing car!'

'I must have missed it. Perhaps I was here too early?'

'Why don't you have a car, Harry?'

'I don't need one.'

'But you ought to have a car. Everyone needs a car. A man like you shouldn't come to work on a bus.'

'I like the bus. And there's nowhere to park.'

The youth continued to peer down at the street. 'Jesus, these blinds are filthy.' He blew along the slats, sending a little puff of dust against the glass. 'Shall I ring Maintenance?' He turned to Harry, 'I could get Maintenance to speak to the cleaners.'

'I'd rather you started work.'

'I mean, it's not healthy, is it, all this dust?' Darren sauntered to his desk, wiped his hands on an unpressed handkerchief. He removed his jacket, revealing a pink striped shirt and a green tie. Without the padding of the jacket, he had the body of an adolescent.

'You must try to start work on time, Darren.'

'Sorry, Mr Crane. Got my mind on something else this morning.'

'Well, whatever it is, put it aside. You're here to work.'

'Don't you want to know what's on my mind?'

'Not now.'

'Later then — but don't say I didn't offer to tell you first.'

He sauntered out. Harry watched the door swing closed. Darren was no worse than the last, he thought. All these young men with their vanity, their coarseness, their . . . he searched for the word. Wisdom? Yes, it was that. Wisdom. They were of their time; their dress, their manner. It was the manner of survival.

And David — in your desert? Are you like that?

He tapped his knee, piano style, counting the years as if he didn't know the answer already, as if he had not counted every one of them, almost every day, over and over, unable to believe how many had passed, how much of his life had gone by. Twenty years since they had asked their questions.

'Did you know the woman who stood at the gate?'

Nine years old, and so small, so quiet, speaking out from the witness stand in his clear boy's voice.

'She is my mother.'

'Do you call any other person your mother?'

David had turned, looked across the crowded court-room. A moment's silence while he had looked at Harry, steady-eyed.

Then the reply. 'Yes. Mummy — the lady on the verandah.'

'And your real mother, the woman who stood at the gate, is she here today? Do you see her?'

'Yes.' David's voice rang clear across the hushing of shoes and the scraping of chairs, and the clearing of throats, women at the back in tears. 'She is there.' An arm, short-sleeved, raised to the horizontal, an unwavering finger.

'You want this coffee, Mr Crane?' The face of the tea lady peering round the door.

Harry grunted.

'Here we are, Mr Crane. I put three sugars in, how you like it.'

'Thank you.'

'I've got doughnuts and Chelseas.'

'I'll just have the coffee.'

'What about young Darren? He'll be wanting a doughnut I expect?'

The woman laid a square of serviette on Darren's desk, a brown ball of doughnut oozing red syrup. 'Tell him I'll catch him tomorrow for the money.'

Harry made no answer. She didn't quite close the door. He could hear her in the corridor, the rattle of her trolley like the sound of a hospital trolley, and her humming.

Eugenie Jones turned. Her eyes, that had been fixed upon the boy as though his life depended upon her look, dragged themselves away. She stared across the court to Harry. 'Why?' she seemed to be saying. 'Why did you let this happen?'

You ought to tell her sister.

A request — command? — on the second page of Jessie's letter, Harry had skipped it at first, skimmed through.

Someone should tell her — and Eugenie too. I cannot do these things from here. I'm too old, it's too far. But you, you were always a good

91

man, Harry Crane. I never doubted it. You will do what is right.

Harry rubbed his face. Was it possible? Could it possibly be up to him now, to do as Jessie Bell asked?

She gave no hint as to how it would be done. How to find Regina, how to tell her. And for what?

The door in front of him flew open.

'Cake!' Darren had seen the doughnut on his desk. 'I didn't pay for the one she left yesterday.'

'The woman said she was keeping a tally.'

'She's leaving on Friday.'

'Who is leaving?'

'Connie, the coffee lady. There's a collection going round for her.' Darren filled his mouth with doughnut and took a gulp of coffee. The doughnut was still there to be chewed when the coffee had been swallowed. Harry looked away.

'She's got a job in a hospital.'

'Who has?'

'Connie.' Darren took another bite of doughnut. 'She's going to be an orderly or something. She worked in hospitals before — in Jamaica. I shouldn't think it's the same, though — there as here.' Darren put the rest of the doughnut in his mouth. 'You were somewhere like that, weren't you? One of these other places where they have blacks and that?'

'I was in East Africa.'

'Hospitals any good there? I've never fancied being in hospital abroad, myself. You don't know what you'll pick up.'

'No.' Harry turned back to the papers on his desk. He had developed an ability over the years, to look absorbed in work while his mind wandered away. Harry indulged his memories as others indulge their fantasies, but without the pleasure. All his memories, even those that began in joy, were coloured, stained by the events that followed.

★ ★ ★

David had caught something at school. The first sign was in the car going home. June saw it.

'You look pale, sweetheart, is something wrong?'

'I feel hot.'

They stopped for petrol and she bought him an ice-lolly. He let it melt, an orange puddle on the floor of the car.

'What's the matter with you, David?'

'I'm all right.'

'What would you like to do until supper time? How about the drawing book?'

He was good at drawing. 'Promise', the school master had said. 'He has considerable promise.'

Harry and June tried hard to be pleased; to acknowledge a talent that was not something they had given; not a consequence of their son's orderly, educated home, but a gift of genes, of parenthood. Harry had watched June struggle to accept it. And — bless her, bless the gentle heart that he had first loved — when the pictures came home from school she had pinned them up on the kitchen wall without a murmur — all of them — even the one entitled 'My Family'. Harry and the dog, and two women — 'Mummy' and 'Mummy'.

At the teacher's suggestion they bought drawing books that had squared paper with pictures of trains and ships to be copied. David had drawn a ship the day before. Harry had watched the delicate ease with which he had held the pencil in his ordinary, slightly grubby boy's hand. Today he was clumsy, his outlines were ragged. After ten minutes his head lay on the table. 'Mummy, I don't feel well.'

Dysentery. June shuddered. A disease of the poor. How could he have caught such a thing, after all the care they had taken? A private room in the city hospital. A window on the garden and a bright coloured cushion on the wicker chair for visitors. The expense was not even considered. A raging fever, dehydration, nappies again — at six years old — and blue marks on his bottom from the hypodermic, four times a day.

'No cause for alarm, Mrs Crane. He'll be as right as rain in a week or two.'

June was mad for the first time.

Was that too strong a word? Mad? Perhaps it was, in the light of what followed. Disturbed, then, distressed. Inconsolable.

Night after night, Harry had paced the verandah with her, back and forth.

'Come to bed now. You'll make yourself ill.' Tiredness hanging from his limbs like a drape.

'Why won't they let me stay there? Why won't the hospital let me stay with him? I'm his mother!'

'You will disturb him, darling. He must rest. He won't know you aren't there.'

'But she's there. Eugenie is there. She's on the

94

night shift. She's been on it for months — she volunteered — so that she can be around in the day. So that she can spy on us!'

'Hush now, darling.'

'She's there. She can go in. She will see his name and go in.'

'She won't harm him.'

'How can you say that? How? When you see the harm she does with those cheap little presents and 'I'm your Mummy. I'm your real Mummy!' all the time?'

June's outburst set off the dachshund in the neighbouring house. Its sharp yapping roused their own placid labrador and soon the whole valley rang with the barking of dogs. The pillars of the verandah were stark and black against the sky. Small hushing sounds were all Harry could manage.

June turned on him, pointing her rigid finger into his face. 'It's only me she denies. Never you. What is it between you two?'

'June!'

'I can see the guilt in your face!'

'What are you saying?'

'It's what she says: 'I'm your Mummy, June isn't your real Mummy.' Filling our little boy's head with lies. But never you. Never, 'Harry isn't your father.' Never that, never anyone else for a real father!'

She pulled away from him, lunged across the verandah, hurled her arms around a pillar.

There was no truth in it. Her accusations were wild, unfocussed, searching for a target.

Transquillisers were prescribed. She became

calmer. David recovered, bright-eyed again, almost himself. Harry found them at visiting time, playing Scrabble. June on the wicker chair with the colourful cushion, the boy sitting up in bed. He held his arms out to Harry. 'I'm beating Mum. She's twenty points behind.'

June looked up, slow-eyed as the drugs had made her. She smiled. At the end of the visiting time when the nurse came in with a hypodermic on a tray, she left without a fuss, holding Harry's hand. In her other hand a dhobi bag, David's pyjamas and towels for the wash.

Later, when their supper had been cleared away, she brought the bag into the sitting room and without a word spread the contents on the floor. There was more than towels and dirty pyjamas. There was an empty sweet packet, a broken toy car, a half-eaten orange.

'You see,' she said, in the new, calm voice of her tranquillisers. 'I am not wrong. Eugenie has been in that room.'

★ ★ ★

'You've been staring out the window a long time, Harry.'

'What?'

Darren was sitting at his desk, cleaning his nails with the end of a paper knife.

'I said, you've been staring out for a long time, Mr Crane. I don't know what you're looking at — the Testarossa isn't there anymore. Won't you let me get Maintenance to clean those blinds?'

11

The railway station was a market place, crowded, dusty. Cartons of tomatoes were thrust into Michael's face, electrical fuses and enamel plates, bolts of cloth and boxes of matches; a mêlée of voices, 'Lookee, mister. Just one look! No price for looking!'

'N . . . no, thank you. No, no thank you.'

He had spent the afternoon shopping in the part of the city known as the bazaar. Like everywhere else, the place swarmed with people. Twice he was jostled, felt a hand feeling for his wallet. They took nothing, his wallet was in a body belt, but the incidents added to his growing feeling of hatred for the place, for the broken paving stones over which he stumbled, for the poor quality of the shorts and tee-shirts that he purchased, for the feeling he had of utter isolation, uselessness. He was going to the coast because Ojekwo had told him to; because the policeman was tired of him. It was a mad idea, to go south, to be further away from the place where she had gone missing, but what did it matter? He could not find her himself, he could not search thousands of miles of empty desert. She had been to visit Jessie. Jessie was part of her childhood. There would be something of her there, some part of the truth.

A railway porter took his suitcase and made off across the station at great speed. Michael caught up with him at the notice-board where lists of names indicated the allocation of berths.

'What is your name?'

'Ballantyne.'

'You are First Class?'

'Y . . . ye . . . yes.'

Michael saw his name on the list and pointed to it. The porter set off again.

The platform was at ground level, so that it was necessary to climb steep steps to board. The dirty rusted underside of the carriages was clearly visible between the towering wheels of the train.

'This one is yours.'

His case was deposited on the seat of a compartment that was narrow and shabby, its open window covered with rusted mosquito mesh. Out of breath, Michael thrust a five shilling coin into the man's hand and sank down onto the seat.

'Not enough.'

'Wh . . . what? He looked up. The porter was still there, standing in the doorway.

'Five shillings is not enough.'

'Oh, for . . . for God's sake. I could have carried it myself.'

The porter remained, still holding out the coin. Feeling irritably stubborn, Michael stared fixedly out of the window. After a moment there was a noise. The porter had gone. The bright silver coin lay on the floor.

Michael rubbed his eyes. Now the man was gone he felt ashamed. What sum should he have given? He wanted to go after the porter, to ask how much would have been enough? The words of the dead driver's brother rang in his ears. How many children were there, to be fed from these tips? But fear of the train leaving him behind, of the crowded chaos of the platform, held him back.

He looked around. The walls of the compartment were lined with some kind of linoleum. In the corner a metal wash basin with a recess above it had a small tap and a dirty sign, 'NOT DRINKING WATER'. Engraved on the basin was the name of the manufacturer and 'Made in Birmingham'; below, the letters EAR had been partially erased. There was no plug.

At last the train began to move. He went into the corridor and watched as the low red roofs of the station slipped slowly out of sight; like a long, rust coloured snake the train wound through a maze of industrial buildings, acres of mud-splashed concrete, heaps of sand and twisted metal.

An attendant appeared, brass buttons shining on a starched white suit.

'Jambo, bwana. You want beer? Very cold beer?'

'Yes, please.'

The little man scuttled away and returned almost immediately with a glass and a large brown bottle on a battered metal tray.

Michael eyed the bottle suspiciously. 'I'd rather have Premium . . . '

The attendant shook his head. 'No Premium on this train. Only Tusker — is the best.'

'I was t . . . told Premium is the quality beer.'

'Tusker is the best!' The attendant tapped the bottle. 'Is the biggest!'

He brought Michael a roll of bedding and, at the

sight of a ten shilling tip, grinned with all his teeth and showed him the way to a sticky-floored lavatory and the sign for the dining car. The latter was at the other end of the train, past a galley, men in green aprons, vats of stew over glowing charcoal. Michael ate soon after dark, minestrone with soft bread rolls, fatty stew and mashed potatoes, pineapple crumble and custard.

Late in the night he pulled the mosquito mesh aside and leaned out of the carriage window. The train was crawling between two hills, the carriages festooned with lights. He rang for the attendant and asked for a cup of coffee.

'Why the lights?'

'Elephant!' The attendant grinned, pointing through the window. 'Is Tsavo.'

'The train is going th . . . through the game reserve n . . . now? But we won't see a thing.'

The attendant bustled forward and made a show of dusting the window.

'But it's not dust, you fool, it's dark!'

'Yes,' the attendant nodded energetically, 'is very dark!'

Far ahead, the train driver sounded the hooter, long slow blasts into the night.

★ ★ ★

Jam jars of insects. Moth-wings battering the glass. Regina caught a praying mantis but its stillness bored her.

Centipedes were the best. The totoes found them by the cactus fence, under the old crates. Regina was Toad in a green curtain; the totoes her silent, astonished audience. She said they must sit down because their legs were made of chocolate, hollow like an Easter egg. Be careful with those crates. Dennis cut his hand on a rusty nail; there was blood on his shirt; the neighbour sent him to the hospital for five stitches and an anti-tetanus jab. A police car brought him home. Eugenie screamed at the sight of their uniforms. 'Harry Crane sent you! He sent you to spy on me. Harry Crane wants to steal all my children!'

Centipedes were rusty nails rattling in a jar.

Friday afternoons playing on the stone lions outside the library. Eugenie inside, prowling the shelves and bays. Olivia aboard the lions, her legs spread wide over their flat granite bodies. From that height she would see them coming. David running to keep in step with the high-heeled shoes. Sometimes they came every week; sometimes not. Sometimes a month would go by — four Fridays in a row.

The coolness of the lions travelled through the blue serge of her school dress. Eternity and then her mother's voice, pitched high with disappointment if she had seen the boy, rage if they had not come. Either way, Olivia's legs were slapped, her hair pulled as they hurried to the bus. Supper was macaroni cheese, stained pink with tomato sauce. Silver-haired Samson waiting in the kitchen, his totoes turning up at the back step to play in the crates until bed-time.

★ ★ ★

She drew maps in her mind; talked to herself. They drove this way . . . the lake is on this side. This is where they were stuck in a pot-hole. This is where they stopped to look in her bag, rifled through her clothes to find only the cheap camera, her medicine box, a few pairs of shorts and a sweatshirt. So disappointed she wanted to apologise. Only the fuel pleased them; the secondary tanks strapped along the sides of the chassis.

She pointed a finger into the dust. This is where they threw me out. Why? Why not shoot her? Putting her out into the desert was more cruel than a bullet in the head.

She lay down again and closed her eyes. Flies buzzed around her ears, settling, licking she supposed, the wounds where Michael's ear-rings had been torn from her ears.

They had laughed at the glitter, giggled: stilled for a moment by the clear cut stones in their dusty brown palms. Ballantyne sapphires. The only kind of love he knew. The language of his kind, useless for the desert, for the children of Eugenie.

She put her head back. The pain of her ears, ripped flesh and the pulse of infection, no more and no worse than the other agonies.

12

Regina sat bolt upright, listening for the sound that had shaken her out of sleep. The room was filled with the yellow glow of Thanos's bedside lamp. His eyes were closed. His book lay flat on his belly. She could hear the cars on the main road, a distant siren. She looked at her watch. It was half past two. The bedroom felt empty and cold. Pulling the flimsy collar of her nightdress closer round her neck she knelt on the mattress to move his book and turn off his light. As she leaned, with half the weight of her body lying across him, she heard the noise that had woken her; a long gurgling sigh.

'Thanos?' There was something not quite right. 'Thanos, wake up!' She patted his face. His mouth, instead of closing — as it would when she disturbed his snoring, with a little smack of tongue and teeth — lolled further open.

'For God's sake, what's the matter with you?' She patted him again, harder. 'Are you playing games with me?' She shook his shoulders, lifted the upper part of his body as high as she could and shook him harder still. His slack, open jaw flopped from side to side. The lower lip had dropped, revealing his bottom row of teeth, uneven, darkly stained.

'Thanos, wake up!' The last word came out as a shriek. She hauled back the bedclothes. His calves, his fat slack limbs, bounced lifelessly on the bed. Regina was breathless, her alarm mixed with outrage. 'You won't do this to me, Thanos. You cannot do this to me.'

He lay flat, inert. Dimly recalling a first-aid leaflet she had read somewhere, she tore his pyjama shirt aside and pummelled the hairy flesh of his chest. She sat on him, straddling his hips.

'Thanos! Please, Thanos!'

Using her whole weight she jumped on him. The response was another of the long rattling sighs and a stringy mess of spittle running down his chin. With a cry of panic she clambered off him. Her feet scrabbled blindly for her slippers but finding only his she flapped across the room like a clown and ran awkwardly and dangerously down the stairs to the telephone.

The rest of the night was confusion; telephone conversations, unfamiliar faces. When the morning came and the ordinary light of day filled the house, she could remember only snatches: a doctor with his bag, a stretcher, men with long grey expressions who addressed her as 'madam' and asked horrifying questions in voices that were gluey with sympathy. It was a policewoman who telephoned Vasillios. 'You must have your family around you, dear.'

Vasillios brought the other brothers and, later, their wives arrived, with the old mother and shopping bags of food. They cooked in her kitchen, on her cooker, and set the table for a workman's breakfast. Packing crates and boxes appeared. Regina tried to intervene. She was hustled to the sofa. They babbled at her in Greek, scorn in their voices, scolding her dry, tearless face. She sat on the sofa beside the broken-toothed mother, who was wailing at the fireplace, dabbing yellow rheumy eyes with a handkerchief as black as her dress. There was a moment, Regina recalled later, when she admired the mother, the ease with which she played her part, as if, in her old age, death had become a kind of career for her, following the coffins of the family, wearing her shapeless black dress with her matching handkerchief and mantilla.

The brothers shook ketchup over their eggs. On the table was a bowl of olives and bread speckled with seeds. The wives ate their meal in the kitchen. Refusing to eat Regina went upstairs. All over the house the walls had been stripped. Pictures stood propped against doorways and furniture, even laid across the bath. They had taken down her portrait from over the bed. Blankets were being used to separate one frame from another. The portrait was on top of a blanketed stack. She peeled the covering away and her own face stared back at her; a brainless, empty model's face.

'What have you done, Regina?' she whispered. 'What have you allowed to happen here?'

In the kitchen below she could hear the clatter of crockery.

At the end of the day, when the brothers' van had taken the last of the crates, the dining plates stood neatly in a rack on the draining board; uneaten olives in a bowl beside them. There were crumbs on the carpet where the table had been. Hooks and nails protruded like thorns from the bare walls. They'd left his dressing gown. It hung as it had always hung, like a tired coat behind the bedroom door. Hugging it about herself she crawled onto the bed. His pillows were left too, and the deep pit in the mattress where his short, fat body had lain beside her. Eighteen years? More? She counted back on her fingers. Had it been so long?

Rolling into the mattress she buried her face in his pillow. She could smell the pomade he used on his hair, and garlic, and the other indefinable smells that she had so detested when he was close. Now they filled her with sadness.

Are you weeping, Regina? Are you weeping for this old Greek?

You did not love this man.

There is nothing to weep for.

I can weep for myself. My cooker is gone. Soon they will take away the house.

She slept. When she awoke, the house was quiet. She lay for a while, her tears dry, tightening the skin around her eyes.

You can get another cooker, another house.

Brushing aside her hair she felt for the little fold of skin under her chin. Tentatively she tapped it with her hands. Tomorrow she would get into her leotard — if it would fit — and remember the old routines. With satisfaction she recalled that she had eaten nothing all day. It was a good start. By the weekend she would begin to be slim again.

13

A day passed. A night. Another day, perhaps a third. The exposed parts of her body burned the colour of poppies and blistered. Her thirst was a physical pain, the skin of her tongue like some dry alien thing in her mouth. The sores on her feet congealed, crusted with sand and blood and the glistening bodies of insects.

She had ceased moving, made a kind of bed where soft powdery sand had heaped against a rock. Michael. There was no-one else to hope for and no-one less able, less equipped. For what purpose could they serve here, the things he valued? The yellow car, the silver candlesticks? 'Michael.' The words cracked from her throat. 'Michael, look for me.' The sand folded softly around her, cool and sharp. The yellow car hovered above her head. A hearse of bright colours.

Threads of her clothes lifted in the wind. It was over. No hope to cling to. No deliverance in a yellow car, no water from the faucets of his bathroom. Nothing but the unwanted memory of his fireside, the safety of an autumn afternoon, the strong, hopeless certainty of a city man, useless and irrelevant to her burning limbs, to a tongue swollen, bleeding, invaded already by creatures whom she could not see, death finding its way inside her, remorseless; a frail cluttering of flesh on the desert sand.

Movement. She had seen many such. Mirages, aircraft flitting, yellow cars, pools of water, men who did not exist.

This movement persisted. Hazy as a ghost. A boy or small man. Michael? The wind carried his song; a tinkling of bells. He twisted and shimmered, dancing in the uncertain, heat-stained air. Olivia closed her eyes. Death now. An angel dancing. Had she thought of such mockery?

And then flesh and blood; bright black limbs standing by her face, a head in front of the sun looking down at her. A kid goat wriggling in his arms and, by his side, shy in the huge silence, a smaller boy picking his nose. The tiny kid bared, a noise so clear and stupid she wanted to laugh, she croaked, cackled at them, from the dry hollow of her throat. Into their silent stares she cried, tried to speak. Nothing came but a noise that echoed the short, whinnying hoops of the kid, a sound from a tongue, huge and swollen, a thick, wordless sponge.

★ ★ ★

The taxi had gone, swirling away into the dust. The quiet of the garden, warm and still, was creeping back as the servant stooped to lift Michael's suitcase from the step. He had a scar on the dark skin of his neck. The collar of his long, white garment flapped open as he bent down. Michael saw that the scar was long and deep, extending, ragged and haphazard, down into the muscle of his chest.

'My name is M . . . Michael Ballantyne. M . . . Mrs Bell is expecting me.'

The servant did not speak. The white garment fell back into place. With Michael's bag in his hand, he stepped aside to let the white man go first into the house.

Carved double doors into the hall were matched by a pair at the other end. Dimly, after the brightness of the garden, Michael made out a square, bare walled room. Such light as there was came through half moons of glass, flecked and dusty, above the doors. The servant pointed to a chair with a high seat, the back ornately carved, arm rests that ended in heads of serpents. Obediently Michael moved towards the chair. The servant opened the second pair of doors. Briefly there was light, a glimpse of blue sea, flickering shadows and then Michael was alone.

He looked around. The room was not as bare as it had first appeared; a rug lay across the floor. Even in the gloom he could see the richness of the pattern, the places where it was worn through. Beside him, within reach, an ancient black telephone rested on a table carved in the same style as the chair. He sat back. A serpent's head fitted neatly into his palm.

'I see you like my Mombasa chair.'

He had closed his eyes, missed the shaft of bright sunlight as she opened the door.

'M . . . Mrs Bell?' He stepped down. The high seat made his movement clumsy.

'You can't buy them like that now.' Sandy-white

hair framed her head, like a ruffled halo against the light. 'Years ago there was a man in Malindi who would make you one for a song. Nothing like it now. They're all made by machine.' She was shaking her head. Michael had the impression of a complaint that was automatic, something recited out of habit.

'Hell to sit on, though.' She held out her hand. 'Come through. Joseph will bring us tea.'

He followed her along a verandah that looked over the sea; white sand and blue water, palm trees leaning, their fronds blown forwards like the scarved heads of women in an English high street.

The verandah served as a corridor between rooms. Jessie Bell led him to the end, through a glazed door and into a room crowded with furniture, ornaments, photographs in tarnished silver frames.

She faced Michael for the first time. He saw how old she was, how sun shrivelled, her creased yellow skin like worn out chamois.

'You've heard nothing?'

He shook his head. 'Every t . . . time I ask they t . . . tell me the same thing. They won't admit that they can't find her — that they've s . . . stopped the search.' His voice wavered. Tears of anger and frustration were gathering, vinegar-sharp, in his eyes. 'I cannot bear to think of her, of where she m . . . m . . . might . . . '

Jessie raised her hand.

'Stop that. There is no point thinking of that.'

She spoke like a parent, or an old friend; as if, in their loss, the rules of first acquaintance could be discarded.

'I want to do something — I must — '

'What can you do?'

'There must be something they have overlooked.'

'They have searched by air. I wrote to the Minister — '

Michael nodded. 'Ojekwo showed me your letter.'

'Ojekwo?'

'The Police Inspector in charge of the investigation.'

'Ah, yes — youngish — his picture was in the paper.'

'I can't tell if he cares or not — '

Jessie interrupted him. 'They didn't answer my letter. I don't know if they've done as I suggested — if they've seen David.'

'They have.'

Jessie smiled. 'I doubt it.'

'They interviewed him — I saw the report.'

Jessie shook her head. 'You saw a report which said they had interviewed him. I doubt they even bothered to trace him.'

His hand was held for a moment, half in kindness and half for support as Jessie lowered herself into the most used of the armchairs. 'She came to see me you know, before she went up there. It was wonderful, simply wonderful, to have her here again. All those years just rolled away.' Jessie nodded, scrabbling in the pockets of her dress for a handkerchief. 'She looked so well, so . . . whole. I thought perhaps we were coming to the end of it all.'

'The end of . . . of . . . what?'

'All the suffering — all those years.' Jessie blew

111

her nose. 'I've written to Harry Crane. I don't know why. But there is no-one else.'

'Who, pr . . . precisely is Harry Crane?'

'She didn't tell you?'

'Not properly.' Michael thought for a moment, remembering Olivia's words. 'She said he was the best and worst thing that happened.'

Jessie smiled. 'You could describe him that way. But he was a victim really. Just like the rest of us.'

'Will you tell me what happened? I mean the whole story?'

'You really don't know?'

'I know almost n . . . nothing. That's why I've come to you. Ojekwo sugg . . . gested it, he said that I would learn something from you.'

'Learn?'

'About David, about what happened to Eugenie. All the m . . . mystery.' Michael held out his hand. 'You will tell me, Mrs Bell, won't you?'

'Sit down, dear. It's too long a story for you to stand.' She settled herself deep into the winged armchair.

Michael hesitated. 'But I can't stay long. I can't waste any time.'

'Then why have you come?' Jessie's voice rang out, deep and harsh. 'Why have you come all these miles south when she is north?'

'I told you — the p . . . police suggested it. I wanted to go up there, to see David. Ojekwo p . . . practically forbade it. He told me to come to you first. That I am useless, white, English. Th . . . that I would learn more from you — '

Michael tried to pause but found himself unable to stop the words that babbled from his lips. All semblance of the merchant banker had vanished. He was a child again, crying to his mother or his sister, in need of female solace. 'I need your help. This is my first time in Africa. I don't know how to begin. B . . . before I left h . . . home, I thought it would be simple. I would just hire a vehicle and go up and look for her myself. B . . . but they say that the area of search is almost limitless. There are no roads and no water. I wanted to charter a plane and ov . . . over-fly the area, but no-one will do it, everyone s . . . says it would be a waste of t . . . time. If she is alive then she is in someone's care — or capture. There will be nothing to see from the air. Even the commercial pilots are unwilling. It's as if they've been stopped. As if some off . . . official has leant on them, as if they don't want to discover her dead, for the effect it would have on . . . on their tourism.'

There was a noise on the verandah. The servant entered through the glazed doors, a tray balanced on his hand. Michael saw the spin of eyes in his brown face, at him and then at Jessie, looking not at her face, but her hands, at the flutter of fingers, indicating the table on which the tray was to be placed. There was a confidence in the exchange, a familiarity that required no words.

Jessie patted the sofa next to her chair. 'Sit here by the window, you'll catch the breeze.'

Michael settled back into the sofa, he could feel a flutter of air, wind off the sea filtered by a layer of mosquito mesh and wooden shutters. He peered between the slats while she poured the tea. An image truncated, a line of sea and sand and in the space between, a brown lawn, speckled with shaded, stringy grass. A boy was hacking at a bright mantilla of bougainvillaea that hung over the roof of a wing of the house that extended towards the beach. Flowery branches lay on the ground about his feet. As Michael watched, the boy paused to wrap a purple frond, Hawaiian style, about his neck. There were girls on the sand. The boy waved at them, and did a little dance. The girls waved back.

A rattle of china made Michael turn. Jessie was holding out a cup of tea, the colour of thin gravy.

'Your policeman was right,' said Jessie. 'You'd do no good rushing up there on your own. If she has survived until now then she will live. If not, then it will be too late anyway.'

'Tha . . . that's what Ojekwo said.' Michael leaned forward. 'Do you b . . . believe she's alive?'

Jessie spread her hands and sighed. 'She is young and healthy. She has a chance.'

Out on the lawn, the necklace of flowers lay discarded on the grass, the boy was running back towards the house.

'Is that shamba-boy working?'

'He is now,' said Michael.

The boy picked up his panga and hacked fiercely at the creeper.

'Is Joseph there?'

In the corner of the verandah Michael could see

114

the white skirt of the servant.

'I think so.'

Jessie stirred sugar into her cup. 'You can't rely on these boys any more. They want to work in the hotels. They want money and girls. There's no status in being a shamba-boy for Jessie Bell.'

Michael sipped his tea. 'Will you tell me — right from the beginning? . . . There m . . . must have been a beginning?'

Jessie sighed. 'We used to go to the pictures every week, before the war. Errol Flynn, Douglas Fairbanks. Now, they were what I call handsome.'

'Did Olivia live here with you? Was th . . . this where she was born?'

Jessie would not be diverted. 'Gareth Jones had the same looks. Like a film-star. We all said so, with his moustache and his smart clothes. There was a run on lipstick. Rimmel we had then, it was the best we could get.'

'Who was Gareth Jones?'

'Who was he?' Jessie looked up in surprise. 'Why, he was Eugenie's husband.'

'He was Olivia's f . . . father?'

'Yes, dear.' Jessie drained her tea cup and put it down on the saucer. 'Of course.' The old lady frowned. 'Did she really tell you so little? Have you really come all this way, knowing so little?'

'I know almost n . . . nothing. I could never keep track.' He paused to finish his tea and put down the cup. 'Olivia t . . . took me there — ' He paused again. Should he tell her this? Would she want to hear?

'Where, dear?'

'To Castleton. To see Eugenie.'

Jessie touched her collar, smoothed it flat against her neck. 'Is it a nice place? I've heard it is.'

'Nice?'

'I mean she's not kept locked up.' Jessie Bell raised an eyebrow. 'Olivia told me they have a garden. Eugenie is allowed to grow flowers, she said.'

'I didn't see any flowers.'

'It must be better than the place where she was out here. Here she was kept behind bars. And such lunatics with her — blacks as well. It broke my heart.'

They sat in silence for a moment and then Jessie said, 'Would you like some more tea?'

'No. Thank you. Why did he come here?'

'Who?'

'Her father. What was he doing in Africa?'

'They were building the bridge over the creek. He was studying engineering — far too old to be still learning. But so they all were then, in the years after the war.'

Jessie smiled. ' 'That boy will break a few hearts.' We all said it — we said it from the day he arrived. He was a handsome man. No doubt about it.'

She sank back into her chair. 'No-one thought of Eugenie. She was still a child — just out of school. Still running about. 'I'm growing my nails,' she would say. As if she could will them to grow. She meant to stop biting them, so that she could use her mother's varnish, just as she used her lipstick. Her mother was my brother's wife. I didn't approve of lipstick. Nor did her mother. But there seemed little harm in it. She was only a child.

'Then she started staying out. She painted her nails and came home with beer on her breath. When my brother — her father — threatened to beat her she didn't cry; didn't try to run. She turned her face and stared him out. That was when we knew we'd lost.'

Jessie paused. Michael waited. He could hear her breath, a bubble of saliva on her lip. Down on the beach someone was laughing.

'Eugenie stared her father out. Stamped her feet in front of her mother. She wore us all down with her wilfulness, running round in a tight skirt, scarlet nails, people saw her going off into the bush with him. She would come home late and sometimes not at all. The wonder was that they got engaged. He'd had his cake, as far as we could see. There was no reason for a wedding, but he bought her a ring — a little opal of all things — an unlucky stone as everyone knows, but she wouldn't hear a word against it. Only when it was too late, the whole disastrous process too far gone to stop, did she see the folly of it, sense the dismay behind our brave wedding faces. She cried in her father's arms. Right here in this room. They came over, my brother and his wife. We had planned a little night-before get-together — to have her as our little Eugenie once more, before she became Mrs Gareth Jones.'

Jessie's voice faded. 'The child was crying before the sherry was poured — little sobs that would tear your heart. Even now I hear them. Casserole of chicken and rice, we had. Rice was a luxury then.

117

And trifle — real trifle — I baked the sponge myself. Three fresh eggs. And tinned cherries, and mango and chocolate drops on top in the shape of an 'E'. I remember it as if it were yesterday. And little Eugenie starting to cry. Something her mother said. A daughter's a daughter forever — that kind of thing. Harmless words but it set Eugenie off crying. A pitiful sound. We told her she needn't go through with the marriage. 'We'll stand by you.' Over and over. My brother grew impatient with it all. He sat out there with my husband — ' Her hand extended round the chair, pointing to the long verandah. 'They said they would leave it to the women — to her mother and me.'

Michael got up and walked across to the verandah door. He tried to picture the scene she described, the child bride weeping, the men on the verandah — and out in the kitchen the waiting servant, bowls of chicken and rice drying in the oven.

Behind him, Jessie had taken up the story once more. He stood with his back to her, listening, his eyes on the stones of the verandah wall; a centipede was moving vertically down the brick, its long body rippling and bulging like a tightly packed sausage.

'You can never know, can you?'

He could see Jessie's face reflected in the glass door. 'You can never foresee what will happen. 'Do you want me to forbid it?' my brother — her father — asked her. 'I can simply forbid the wedding.' She was below the age, you see. But it was no use. Despite her tears, despite the fear I believe she had already for the man, Eugenie wanted her wedding. She didn't want to give up the dress.'

Jessie shrank back against the chair, shaking her head. 'A whole life wasted, four children, years of misery — all for a twenty guinea dress.'

Minutes passed. The story wasn't finished. Jessie talked around it, gave glimpses of history, stories of people who had no interest for him. The elderly, wavering voice went on and on, the murmuring of a litany, as if she told these stories every day, regardless of her audience; as if, no-one else being there, she would have summoned the 'boy' Joseph, to sit where Michael had sat, or, more likely, stand, hovering in the shadow, himself a shadow in the long white robe, listening, waiting for his part, pieces of his own history to be gathered like pages scattered from a book.

There was a noise like the snuffle of a dog, a grunt. After a moment he realised that what he could hear was not a dog, but snoring, the old woman had fallen asleep.

His shoes squeaked on the tiles. He left the room and went down into the garden.

Below the lawn was the beach. Lines of seaweed on the sand marked the limits of the tides. Here, like brightly coloured litter, lay the tourists' playthings; the Africa his friends had described, glass bottomed boats, a fibreglass catamaran hauled up beyond the reach of the tide, shoals of wind-surfers scudding across the shallows, their sails like bright fins. Further out, the water was shadowed, smudges of grey and black, dappled with pools of pale green where beds of sand lay between ridges of seaweed and coral. The reef lay on the horizon, a streak of white paint between sky and sea.

Sandbags buttressed the end of the lawn, dividing the grass from the sand. Three or four hawkers had gathered near the water, crowding round a couple of tourists. They carried their wares in their hands: bracelets and necklaces, carved elephants and rhinos.

Taking off his shoes, Michael stepped down. Like fine white flour heaped upon a pastry board, the sand accommodated the push and twist of his feet. He circled the bargainers, moving quickly. Close to the water the sand was coarser grained. He stood in the shallows, letting his feet sink in. The sun was like a hot dry towel against his back.

Olivia had been here. She had been here with Jessie; stood here on this very spot, perhaps, her hair blowing freely, her skin turning brown in the warm sun.

He knew her so little! They'd had so short a time. Even to say he had known her was wrong. It could mean so many things. In the biblical way, it could mean he had known her body, had knowledge of her; this he did. In the cool of his bedroom, in the grey shady light of an English afternoon, he had known her, followed the curves of her limbs with his eyes and hands and tongue. But he had not 'known' her. The time had been too short. It took too long to start, to make the smallest progress towards knowledge — and yet he had drowned a little, lost himself in the deep well of her person, her senses, her history, finding with her, through his urgent, breathless need, a kind of communion, a relationship, a way of being utterly unlike anything in his experience, awakening a self he had never known or acknowledged.

'Jambo, bwana!'

Michael turned. A pair of hawkers had detached themselves from the other group. Metal bracelets were thrust into his hands, brass and steel and copper wire intertwined and polished — pretty things, too pretty for a man. He shook his head, tried to hand them back.

'Just have a look. Just lookee!'

'It's very pretty, but I don't want it.'

'Buy it for Mama.'

'Ma-ma has one already.'

'Mama has one like this?'

'She has t . . . two or three like this.'

It could have been true. Olivia could have bought one for herself from this same hawker — while she was staying with Jessie, while she was still safe.

He thrust the bracelet back into the man's hands. 'P . . . please take it back. I don't want it.'

The other one came forward, showing him how the tusks of a carved elephant could be detached for packing.

'Is that ivory?' Michael asked.

'Oh, no!' cried the hawker, his eyes wide with horror at the idea. 'If I sell ivory,' he made a gesture, bringing his wrists together, as if to show manacles. 'Many years.'

'What is it then?'

'Is bone, cow bone. Is like ivory, yes?'

'You take for your children?' said the other.

'I have n . . . no children,' said Michael.

'No children?'

'Where is Mama?' asked the first man.

'She is g . . . gone.'

'Mama is gone?' The hawker's face grew long, smiling lips pulled down over his teeth. 'Where is she gone?'

Michael shrugged. The persistence of their questions, their blunt, innocent enquiry, dragged the answer from him. 'I don't k . . . know. She is lost. I have lost her.'

They looked at one another and then at Michael. Their hands were held out to him, burdened with merchandise, the gesture showing their dismay, their sadness.

'Where are you looking?' asked the first.

'Everywhere,' said Michael. 'No-one can t . . . tell me where to begin.'

The hawkers responded together, a 'tusk-tsk' sound.

'Is a bad thing,' said the younger one.

'But I will find her,' said Michael.

The hawkers smiled once more. The first man, using his free hand, tapped Michael's shoulder. Michael found himself smiling in return.

'If she is to find,' said the younger hawker, 'Jesus Christ will help you.'

The other one nodded. 'Bahati nzuri!'

Michael shook his head. 'I d . . . don't understand.'

'Bahati nzuri. Good luck. God goes with you.'

Michael smiled again and they left him, hastening to approach a pair of girls, shiny with sun oil, wading through the shallows. Michael went on into the sea, continuing until the water came as high as his shorts. Olivia was here, he thought, such a little time ago, here in this almost-paradise, here she had been safe.

★ ★ ★

Late in the afternoon, Jessie resumed as though she had never ceased, as though the interruption had never occurred, not the dog-like snore, nor the coming out to find Michael walking back across the beach-lawn with sand clinging to his wet feet. 'I think it's time we had another cup of tea.'

He walked towards the house.

'No. Not there. We'll have it out on the grass — in the shade.'

Joseph carried the chairs out, settling them with the backs to the sea breeze so that, sitting beside her, Michael could see, not the beach and the sea and the white line of the reef, but Jessie's house, the overhang of bougainvillaea, showing fresh scars from the panga.

She leaned forward, shaking her finger. 'They were crazy by then, of course, both of them.'

Michael frowned. 'Who?'

Her finger touched his face. 'My niece Eugenie. She was as crazy as the other one that day, screaming for the boy to shut the gate.'

Michael settled back, rested his hands on his knees.

'She went for the blade with her hands — as if it could not harm her. It was the dog who turned on Joseph. Trained only to bite blacks, you see. All the screaming frightened him, made him vicious. Joseph went to close the gate as he was bidden, the dog went for Joseph and Eugenie took the panga.

'You can see it, can't you? That blade leaping in the sun? But it is this — ' Jessie's finger waved in front of Michael's face. 'This is the part that we found so hard to bear. David went to the aid of the dog. He did not try to help his mother. Just a nine year old boy — the dog was something he could understand. He pulled on that silver stud collar until the dog let Joseph go.' She paused for breath. 'Joseph has the scar still. Did you see it?' She twisted round in her chair to point to the base of her throat. 'Here, a big bite mark.'

Michael nodded, not wishing to interrupt. Patiently, resisting the urge to speak sharply, to insist on chronology, he prompted. 'So David went to help Joseph, and not his mother?'

'Neither of his mothers.' Jessie's head waved slowly against the back of the chair. 'Neither June nor Eugenie. He helped pull the dog off the servant while his mother lay dying.'

The verandah door banged. A rattle of cups. Afternoon tea. Joseph came across the lawn with a tray. A teapot, cups, sugar and milk. Returning to the house, he came back with a plate of drop scones, still warm, spread with butter.

Jessie folded the white circles of dough to fit them between her lips.

'Eat something, young man. These are the only cakes he can make.'

'Did you teach him to cook?'

'No.' A mouthful of scone. 'It was June. But she never was one for cakes. Fattening.'

'June was David's mother?'

124

'No!' Butter dropping onto the grass. 'No. June was not his natural mother.'

Jessie pressed the napkin to the corner of her lips. A smear of lipstick and butter appeared on the starched cloth. 'Eugenie gave him birth. It was my niece who gave him birth.' She pointed to the house. 'I have the certificate.'

Michael sighed. 'I wish you would tell me from the beginning.'

The last of the scones disappeared.

'Would you like some more tea?'

Michael shook his head.

'I will tell you, right from the beginning. But you'll have to be patient. I have guests for dinner. Two of my oldest friends — practically the only ones still alive. They'll be here as soon as the sun goes down.' She put her empty cup on the tea table. 'I hope they won't bore you. There are so few people left.'

During the interval before dinner Michael wrote a letter to his father, an epistle of hopeless complaint — the shortness of the sheets on his hotel bed, the sickly sweet smell of the local soap. *I have never felt so useless, so entirely out of my depth and unable to make any difference. I no longer know why I am here.*

14

'Good morning, Harry!' Darren let the door slam behind him.

'You're late again.'

The boy moved towards him, grinning; utterly indifferent to Harry's feeble reprimand, he pointed to a pink carnation in his lapel. 'What do you think that's for?'

'I've no idea.'

'Carnations? Buttonholes?' Darren clicked his fingers and did a little pirouette. 'Top hats and monkey suits?'

Harry put down his pen. 'Are you — is somebody getting married?'

'Right first time!'

'You, Darren? Are you getting married?'

'Don't look so alarmed.'

'But you're so — young, I — ' Harry stood up. 'Forgive me — ' He held out his hand. 'Congratulations!'

Darren grinned. 'I told you I had something on my mind.'

From the breast pocket of his oversized suit, he extracted a photograph in a heart-shaped cardboard frame. Harry was shown the face of a girl, smiling. 'Her name's Debbie.'

'She's very pretty, Darren . . . I hope you'll be happy.'

'They're Catholics — that's why it's a bit of a

rush.' Darren came round the desk. 'She's a bit
— in the family way. You know?'

'I see,' said Harry, coughing lightly to hide his
dismay.

'Will you come then?'

'Come?'

'To the wedding. Three weeks on Saturday. I've
told her all about you.' Full of confidence, the
boy sniggered, 'I've told her you growl but you
never bite.'

Awkwardly Harry rose to his feet and held out
his hand. 'Thank you, Darren. I'd be delighted to
come.'

'What about — is there a Mrs Crane?'

Harry shook his head.

'Or someone you could bring? It's Debbie's
mum, you see. She wants to keep the tables
even.'

'I'll try and think of someone.'

'Great!' Darren swaggered out. Harry slipped
back into his chair. He rubbed his eyes. A wedding
in haste. He could hear Darren's voice in the next
room, high and coarse with excitement. The print
room boys were laughing, as they would laugh at
the wedding, at the speeches, the well-worn jokes.

May all your troubles be little ones.

To the patter of tiny feet.

Over and over.

★ ★ ★

How inevitable it had seemed, that children would
follow. The bridal veil ready for the christening, the

top layer of the wedding cake preserved in a tin.

'It'll get better. Fruit cake keeps for years. All the better for waiting.'

June's wedding cake had developed a fine dusting of mould. For years it had waited, a tin perched on the top shelf of the larder, mocking them; spoiling their happiness. It was as if, with the layer of the cake left uneaten, the wedding itself was incomplete, the perfect day suspended, unfinished. The wedding portrait showed a pink, breezy carpet on the steps of the church; sunlight through the pure white lace of June's dress. Blossom instead of rice. June had turned to him, her veil billowing around her face, oblivious of the aunts, of his mother's hat poking itself between them, oblivious of all but the smile she had to give him, the smile of a bride holding out her hand, newly beringed, nails and lips in the same bright innocent pink. This is all of me, this is our beginning.

Harry rubbed his eyes again. So sweet she had been, pausing at the threshold of that first house in Kileleshwa, a roof of corrugated iron, no garage and just a stable door from the kitchen to the garden. He had carried her inside, laughing, careless. Even the cockroaches had made her laugh. They were married, they loved one another, what could harm them?

Six years. People stopped asking.

They went to the family doctor. To a specialist. Another specialist. Home on leave. Two days in a private clinic. Presenting himself behind a drawn green curtain, a test-tube of hard work and stifled shame. Thermometers, calendars. June's voice in the darkness, demanding: 'It has to be today! Today is the day. How can you fail me today?' The test-tube became easier than his wife.

The fifth long leave saw the end of it. June was thirty-nine. The last specialist. The last course of drugs, of investigation, his body failing on the rubber sheet.

And then the girl on the boat. Another mouth on the way that she could not feed. The idea turning in their hearts, separately. 'So much better than an anonymous baby.' It was June who said it. 'So much better to know who the parents are — to see the other children of the marriage healthy and strong — and white.'

She urged him on. 'There'll be no formalities — interviews. No-one to tell us we're inadequate, or too old, or that if we were real Christians we would take a child of mixed blood.'

Anonymous adoption would have been easy. The colony had hundreds of children. The flood of new arrivals had produced a crop of unwanted, half-white children. It became June's special horror. 'We could take one and not know. It doesn't always show. Sometimes the features develop as the child matures. There've been cases down South, families divided. It can even skip a generation. We could get brown-skinned grand-children.'

★ ★ ★

Darren came back, leered close to Harry's desk. 'The boys and me are going down The Lamb at lunchtime.' He grinned, eyes bright with friendship. 'Are you coming?'

Harry blinked. 'The Lamb?'

'The pub on the corner. They do ploughman's and that. We'll have a bite and a pint — to celebrate.'

Harry forced himself to smile. 'You won't mind if I don't will you — ?'

'You don't want to come down the pub?'

'Not today. I've really got too much to do, but here — ' Harry extracted a note from his wallet. 'Buy a round of drinks for me. And take your time. I won't watch the clock.'

'Thanks, Harry!'

The boy went out whistling . . .

★ ★ ★

Her wedding ring had been returned; a brown envelope, sealed and, as if someone at the mortuary had given a thought to its value, stapled, so that Harry pricked his finger prising it open. Her clothes too, were returned. A paper parcel, a printed tag. Like a present. All the parcels of childhood, the excitement of string and Sellotape but inside, just the wedding ring and her clothes, laundered.

The servant's wound took weeks to heal. His hospital bed had Harry's name on the clip-board at the foot, in case anyone should challenge the boy for payment. When at last he was discharged, Joseph joined the throng who slept on the grass in City Park, unemployed, without a reference, until one day Jessie took pity on him, gave him a job in her own home at the coast, a world away from Lavington Green. The gardener too had gone; hurried away across the valley, afraid of the bad blood of Harry Crane's house. The grass grew long, trampled by feet that paused to stare and, seeing no resistance, trespassed, staring, pointing at the verandah, the gate, the long-obliterated marks in the dust; noting with a certain glee Harry's shirts on the line by the kitchen door, inadequately washed.

They came for her clothes; the young ayahs from the Green, hovering at the back door, shy at first, like young does. Her wardrobe was handed out, dresses and nightclothes, her slippers, even her thick winter coat that she kept for the journey Home. David's ayah took a month's pay in her brown fingers, tucked the notes into a hidden fold of her dress and slipped off without a word, without a single inquiry for the boy whom she had nursed from his first days. Slipped off with the other women and then dawdled, the shyness gone, by the gate, June's handbag dangling over her arm.

'Personal call for you, Mr Crane.' He remembered his slight irritation. He had asked June not to call him at work.

A phone call in the afternoon. All the structures and order of his life unravelled by the simple ringing of a bell. The mad, helter-skelter drive through the outskirts of the city. Swinging blindly into Lavington Road, a boy on a bicycle, almost run down, his pedal clipped by the white man's car fishtailing onto the grass verge. Running in, through the open gate, past the labrador, growling, muzzled, demented eyes on Harry; past the crowds of men — the servants of neighbours, ayahs, people from the compound, as if the whole district had abandoned its life for a glimpse of the police car, the ambulance, a panga in a plastic bag, the bag as bloody as a bag of lights from the butcher for the dog. A chalk outline on the verandah floor.

Pieces of Lego in the dust; red and white bricks half trodden in, an open box, a torn paper bag.

David sitting on the step, resting his chin in his fists.

'Hello Dad.'

Harry sat beside him on the step. Afterwards he would find a circle of red polish on the seat of his trousers, and splashes of another, darker colour.

'It wasn't her fault, Dad. It wasn't Mum's fault, it wasn't . . . I should have said: No, thank you. She told me I should be polite and say: No, thank you. But — ' David looked up, his eyes screwed against the sun. 'I wanted the Lego. Everyone talks about it at school. James got it when they went to England. He's built a big garage, with a car wash and everything, like they have in America. I wanted it, Dad. James always has everything first.'

Harry smoothed the boy's head, the dark, curled hair that was neither his nor June's but a relic of Gareth Jones, just as the eyes that looked so fierce now, with fear and fright, were the eyes of the girl who had been waiting that day when he had gone back about the guns.

David had a piece of white Lego in his hand, biting the corner. 'It wasn't her fault, Dad. It wasn't Mum's fault.'

Harry's courage failed him. He did not ask the question that begged itself. 'Which Mummy, David? Which of your mothers is not to blame?'

Harry went back into the sun; through the scatter of people on the drive, eyes that turned away as he approached. The box lay in the dust by the unclosed gate, its contents spilled like a scatter of sweets. He knelt in the fine red murram and gathered the plastic bricks, one by one, placing them carefully in the box. When he could find no more he replaced the lid and carried it back, through the white-eyed crowd to the little boy waiting on the step. Late in the night, when the crowds had gone, the police with their notebooks and their bloody bag of evidence, Harry wept; long racking tears for his June, his beloved girl. And through the silence of the house there came the rattle of model cars on the wooden floor and a hissing sound imitating a car wash, like they had in America.

Dolland and Black wanted a fight. Harry Crane became a familiar visitor to the offices of the lawyers in Government Road. The case of the white woman, the 'ex-pat' murdered by another, had advanced the practice — and that of the young barrister sweating in his robes.

'We'll keep your son for you, Mr Crane.'

'I do not want a fight.'

Disappointment in the young barrister's eyes. Dolland's hands shifting.

'But surely — ?'

'David is not my son. It was wrong from the start. I was wrong to permit it.'

'But what is to become of him?'

It was Dolland that spoke. Grey haired, the lawyer had seemed so old to Harry then, the jacket of his suit on the back of a chair, a sweat stain just visible on the lining of the armpit. 'He is your adopted son.'

'No,' said Harry. 'The adoption was a fraud. You said so yourself. He has a father of his own.'

'Jones?' It was the young barrister, forgetting himself, as so many did in the course of the trial, blood running high in the court-room. 'Jones has forfeited any right — '

'It is I who have forfeited the right.'

'But you have a strong case. The Court will rule for the boy's best interests. Yours is the only home he has known. You have been a good father to him. A drunk father and an insane mother cannot compete with you.'

'No!' The palms of his hands stung from the impact. Meru oak, french polished. 'I have been no father to him. Only a keeper. It is all we were doing, really — keeping him for Eugenie.' Harry put his stinging hands against his cheeks, felt the stubble there, the slip of appearances. 'I have no servants, no gardener. My swimming pool is covered with leaves.'

'But these are small things, Mr Crane. The servants will come back once the trial is over.'

'But not the boy. He will not come back.'

'Of course he will. He told his Case Officer — '

'What?' Harry's voice was harsh. 'That he liked the swimming pool? That he loved his dog? That we gave him everything he wanted?' Harry sat down again, slumped in the chair. 'Except Lego. Did he mention the Lego?'

Dolland raised an eyebrow. 'Pardon — ?'

'That was what she brought. That was what he wanted. And we didn't know! We did not know the smallest wish of his heart. But she did.'

'Yes, but — you would not have wanted to spoil the child. You would not have bought him the Lego simply because he asked for it.'

'That isn't the point. The point is that we didn't know it was important. But Eugenie did. His own mother knew. She saw the gap in all the good things we showered upon him. The school fees, the toys — in the end it was she who knew what he really wanted.'

'His mother is on a murder charge. His father is a drunk. If you will not have him the boy will be made a ward of court.'

The lawyers watched him pace the room. 'I am to be posted back to England — I am an embarrassment to my employers. The boy will stay here. Eugenie is here. That at least I can do for him and for her. I shall sell my house. The money can go into trust for him. He can stay here and go to school. He will want for nothing and when she is better, when she is released, they will be reunited.'

The papers made much of it.

UNWANTED BOY — WHO WILL TAKE LITTLE DAVY JONES?

Davy Jones. The name rang better than 'Crane'. Fitted better with the story. CRANE ABANDONS LITTLE DAVY.

There was no mention of the money, the proceeds of the house that Dolland and Black held as trustees; money for the boarding school, for the priests. Harry received an annual report. Invested in gold mines and Government stocks, in the manufacturers of washing machines and household soaps, the trust fund prospered. The reports came on airmail paper, typed on a manual machine. Erasures made a hole in the paper.

Later, when the boy went into senior school, the accounts became more formal, bound in coloured card, with a covering letter from the senior assistant solicitor, James Karanja LLB.

Recently Harry had seen an obituary in *The Times*. Dolland was dead. Black had gone south. The firm of Karanja and Co (incorporating Dolland and Black) had taken another floor of office space in the building on Government Road. Now the accounts were sporadic. The paper faintly dusty. The gold shares languished. A letter came from James Karanja LLB. What should they do? David had moved up north. Messages were received, occasional letters, asking for money; sometimes a shopping list as well . . . 'We cannot provide this service, Mr Crane. You must make another arrangement.'

15

Laughter, church bells: rose petals scattered for Corpus Christi, a procession of little girls in white, silver bells ringing.

Fingers pinched her skin. She screamed. The bells were tin cans; a sea of goats, hundreds, even thousands. Three boys laughing at her. She held her hands out to them, begging: white hands smeared black with ashy dust.

Milk from a gourd, thin and sour. At first it came back, spurting from her throat onto the ground. She drank again and it stayed, a warm sticky liquid soothing the parched places of her mouth, running down, like a cold fire into her stomach. The boys moved away from her. She drifted asleep to the sound of their voices, arguing. Then they came back. A rattle of bracelets. She was lifted and bundled, her face against a blanket that smelled of grease and dung. The one who carried her walked very fast, as if her weight on his shoulder was nothing but another blanket that slipped from time to time, pushed back, ignored.

Intermittently she slept, descending into dreams, periods of blackness from which she woke to a pounding pain in her head, the world seen through a red gauze, sweat in her hair.

'Please put me down. Let me rest. Please.'

The boy sang to himself, a long monotonous ballad. And there were times when he whistled, *the high sound of it merging with the sounds in her head, her thin, tight screams.*

When darkness came she was laid on the ground. The boy lit a fire and sat watching her, his stick propped between his knees.

Early on the third day he patted her face until she opened her eyes. He pointed. In the distance a cluster of huts. Relief drained the last of her energy. By the time of the coming in she had slipped back into sleep. She did not see the bed that was made for her on the packed earth floor; the lighting of the fire, a glow of charcoal in the corner. She was brought to consciousness by the sprinkling of strange bitter tea on her skin. It burned and she cried out and the old woman who nursed her, hissed. Then the feeling went and she became numb. Time floated away.

★ ★ ★

Jessie's guests arrived at sundown. Flora's hair was the same as Jessie's, grey-white and thinly curled; her dress too, was the same, a shapeless shift of printed cotton. Michael had the impression that Jessie had summoned them. Look, I have someone to show you.

Colonel Bingham took charge — as if Jessie herself was the guest.

'What are you drinking, young man?'

He had no chance to answer. Flora was coming towards him, her lipstick had spread into the fine creases above her lips. The effect was of a bloody starburst.

'We read about you in the papers!'

Michael nodded.

'Have you been up there? Have you joined the search?'

'The p . . . police won't let me. They s . . . s . . . they said they didn't want the liability.'

'But have they looked — really?'

'There have been three aerial searches — ' said Jessie.

'Three? They sent up three planes?'

'That's what they say.'

Michael rubbed his face. His throat felt constricted. 'They found nothing. Not even a trace. They think the van has gone over the border.'

'And Olivia with it?'

'They don't know. They have searched on the ground. Interviewed people. There is nothing there. Nowhere to begin the search.'

'He has come to me for a rest.' Jessie clapped her hands lightly, as if to indicate the end of the topic. 'He came down on the train — didn't you, Michael?'

'First class?' asked the Colonel.

Michael nodded.

'Not quite what you thought it would be?'

'It was all right.'

'It used to be something, that railway. Everybody travelled on it,' said Flora.

'It was — interesting.'

'Filthy, though.'

Michael paused. There seemed, in the Binghams' remarks, an obscure conspiracy. As if, in any services provided by Africans, he should acknowledge nothing but failure. The attitude was familiar, he knew dozens of people who thought like the Binghams. His own father, his sisters. He himself had objected when the first black trainee had been recruited by the bank. And yet faced with these old memsahibs he felt a curious surge of rebellion. 'The sh . . . sheets were clean.'

Flora nodded. 'You still get the linen all right. It's the trains — should have been in a scrap yard long ago. That rolling stock came second-hand, from India. From India!' Her voice rose. 'India that never threw away the smallest thing until it was used beyond use. These fools paid money for second-hand carriages. Imagine how many palms were greased?'

Michael was silent. She was wrong. The basin in his compartment, worn as it was, with base metal showing through the chrome, still had the initials of the old East African Railway stamped between the push-down taps. The basin was as old as the compartment. He wondered where the Indian story had come from, and why they told it. Were all these people's stories so flawed?

Once again, Jessie redirected the conversation. 'He wants to marry Olivia.'

Flora beamed.

'I have to find her first.'

The Colonel patted his back. 'You mustn't wait for the police. In this country, if you want something put right you've got to do it yourself. Why, only last week . . . '

'And she jolly well should marry you,' Jessie interrupted. 'After all you've done.'

'I don't think she'd see it quite like that,' said Michael.

The Colonel thrust a glass into Michael's hand. It was almost full of whisky to which the merest drop of water had been added.

'Bad business. All those Jones children — trouble with every one of them.'

'What do you mean?'

The Colonel took a swallow of whisky. His moustache was wet at the ends. 'She used to stay with Jessie here, in this very house. A nervous little thing. A row of dolls on the verandah, that's what I remember.'

Flora Bingham laughed. 'With a neat piece of lavatory paper over each one for a sheet. Eugenie liked to play hospitals. It was what she always wanted to be — a nurse.'

Jessie held out a dish. 'Cashews?'

Michael shook his head.

The Colonel took a handful of the nuts and began to flick them, one at a time, into his mouth. 'Then she got married. Barely sixteen, it was a scandal.'

Jessie wagged a finger, swallowing a mouthful of whisky. 'I've told Michael already how she cried that night. Sitting just where you are now, a little slip of a thing.'

'But it was a lovely wedding.' Flora's voice was hushed.

Jessie swallowed her drink. 'Then there she was in the morning, after all those tears, looking as fresh as a rose.'

'Pregnant,' said Flora.

Jessie cleared her throat. 'It's the truth, though none of us knew it at the time.'

'There were those of us who suspected it.' Flora held out her glass to the Colonel. 'Do me a refill, will you?' She turned to Michael. 'Seven months later that baby was born.'

'David?'

'Oh, no,' said Jessie. 'David was the last. She had three before him. One after another, Regina and Dennis. Your Olivia was the third. Poor little mites.'

The Colonel poured an inch of whisky into Flora's glass. 'The man was a brute,' he said. 'Though I dare say she provoked him.'

Flora shook her head. 'The children had bruises too.'

'Not as bad as their mother's.'

'I used to say I'd go to the police,' Jessie sighed. 'But I never did. No-one likes to interfere.'

'He was a drunk.' The Colonel bit into a nut. 'There's no point beating about the bush. Gareth Jones was a drunk.'

Jessie's voice rose, as though she was answering an accusation. 'We clubbed together, all the family, to pay the fares back to England. We thought she should get away, that the children would be better off if she went home. And she was! She was all right! She finished her nurses' training. Nice little council flat off the Walworth Road, a job in Guy's Hospital. But she threw it all up for him. That was the power he had — '

'When he was sober!'

'Yes, when he was sober. She threw it all up.

Wrote to us that he'd found another job out here, that they were reconciled, that she'd never been so happy. She took the children out of the free school, surrendered the council flat. All for a promise.'

'And another baby.' Flora let out a sigh.

'David?'

'Yes,' said the Colonel. 'But it wasn't Eugenie who named him. It was Harry and June Crane who named him David.'

Michael leaned back, distancing himself from their voices, the stridence of Jessie, the continuous interruptions from her guests. He tried to unravel the story, the names he had heard. Eugenie — Olivia's mother. Dennis and Regina and David — her brothers and sister; her father, the father of them all — Gareth Jones. Then Harry and June, about whom there was no information.

From the dining room came a clatter of plates.

'Joseph?' Jessie's call was loud and harsh.

'Memsahib?'

The servant had put a red cummerbund around the white robe, white cotton gloves, and on his feet, green plastic sandals.

'Is it ready?'

'Soon.'

'Hurry up then, we don't want it at midnight.'

Joseph inclined his head and withdrew.

'Did Jessie tell you Joseph still has the scar?'

'Yes.'

'Right across here.' The Colonel spread his hands over his chest, leaving a trail of nut grease on his white shirt.

'I thought it was his throat.'

143

'His throat — that's nothing. It's his chest you should see.' The Colonel leaned forward. 'If it wasn't for young David, it would have been curtains for the boy.'

'But David should have gone to help June,' said Jessie. 'He should have tried to stop what happened. June was more important than the servant!'

Joseph reappeared at the door.

'Is it ready?' Jessie eased herself out of the armchair. 'I hope you haven't burnt the lamb. I keep telling him it's not pork, we don't want crackling, but he will turn up the stove.'

Michael sat beside Jessie. Flora was opposite, the Colonel took the place of Jessie's long dead husband, at the head of the table. They continued to talk, interrupting one another; each following his or her thread of the story. Michael could hardly bear to listen. There was no love here, for Olivia. These people were centred upon the past, on a Eugenie who was no more — dolls on the verandah, a tangle of lives and a twenty guinea dress.

The lamb was burned. Michael turned over the slice on his plate. Charred on one side and raw pink on the other. The Colonel pulled a piece of gristle from between his teeth.

'You can't buy good lamb these days,' said Jessie. 'The hotels take it all — so the visitors will go home and say the country is doing well. The people who live here can't get it — that good lamb that we used to buy.'

'It's the same with the water. The hotels along the shore have auxiliary pumps. All the fresh water goes up there; the local people are left high and dry.'

The rest of the food went cold while they talked, the joint on the side-board congealed. Joseph was summoned to take away the plates. Pudding was puree of mangoes with cream.

'Thank God for the garden,' said Jessie. 'At least he can't ruin a mango.'

Why does she do it, Michael asked himself, rolling the chilled fruit against his tongue. Joseph was the most important person in her life; her best friend, it could be said. But she had begun to complain as soon as the guests arrived, speaking of the servant as if he were a child, errant, unteachable. At the end of the meal Jessie made a show of giving Joseph the remains of the lamb.

'You shouldn't spoil him,' said Flora.

'He knows how far he can go,' said Jessie.

They trailed back into the sitting room for coffee. A string of meat had lodged itself between Michael's teeth. As he tried, discreetly, to pull it away he looked up to see Jessie watching him, chuckling.

16

Olivia dreamed, shivered, sweated. Every part of her body was on fire. The thin sounds of the desert reverberated in her head as if her head were the box of a fine violin: a cicada in the hump of yellow grass that grew beside the hut; the cry of goats tethered inside the stockade. The woman brought her herbal brews, shreds of leaf lingered on her tongue.

'Marie-Therese. Marie-Therese.' Long, crack-nailed fingers thrust the mouth of a gourd between her lips.

The bibi's name had come lately to her ears — singled out of the gabble, the natter and babble that accompanied the old woman's coming in, the handfuls of fine sand that were used to gather up, as matter-of-fact as a nurse, the mess that Olivia made; to give her a kind of bath, a rub down with the sand, and feed her, like a baby, warm goat's milk, mixed with blood, a drop at a time from a plastic beaker with THERMOS imprinted on the base.

It was Eugenie who brought her tea. Her head shaved, patches of plaster on her scalp.

Mummy?

The tea came out of her mouth coloured pink and brown, crushed strawberry creams.

Regina was behind the dukha, her blouse undone. There was a line where her bra had been. A man had his hand inside. A spiral notebook jutted out of his hip pocket. When he saw Olivia he offered her a piece of gum. 'Did your Daddy ever hit you, dear?'

Aunt Jessie's breath smelled of tea. Scones cooling under a tea towel. 'Your mother isn't herself, dear.'

If not herself, then who?

Telegrams on the mantel-shelf. Doves cooing in the neighbours' gardens; breathy, woodwind music, endlessly repeated.

'We should sue that teacher. He had no right to encourage the boy.'

Regina's sharp voice, gum like a false tongue against her teeth, eyes as red as her lips. 'It wasn't the teacher who made him jump ship.'

'That's enough from you.'

'My brother is dead. I shall say what I like.'

A pin-board in the kitchen. 'That's your little brother, David. Isn't he a lovely boy?' As if David was a film star.

'Dennis is my brother,' said Regina.

'Dennis is gone, dead. He went to your father. He went bad and was punished for it.'

The motorbike posters still hung in his room. The crash-helmet hanging on the wall was Dennis's empty head. Regina said she liked motorbikes. There was hair between her thighs. Olivia remembered the shock. Hair between her sister's thighs and her brother's head hanging empty on the wall.

Bits of leaf and twig banged against her lips. She could not swallow. The tea was a wet stain on her chest. She felt light, floating, all her body flowing

*out of her into the soft sand of the hut, leaving
only her burned empty skin.*

*Marie-Therese came back, hissing and clicking.
The old woman was wrinkled and dirty, like an
elephant that has bathed in dust against the flies.
She brought water; held her head as Olivia was sick,
wiped the sweat from her face with the hem of her
wrap. She kept the other women away. Olivia saw
them intermittently, horrified faces keeping their
distance, one who was pregnant and another with
a child at her breast.*

★ ★ ★

It was past midnight. There was a flurry of kissing,
the Colonel slapped Michael's back.

'I'm sure you'll find her, my boy. I'm sure
you will.'

Flora's lips were wet on his cheeks. 'You'll have
her back for Christmas. I'm sure of it.'

The white dust raised by their car hung in the
moonlight like a mist over the drive. Michael
carried a tray of dirty coffee cups into the kitchen.
The servant sat on a hard chair by the door,
fast asleep. Quietly, Michael put the tray on
the draining board and returned to the sitting
room. Jessie had settled herself on the sofa by
the window.

'You've been very patient, Michael.' She patted
the worn upholstery.

'Joseph is still in the kitchen.'

'He'll go when he's finished.'

'He's fallen asleep in there, on the chair.'

'I dare say he has.' Once more Jessie patted the sofa. 'He's an old cat-napper like me.'

Michael sat down beside her. 'Can't he go to bed now?'

'He will, he'll finish clearing up and he'll go. Now, where was I?'

'You were t . . . telling me about them coming back. Eugenie returning to Africa.'

Jessie stared out at the garden. The windows were open, letting in the warm night air and the distant shushing of the sea. When she spoke, her voice was faint, as if she were speaking from a long way off. 'Eugenie was good to those children you know. She used to make all their clothes. You'd never guess they were so hard up — to see Regina and Olivia in their little frocks with ribbons to match. It was term-time. Eugenie's three were the only children on the boat. The stewards spoiled them with sweets and ice-cream and fizzy drinks from the bar. Dennis was already tall, almost ten years old, wearing a tie to escort his mother into first sitting at dinner. He had his father's good looks, that boy.' She touched Michael's arm. 'Gareth wasn't there with them, of course. He'd gone on ahead, once Eugenie had given her promise — that she would throw it all up for him — the free school and the council flat — that she would come back on the boat and join him. It was Eugenie who did all the packing, worried about the tickets and not having enough cash for all the extras they would need on the trip. They used to come via Suez in those days. The Canal was open. It was something of a holiday. Duty free drink, swimming pools and kiddies' rooms. The only thing people complained of was seasickness — and Italian apples. Ever had one?'

Michael started. 'What?'

'An Italian apple.'

'I'm not sure — '

'They look pretty enough, shiny red skins and so forth. But they taste like cardboard.'

'I'll remember that.'

Jessie nodded to herself. Her fingers drifted to the beads around her neck, counting them, like a rosary. 'She must have known, though. She must have known before the storm they had, crossing the Med, when she was more sick than the others. She would have known before the ship's surgeon told her, this being her fourth — that another child was coming.'

Jessie turned to face him. 'That was why she'd given it all up. The flat and the free school and the job at Guy's. The reconciliation had borne fruit. So she gave it all up. She told me she spent most of the time on deck. You get less sick up there. The children would be out of sight, making mischief somewhere, tanned as brown as little berries. You can see it, can't you, a single woman, still less than thirty, alone on a deck-chair?

'They met after Aden. Years later, when she came down for a week with the children — a happy week, before she was really ill, before Dennis went — we drank a bottle of wine together and she told me the whole story.' Jessie sighed. 'But you can't know, can you? You can't know how things will turn out.'

'After Aden?'

150

'Aden, yes. It was after Aden. The bum-boats had been round, flogging leather pouffes and Rolex watches. She'd bought a watch for Jones, despite having so little. A present for Jones. It was Dennis who wore it. It went with him . . . Genie never saw that watch again. When his possessions were returned to her, just a bag in the post, there was no watch. Perhaps Jones had it after all. Perhaps Dennis had been keeping it for his father all that time.'

Michael rubbed his face, stifling a yawn. The story of the watch was unrelated. He touched Jessie's arm. 'What happened on the ship?'

'Boat, dear. You call it a boat.'

He suppressed a smile.

'They'd left the port behind. All the passengers were on deck to escape the heat. There was no air conditioning in those days, cabins like ovens. Anyway, it was there, up on the deck, that Harry and June befriended her.'

Jessie turned her beads. 'They were coming back from long leave. Nice people. He was some kind of civil servant. They had a house out at Lavington Green. Few people bought in those days. Only the farmers tended to buy. Everyone else rented. There was a lot of moving about — people coming and going on leave. But June Crane had a little money — from her parents I believe. She was the type to have parents with money. They bought a house. Not too big, but it had a wonderful garden. Harry had plans for a swimming pool, if he got his promotion.'

Jessie paused, nodding. 'Nice people. No-one

151

would have said otherwise, not then. Later they did. Later they called Harry Crane everything under the sun — heartless, cruel — you name it. But it was unfair. They were as much victims as Eugenie. And on that boat they were nothing but kind. June bought Eugenie fruit juice and little nibbles to tempt her appetite. Harry played cards with Dennis and Regina, and badminton. It was Harry who taught Dennis to swim. They were so kind, so pleased at her news, encouraging her to be pleased though she was less than — even despite buying him a Rolex, despite his promise.

'I did believe — I still do — there was no malice in the Cranes; no envy. Even when, innocently enough, Eugenie asked about Harry and June having children of their own. Even after that they were kind.'

Jessie pushed herself off the sofa. 'This talk is making me thirsty. Joseph!'

'I'll get it. He must have gone to bed by now, it's one o'clock.'

'As late as that?' Jessie puffed. 'Even so, Joseph can bring it. He sleeps as little as I do these days.'

'I'll get it for you. What would you like?'

'Brandy.'

'Anything with it?'

'Soda, not too much.'

Michael poured the drink from a collection of bottles on the sideboard. He put the glass in her hand. 'Go on.'

Jessie was working her jaw, as if she wore false teeth that did not quite fit. A small clicking noise confirmed it.

to her own mother down here, who telephoned me. 'She's had a boy.' Her surprise even greater than mine. A fourth grandchild that we hadn't known was coming.' Jessie started to cough. 'We never understood why she made that call, why she broke the secret she'd been keeping. Perhaps she just wanted him acknowledged. Even knowing the agreement she had made, the pact. Perhaps she still wanted us to know.'

Coughing, Jessie turned to Michael, waving a hand, as if what she would say next was an aside, set apart from the main stream of the story. 'They're dead now, of course, my brother and his wife. I thank God — ' she coughed again. 'I thank God they did not live to see the rest. The shame would have killed them. Those press men were merciless. Pictures of the panga, the bloodstains, the white outline on the verandah. They even came here, wanting to know was this where she grew up? Was she a violent child? Did she have fits? I ask you. That harmless little Eugenie, playing on the verandah. Did she have fits?'

Jessie's voice had become hoarse. 'Seven and a half pounds. We never saw him. I never saw that boy close up until the day he gave evidence in court. She gave him away, traded him for a bungalow near the Drive-Inn; she signed the papers and put him into June's arms.'

'What about the father — Jones?'

Jessie shook her head. 'He never turned up. Not a word from him — June Crane had it all worked out. She showed herself to be a shrewd woman. Eugenie made a declaration to the registrar, that her husband had deserted her; that he was not the father of the child. There was no one to challenge her. A woman had come out on a ship, pregnant, with no man. She said 'Father Unknown' and so it was: 'Father Unknown'.

'The bungalow was fine. Harry had it painted, a lawn laid. There was furniture, simple but sufficient. The Cranes had kept their side of the bargain. But not Eugenie. The child flourished.

'We went up there. Her mother and I. We went up there for a month. I'll never forget it. There was nothing to be done, nothing but watch. She had begun a kind of madness. Our little Eugenie, my little niece, was living in squalor; the three children running wild, out of control. Regina was more out than in — short skirt, high heels, painted nails. She reminded me of Eugenie before the marriage — as if behaving badly is in the genes. But I guess the poor child just wanted attention, affection and she was finding it outside — among the lay-abouts and tearaways, even blacks. Her mother had no time for her, no time for Dennis either. His bedroom walls were covered with posters — motorbikes! He just couldn't wait to be sixteen. Eugenie ignored him. Ignored us too, her own mother and I who had come three hundred and fifty miles to see her. She thought only of David. Spoke of him non-stop. Piles of photographs. Somehow she had got herself a big lens for the camera.' Jessie gestured into the room, 'You know the kind, the ones that bring the details up close.'

Michael nodded.

'Some of the photos were taken from a long

158

way off. As if she had prowled around the Green. Pictures of little David with the ayah. In the Crane's garden with the criss-cross of the fence a blurred line on the picture.

'It seems she went every week. Took gifts. Slipped in from the back with presents for the ayah's own children, a joint of beef for the houseboy. Harry Crane bought a dog. I saw it once as we drove past — she was always making us drive past, though the road led nowhere; a ferocious-looking animal, snarling black jaws, shoulders like a prize-fighter.

'David loved the dog. You could see it gentle as a lamb with him. We watched him on the Green — she begged us to come and watch with her. The dog was David's friend. He didn't play with the other children. We saw the ayah shoo them off. Instructions from June, no doubt. Only the dog played with him, licking his face, rolling with him on the grass.

'We tried to talk to her. Others had tried. 'You sound like the priests,' she shouted. She'd stopped taking the children to church.' Jessie shook her head. 'We should have tried harder. We should have stayed up there. We should have paid more attention.

'But it's easy to say that afterwards, isn't it? I thought it would pass. She was still young, after all. Perhaps another man — ' Jessie waved her hand. 'Let's be honest, I didn't want to stay in that dirty little bungalow with Regina strutting around. We stayed a month and we'd had enough.'

Jessie began to cough again.

'Shall I fetch you another drink?'

She shook her head between coughs. 'I'm too old to talk like this.' She pushed herself out of the chair. Michael put his arm about her shoulders. He could feel the heave of her lungs.

'I sh . . . shouldn't have kept you up.'

When they reached her bedroom Jessie shrugged him aside. 'I can manage now.'

Michael moved towards his room but after she closed her door, remained on the verandah. His eyes adjusted slowly to the darkness. The moon had set but the stars cast a pale light, defining shadows into shapes. To one side of the garden lay the servants' quarters, a dark hump under the mango tree. No light showed but in the fine pale starlight, he could see the shape of a man squatting on the step in the darkness.

'Joseph?'

'Bwana.'

There was a line, a place in the dust-dry grass where the lawn ended and Joseph's 'place' began. Once there might have been a fence, a row of mealies marking the boundary. Now there was no more than a change in the texture of the grass, just visible in the moonlight.

Michael walked to the line and raised his hand.

A palm came up in answer but the servant stayed on his step. His head was down, as if he was looking at the floor, but the moonlight caught his eyes, rolled up, watching Michael's feet. Michael paused. There was a smell now. A smell, he realised with surprise, that he had come to know; the smell of the place, of burned charcoal and roasted mealies,

160

of sweat and dust and the outhouse at the back of the quarters.

The smell made him pause. The walls of the quarters, that had appeared brightly white from the house, were cracked; moonlight picked out the splashes of mud above the earth line.

'Joseph?'

The man's head remained bent. Michael hesitated. The eyes that had watched his feet were no longer visible. He could no longer see Joseph's face; only the unstirring shoulders, the long black arms hanging forward, motionless, ape-like.

He turned and made his way back to the house.

17

'I have come to see Mrs Jones.'

'Do you have an appointment?'

Harry produced the small card that had been sent in response to his telephone call. Permission to visit, to ask Eugenie the question the authorities refused to answer. Regina's address was not theirs to disclose. 'But you could try the mother.'

The gate in the tall white fence was unlocked. He was taken into a room with barred windows that overlooked a playing field. The curtains had a pattern of sunflowers. A woman in white trousers and tunic said, 'We've not seen you before.'

'No.'

'Are you family?'

Harry shook his head. 'A friend. I knew the family — a long time ago.'

'Eugenie's in here.'

She showed him to a small ward, neat cubicles with curtains tied back. She stopped by one of them.

'Eugenie, here's your visitor.'

It was a moment before Harry recognised her, saw Eugenie in the wizened, bird-like face that turned to him.

He was offered a white-gloved hand — held high, as if to be kissed.

'Would you like a nice cup of tea?'

Harry looked at the woman who had shown him

in. She smiled reassurance. 'I'll be over there at my desk if you need me.'

Eugenie led him to a kitchenette at the end of the ward. He watched her fill the kettle and switch it on. A notice was stuck to the wall: TEA BAGS MUST NOT BE PUT IN THE KETTLE. USE THE TEAPOT. Eugenie tittered. 'Everybody sees that sign. Some people look away. They pretend not to notice. You see their eyes moving along and then away, as if it said something rude.'

Harry opened his mouth to respond but was interrupted.

'We have power in this place, you know — real power.'

There was a small table under the window. Harry sat down and Eugenie settled herself in front of him, straightening the edges of her cardigan with her gloved hands. 'Even some of the nurses are afraid.'

Harry tried again to speak but Eugenie drowned out his words. 'You see, they're not afraid of the things they have drugs for — special jackets, cells lined with foam, plastic spoons. It's not madness they fear, but ordinariness.' She dragged out the word. 'I am ordinary. An ordinary girl making tea in the kitchen that goes for good, ordinary patients. The young orderlies come and chat to me. They forget what I've done. Now and again I have to give them a reminder.' Eugenie giggled. 'Careful or I might do it.'

'Do what?'

'Put tea bags in the kettle!' She grinned at Harry, wide-mouthed, before turning back to tea-making.

163

'I took her out to the garden. We had tea in mugs. I was waiting for her to say why she had come.'

Harry sat up. 'Who, Eugenie? Who came?'

'So few people come.'

The kettle had boiled. Eugenie put a tea bag in a mug and poured hot water over it. She squeezed the tea bag against the side of the mug with a spoon, turning and pressing until the water was dark brown.

'But I have the kitchen, you see, and the garden.' She handed Harry the mug of tea.

'Who did you take for a walk in the garden, Eugenie?'

'They let me keep a patch; stick beans and raspberries, potatoes. Sometimes I have to fight for water — the gardeners keep the hoses on the lawns in the summer. But my patch grows well. You can tell my beans nine miles apart from the ones on the other side. But we never have them fresh. Not once. Always from the freezer; green fingers on unwarmed plates.'

'Who came, Eugenie?'

'She didn't stay long. I offered her a biscuit. I showed her the cream ones and she said no.'

Harry sipped his tea and put the mug on the table. 'Are you talking about Regina, Mrs Jones?'

Still ignoring his questions, Eugenie continued. 'She said, 'You shouldn't keep them in your pocket. They'll melt.' She sounded like a nurse. Nurses say things like that. 'Are you a nurse?' I said. 'No.' She said, 'I've come to see you.' ' Eugenie gave Harry a wink. 'I don't do it consciously — but I know when I do it. You can see it in their faces. As if there was a power cut. They stop in their tracks and don't ask their question or say whatever it is. Even Doctor Morris stops. He starts again, but he does always stop. With him it's a game. He knows just how far he must go.'

Suppressing his irritation, Harry tried another question. 'Is Doctor Morris the consultant?'

'I don't want to be healed. I told her that. She looked so sad. 'I'm Olivia,' she said. Three times: 'I'm Olivia.' As if there was more to it and she couldn't tell me. Do you pick your nose in bed? I asked her. That was when I wanted her to leave. Her hand went to her nose. As if some evidence might hang there. It always works. They always touch their nose and they always start to leave.'

Harry cleared his throat. 'Do you have any other visitors?'

'Yes, of course. My daughter comes every month.'

'Regina?' Harry sat forward. 'Do you know where she lives?'

'Regina?' Eugenie's voice was high-pitched, 'Regina lives in Hampstead.'

'Do you know her address?'

'She's married. Such a nice man. And four beautiful children. Their house has a swimming pool in the garden. She has everything in the world, my Regina.'

'Does she bring the children to see you?'

'You wouldn't bring children to a place like this.' The gloved hands patted his arm. Harry tried to keep still. He could see a bulge of sticking plaster through the white cotton; it was stained yellow, as if the plaster had leaked.

'That's all right, dear. That's from scrubbing the floor.'

Harry put his own hands in his pockets. 'I shall have to go in a minute.'

Eugenie nodded. 'It was kind of you to come.'

She sounded so ordinary Harry wondered if the madness really was a sham.

He bent over her, his face close to hers. 'Could I ask you a great favour, Eugenie?'

She held out her hands and Harry took them in his own. He could feel scabs on the knuckles. 'Will you give me Regina's address?'

'29, Southwater Road, Hammersmith.'

'I thought you said Hampstead.'

'Did I?'

'Yes — a house in Hampstead with a swimming pool.'

'Ah!' The hands pulled away from him. 'Well then . . .'

Harry rose from his chair.

'But don't go yet. It's not often a man comes to see me.' Eugenie held out his mug. 'It would be a kindness if you would stay.'

Harry sat down again.

'Would you like a top-up?'

He shook his head.

'Carriad.'

'I beg your pardon?'

'Carriad. That was his name for me. A Welsh word. Beloved, darling. He was tall and he used his tongue. It made me feel weak. I used to feel the muscles in his back, bending to put in his tongue . . . '

Harry cleared his throat. I haven't come for this, he thought. I don't want to hear it. I shouldn't have come.

Once more Eugenie had hold of his hand.

'Carriad, he would say. When we went upstairs after the wedding he couldn't stop. He told me I was his angel. Auntie Jess came knocking on the door.'

The grip of the cotton gloves was hard, bruising.

'We were happy till Regina was born. She made me into a cow. How could he want me if I was a cow?'

Harry stood up and rinsed his mug in the sink.

'Would you like a biscuit?'

'What — ?'

He turned and she was holding them out — not a tin, but the flap of a pocket lifted, a squidgy mess of pink and cream on the white gloves.

It had grown dark while he had been there. Floodlight glimmered on the wet ground of the car-park. He looked back as the taxi carried him away. The asylum was like a citadel, the fences rising like creamy glass between the trees.

18

Dennis's hand went over her mouth.

'Shut up can't you? You'll wake up Mother.' He gathered the curling bodies in his fist and pushed them through the window, using the end of her hairbrush to push the last obstinate one off the sill.

Wiping their stickiness onto his pyjamas. 'Go back to sleep.' His big hands patting her clumsily in the dark.

'Can I sleep in your room?'

'No.'

'I'm scared.'

'All right. As long as you're quiet.'

The thrill of her brother's room. A crash helmet like a hunting trophy. Sellotape shiny on pictures of motorbikes, cut from magazines and stuck on walls. A low light on the table.

'What are you writing?'

'Go to sleep.'

'Please tell me.'

'You promised you'd be quiet.'

'I will, I promise, but tell me what you're writing. Is it homework?'

'It's a form.'

'What sort of form?'

'I'm going to join the Navy.'

'Ships? You're going on ships?' She sat up. The long hand-me-down nightie wrinkled under her

168

bottom. '*I like ships. Will there be a swimming pool on your ship?*'

'*It's not that sort of ship. These ones don't carry passengers.*'

'*Does Mummy know you're going on a ship?*'

'*No. But someone else does.*'

'*Who?*'

'*Never you mind.*'

'*Mummy will cry if you go away.*'

'*She won't. She won't notice me going.*'

'*I'll cry. Regina will cry.*'

'*There's nothing to cry for. You'll do the same one day.*'

'*Will Regina go on a ship?*'

He didn't answer. His bed smelled of him, of sweat and socks. In the morning he was beside her, snoring. She went into the kitchen and there was the empty jar, crushed leaves and punched holes. Open mouths outside the kitchen door, Samson's totoes asking for the jam jar; disbelief; betrayal . . .

★ ★ ★

She came awake to the rain. First it was a smell. A soft, damp smell on the wind. Then a rustle, a patter on the ground like running feet, a crackle of water on the thatch. Outside, the children began to shout, squealing with pleasure. The shape of the headman filled the gape-hole. He was smiling. Behind him the women ran with their children, dancing and shrieking.

Olivia curled herself into the darkness of the

hut. The rain lasted no more than a few minutes. The torrent slowed to a shower and then nothing but a steady drip, drip, as each length of thatch drained itself, creating a necklace of holes in the mud around the hut. The air was sharp and clean, the strong safe smell of watered earth. Across the compound, one of the wives started to sing.

He was in before she saw him, slithering across the ground, a trail of wet earth on the dry floor.

'Huh!' A grin, gap-toothed, like a damaged keyboard.

'Hello,' she whispered. 'I haven't seen you before.'

'Huh!' The boy crept closer, crossing the floor towards her with a movement that was half leap, half crawl. In the same moment, as he came towards her, the sun came through the rain clouds, low strands of yellow light, shining straight through the gape-hole door. Caught in the light, like a figure on a stage, she saw the boy clearly and thought she saw two. He seemed to be two. One that was normal, one foot, one leg, one hand, one arm, half of a smile, quite normal, the size of a well-fed ten year old. Then the other; the second foot, leg, hand, arm, half a body withered, skin shrunk tight, wrapping the limbs into a tight deformed parcel.

'Huh!' Holding out his good hand.

Olivia swallowed. The child said something. It was a second or two before Olivia realised that he had addressed her in Swahili, the first to do so. All the others spoke a dialect she did not understand. What followed was talk, interrupted by passages of time that she could not measure, periods of sleep or unconsciousness.

'They think you are very sick. The loiboni is coming.'

'Who?' Not a Swahili word.

'The loiboni — medicine man. He has come before. They have given him a goat but you are not better. If you die, the goat will be returned.'

'Where did you learn Swahili?'

'I am at the mission school. In the next class I will learn English, too.'

He held out his hand once more. 'My name is Mosa.'

Olivia smiled. She stretched out her arm. The light from the gape-holed door was blotted out. A hiss. Marie-Therese, the cloth wrap unravelling as she raised her hand to strike. The boy was gone, shooting out, like a snake, into the light, and away. Marie-Therese lowered her hands, tucked back the cloth, muttering to Olivia in tones of reassurance.

19

The key went into the lock. Regina held her breath. It turned. In. Next week they would change it. Next week she would have nowhere to go. There would be a day when the key would not fit.

She left her shoes in the hall, between the marks on the carpet that showed where a table had been. Under the table, they would have been out of sight, nothing to annoy Thanos, or trip him up, if he were still there to be tripped, if the table itself were there.

Past the open door. The long living-room, dining at one end, sitting at the other. Neither now. Only the oldest sofa, with its worn back facing the door. At least the carpets were fixed, nailed down. The pile felt thick and warm under her feet. She pressed the button on the gas fire and it made a *floop* noise as it lit. A lick of flame and the ceramic mesh began to turn red then gold. Holding her toes out to the warmth, she lay back on the sofa. The walls looked filthy, the paint battered and marked. Huge blank shapes, outlined in dust, showed where his pictures had hung.

'You never loved him,' she said, aloud. 'That is the truth. Love could not have endured that couch in the studio, all that garlic, that hairy nose.'

Her thoughts were interrupted by the door bell.

Have they come for the carpets? Even the gas fire?

Her stockinged feet slipped silently to the window. She leaned into the bay, carefully pulling aside one corner of the net. Dust on her fingers. Well, they can wash it now.

A man in the porch. Old. No Greek.

Are they sending old men to bully Regina? She let the net fall. The man saw the movement. He turned to the window, took a step back.

Bald. Something about his face. She pulled the net aside once more. A gentleman. Definitely not a bully boy.

'What do you want?' she mouthed through the glass.

He pointed to the door.

'Just a minute — ' She went into the hall and crushed her feet back into the shoes. She put the chain on the door and opened it as far as it allowed, pushing her face in the crack.

'What do you want? I've no money for anything. I don't owe anything. You haven't come about debts — '

'Please — ' Harry interrupted her. 'I'm not a salesman. It is you I want to see.'

'Why? Who sent you?'

'No-one sent me.' He looked up at her. 'Am I so changed, Regina?'

She kept her hand on the door chain.

Harry smiled. 'Don't you know me?'

'I don't know nothing. The things in this house are mine — what they have left, those bastards. The bed, the sheets, they are all mine. The cooker was mine, I brought it here, fool that I was. You can't take any more away. My lawyer says — '

173

'My name is Harry Crane.'

Regina stopped. Stopped talking, stopped the motion of her mouth. More than mere speech, her talk had been a kind of barrage — something to hold the world at bay. Now it had stopped, the painted lips were still; brown eyes stared at Harry from spiky circles of black.

'Who?' The question barked out, hoarse. 'Who did you say?'

'Harry Crane.'

'I don't know any Harry Crane.'

'You must remember me, Regina.'

'No.'

'But you do remember your sister, Olivia. It's about Olivia that I — '

'I have no sister.' She folded her arms. 'No family.'

Harry took a step forward, moving up onto the porch. She backed away, began to close the door.

'Please don't shut the door. I haven't come to make trouble for you.'

'I don't know about any Olivia.'

'You are Regina Jones?'

'No. Never heard of her.' The confidence was back. She grasped the door with scarlet-nailed fingers. 'You've come to the wrong house.'

'I haven't,' said Harry. 'You must be she. You're the only one who could be.'

'What do you mean, the only one? I'm not in the phone book. Nobody knows that name. I am Mrs Paros.'

'You are on the electoral roll.'

'What roll?'

'For voting at elections.'

'I never voted in my life. Where is this roll?'

'In the library.'

'What library?'

'The public one.'

'I got no books. I haven't taken any books. Those are Thanos's books. He made me go there to choose for him. Too silly for a man, he says, to be with all those women in the library. So I went for him, every month. God knows, I should be familiar with libraries.' She paused, peered at Harry, advanced a step on to the porch. 'You've come from the library, is that it? His books are overdue. Wait there, I'll bring them down. They're just upstairs . . . ' Her voice trailed off. She had almost begun again, almost recreated the wall of words.

'I haven't come about library books,' said Harry. 'I've come about Olivia.'

A moment passed. Harry looked at her. She was staring at his face. Suddenly, she slumped, leaning back against the door frame.

'You look so old, Harry.' Her hands came up, patting her thick, back-combed hair. 'Have we all grown so old?'

The door swung open. She turned her back on him, leading the way along an empty hall.

'I've got no furniture. It's all gone. Just this old sofa.' She turned into the living room. 'Only this and the bed. That's all. They even took my cooker. It was mine. I brought it from my own place when I was such a fool as to come and live with Thanos Paros. Before I knew he would die.

How can you know? One minute he was here, the next he was gone. How could I know? It looked so safe here. The first home I had, you see. Now it's gone. One bed and one sofa and next week I have to go. Out!' She clapped her hands. 'Like a visiting cat. Unwanted. Somebody else's problem. Regina Jones can sleep in the street.' She stood in front of the gas fire and turned to him. 'Would you like a cup of coffee? They left me the kettle, I can make a nice cup of coffee.'

Harry smiled. 'Thank you.'

She called back as she went to the kitchen. 'I've got some brandy — would you like some in your coffee? It keeps out the cold.'

'No, thank you,' Harry called back.

Regina made two mugs of coffee and carried them into the sitting room. Harry was where she had left him, just inside the door from the hall-way. 'You can sit down, you know.' She nodded towards the sofa. 'While it's still here.'

'Thank you — ' Harry perched himself on the sofa. Regina handed him one of the mugs.

'I hope you like it black — I've got no milk.'

'Black's fine.'

She sat on the arm of the sofa and looked at him, waiting.

'I went to see your mother.'

'You went there?'

'Yes.'

'Why?'

'Because Olivia is missing.'

'Missing? What does that mean? Missing where?'

176

'She went up to Turkana. She was looking for David — '

'For David?' Regina swivelled to face him. 'Why do you tell me this? What is it to me?'

'It seems there was some sort of attack — bandits or poachers, I don't know the details. Olivia has disappeared. Her driver is dead. There was a little bit in the papers here — perhaps you read about it?'

'With all the trouble I've got? There's no time for newspapers.'

She stood up and went out. Her high heels clattered on the kitchen floor. There was the sound of a cupboard door and the clink of a bottle. 'You sure you won't have some brandy in your coffee?'

Harry called back, 'I'm sure, thank you.'

He got up and moved to the window. The small square of garden at the back of the house had been paved. Around the edge were flower tubs, remnants of plants, lobelia hanging dryly over the sides.

Regina came back into the sitting room. Harry turned from the window.

'What if she is dead, Regina? Don't you care? Don't you care about your sister?'

Regina shook her head. 'It is all in the past.'

Harry closed his eyes. 'I thought it was too.'

'Then why do you come here hassling me with it? Why drag it all to me?'

'Jessie wrote to me. She asked me to find you and tell you. Just one last thing I could do for her, she said.'

'Jessie Bell wrote to *you*?' She held out her hand. 'Show me the letter.'

Harry hesitated before he took the letter from his pocket.

Regina held it close. Her lips moved as she read. A strand of hair was twisted round her finger, round and round. At last she handed the letter back.

'And you did the other thing she asks? You saw my mother?'

Harry nodded. 'I didn't tell her about Olivia though, it wasn't the right time.' He sighed. 'I was sorry for her — sorry that I hadn't been before. She has had nothing but misfortune.'

'Misfortune?' Regina's eyes flashed. 'She's got everything. She's fed and clothed; they keep her warm and safe. It's us, the ones left outside that have misfortune. There's no asylum for me. For her children. No-one cares for Regina.'

'But she's — ' Harry searched for the right word. None would come except the baldest, the most bleak. 'She's mad, Regina.'

'Huh! yes, she's mad. She's also safe.' Regina wrapped her arms about herself.

Harry moved towards her. 'I would give anything to be able to undo it all, Regina. To go back to the very beginning.'

'What — give back my brother? Would you do that?'

'I don't have him to give, Regina.' Harry held out his hands. 'I'm like you — I am left with nothing.'

20

With the high tide came the wind. Michael woke to the noise of it. The slam of a shutter, palm fronds slapping — a crisp crackly sound, overlaying the call of the crows, the scraak! and shaark! of dark birds swooping between the trees. His room was in the main part of the house. One window looked over the back, over the drive and the servants' quarter. The other looked out to sea. The sun had risen, a wisp of haze separated its orange-brown ball from the grey-glimmer of the water.

He made his way to the bathroom. Broken terrazzo under his feet, a douche of lukewarm water. He let it run over his face, splatter and batter on his back until he felt awake and alert.

Joseph's bleach and scrubbing brush had rendered the shorts he had bought in the bazaar clean and limp.

The garden boy was already at work, raking the thin grass of the beach-lawn. He raised his hand as Michael walked towards the sand. Michael returned the greeting and paused before putting his bare feet on the sand. Pink-skinned early swimmers splashed in the calm sea. Beyond them, in deeper waters, fishing boats lay at anchor. Hollowed tree trunks, outriggers that dipped and waved in a small swell. Further out, a man stood on a raft, poling himself along the reef.

Olivia had been here; she had seen the same

colours in the water, gold and green and scarlet under the rising sun. She had been here as a girl, spent some of her childhood here. He imagined her in the garden. He could see her turning her face to the breeze, letting her hair free.

Olivia.

Did she find him, that brother of hers? Did she find David and forget us all?

It was the only hope left. The alternative was the bleached bones of which he dreamed; flies and vultures and bones, a fragile sculpture on the sand.

He turned back to the house. A row of crows strutted on the verandah roof, their black tails overhanging the gutter. He passed the shadowy hall-room where he had first waited for Jessie. The high, carved doors were propped open with jagged lumps of coral. A display of tall-stemmed, orange blooms had been placed beside the Mombasa chair. The doors to the dining room were also open, and the shutters along the rear wall, so that the breeze off the sea stirred the air.

Jessie was at the head of the dining table, looking out at the sea. Set before her was a dish of scrambled egg and a plate of butter-drenched toast cut into squares small enough for a teaspoon. She blinked as he approached. He caught the pursing of lips, the quick hand raising a napkin. She had forgotten her false teeth. Embarrassed, he cleared his throat.

Joseph glided up behind him, his wide bare feet slipping silently across the floor.

Michael smiled. 'Good morning.'

Joseph inclined his head. A chair was pulled out and Michael sat down. Knife and fork and spoon, side-plate and starched napkin, all of which had been waiting on the sideboard, were laid before him. A plate appeared, heaped with bacon, tomato, eggs that were half omelette, half scrambled; and beside his plate a bowl of small bread rolls, a thermos box of butter, a jar of thick honey.

Jessie had finished her eggs. She rose, clutching the edge of the table.

'Let me help you.'

She waved him down. 'It's only my knee. Arthritis. Always worse in the morning.' She turned away, her bent back silhouetted against the bright light of the doorway. 'I shall be in the sitting room,' she said. 'You can come to me when you've finished.'

The bacon was chewy, the eggs dry, as if the food had been kept warm for him. He ate it all and sipped coffee so strong it jarred his teeth. The servant stacked Jessie's dishes on a tray. Michael tried to catch his eye, to exchange a smile, but there was no response.

A bell shattered the silence. It took a moment for him to realise that it was the telephone, the ancient black instrument beside the Mombasa chair in the hall. There was a hint of empire in Jessie's voice: a harsher, louder tone than she used when talking to her own kind.

'This is she . . . Yes. This is Mrs Bell. Hello? . . . Ah, Inspector Ojekwo, how nice to hear from you. Yes, he is with me. Yes, he arrived safely on the train. Would you like . . . ?'

Raising his head to listen Michael saw that Joseph had done likewise, a fork in his hand held high, as if to improve the carriage of sound. No summons came. The conversation continued for several minutes. Jessie said no more than, 'I see, yes, I see.'

At last she said, 'Thank you, Inspector. I'll pass on your good wishes.'

The bell clanged again as she replaced the receiver.

Michael started to rise. Joseph waited, the fork still in his hand.

Jessie was smiling. 'They have news. A report has come down from Turkana. There is a white woman on a manyatta.'

'Is it Olivia?'

'They don't know.'

'Is she alive? Is she alright?'

'The message says only that she is there.'

'But it means she's alive!' Michael surged from his chair to kiss Jessie's cheek. Joseph began to clap. Michael shook his hand, the African clasped his, there was a linking of thumbs and palms, a ritual of delight that he had seen done in the street, black on black.

'Now.' Jessie put her hands up, as if to quell a pair of noisy children. 'We must make arrangements.'

'If you can order me a taxi to Mombasa I can catch a plane to Nairobi.'

Jessie shook her head. 'Too unreliable. You could wait all day for the flight. The road is serviceable. Tarmac all the way. You could be there before sundown.'

'And then, how will I get up to Turkana?'

'You may find you need go no further than Nairobi. If she is well enough to travel the flying doctor will bring her down.'

Before he could answer she turned and left the room. Soon he could hear the telephone again, the faint tinkle-chunk of the dial and the imperious voice.

'I must speak with Jackson . . . Then please get him from the workshop.'

Listening, Michael walked out onto the verandah.

'Jackson? Jackson is that you? . . . This is Memsahib Bell . . . I'm very well indeed!' The conversation lapsed into Swahili, a rapid exchange, with less hint of empire and much use of the name, Jackson.

The telephone conversation seemed interminable. Michael walked to the far end of the room to look at the photographs on the sideboard. A portrait of a dewy-eyed girl in a twenties frock. The print was speckled and brown — Jessie perhaps? A man in shirt-sleeves smiling beside a white Ford Prefect. There was a more recent picture, in colour, a woman with three children. A boy and two girls, the youngest, unmistakably Olivia, smiling shyly under a halo of ribbons. They had a certain look in common, a tension in the eyes — the mother, the older sister, even the tall boy who leaned back with his arms folded, as if to detach himself from them all. The photograph did not quite fit its tarnished silver frame — as if there had been another, which this one had replaced.

'Alike, weren't they?'

Jessie had come in behind him. Her finger shook a little as she pointed to the photograph. 'Eugenie, Dennis, Regina and Olivia.'

'You have no photographs of David?'

'No.'

She made her way to her chair. 'I have spoken to Jackson. He'll take you up there. Today you will go as far as Nairobi. After that it will depend on the flying doctor, or the roads.'

'Who is Jackson?'

Jessie waved away his question. 'He's a simple boy, but reliable. His father used to be chauffeur for a friend of mine. He has promised to be here within an hour but I don't expect him until noon.'

'What does he do? — I mean for a living? Does he have a job?'

Jessie spread her fingers. 'Odd jobs. Deliveries. At present he is working in a garage. The job is part-time. Sometimes I see him on the beach in the afternoons. He sells the better class of carvings.'

'And how much should I pay him?'

'He'll want sixty shillings a day, all found.'

'Is that enough? It doesn't seem much.'

'It's the going rate,' said Jessie. 'If you pay more than that you upset the system.'

'What about a vehicle?'

'He will arrange everything for you. Jackson is a good boy, you can trust him.'

'And money? How much will it cost?'

'It's hard to say. A lot will depend on the kind of vehicle he gets — and who from. And then there will be equipment — spares and things. I'm afraid it won't be cheap but I'll give you what I can.'

He looked at the tattered furniture around him. 'It's alright, Jessie. I have enough.'

'Go and pack your bag and then come back here. I'll get Joseph to make some coffee.'

She started speaking almost immediately he returned and continued without pause, as if, now that he was leaving, it had become important to tell the story.

'It is what happened to Dennis that gets forgotten.'

'Dennis?' Michael served himself from the coffee pot.

'In all the rest of what happened the tragedy of Dennis, of how it might have turned her mind, gets overlooked.'

'Dennis was the older brother?'

Jessie nodded. 'He was seventeen. He joined the Navy — signed up on his seventeenth birthday. They'd had a cadet group at the school, I've no doubt the teacher meant well, thought it would help the boy. Eugenie must have signed the papers but she hardly noticed his going. She wasn't there with the other parents — at the little ceremony before they departed. She didn't tell us.'

Jessie sniffed, blew her nose. Michael looked for tears but there was only surprise in her face, the wounded look of the uninformed.

'Nobody knew! Nobody knew he was writing to his father. Dennis kept it secret from us all. It was his job to empty the postbox on the way home from school. At least it was he who did it, Eugenie was beyond caring about mail. When the cadets arrived in Southampton, there was Jones. Dennis went off with him. Perhaps he was happy. Jones took him to a public house, perhaps it was what Dennis had needed, a hand on his shoulder, a man. We found a stack of letters in his room. The motorbike was promised to him before he ever joined the ship.

'The telegrams arrived in the wrong order. The first said he was dead and the second reported that he had jumped ship and was A.W.O.L. Jones wrote nothing. A copy of the coroner's report came through. Too big a bike; too much to drink.' Jessie shook her head. 'It's the father I can't forgive. Not a word. Their own son and not a word.'

Jessie touched a finger to her lips.

'From that day, the day of the telegrams, Eugenie lost herself entirely. The damage could not be undone. She became obsessed. Olivia would have starved but for school — and what Regina brought home, stolen or otherwise. Their mother started going out to Lavington every day — skipping work, slipping out of the hospital before her shift had finished. Going round to the back of Harry's house with presents for the servants — meat for the ayah, for the houseboy — and sweets for her son, for David.

'Something was going to happen. All of them knew it. Joseph has told me the story so many times and always it begins like that — that they knew something would happen; that the days before were like the days that precede a storm. The heat was intense — much hotter than they are used to up there — hot and oppressive. Only that morning Harry Crane had shouted at the shamba boy, something about the geraniums.

Harry is the mildest man alive, his shouting was out of character, added to the unease.

'It happened in the afternoon. The servants went off for their mid-day meal and had eaten it and were sitting in their quarters when they saw her. Joseph says it was no pleasure for them, even though there would be gifts, it was no pleasure to see the other memsahib coming down the path — by the quick route from the dhuka — the servant's way — coming down that path with her parcels.

'June was in the bedroom, mending a buttonhole — Harry's shirt was found on the bed, a reel of cotton on the floor. They reckon it was the dog she heard first, the beginnings of a bark, quickly hushed. You get to know the sounds here, the silences that mean more trouble than noise.

'June called to David. Everyone remembered that. She called to David and her voice sounded strange. The servants saw her face at the bedroom window, peering out into the garden. They heard her shriek as she saw Eugenie at the gate.

'She shrieked for the ayah and the houseboy. She shouted for the shamba boy. No-one came. It was their free time. And besides, they were afraid of June, of the quick, fierce rage that had become a part of her. She came through the house barefoot. Her slippers were found on the rug. Past the bathroom, she must have come; they had a mobile of mirrored fish that they'd brought from England and a plastic hippo. All these things were referred to in the trial, to illustrate what good parents the Cranes had been. Through the sitting-room — the

187

curtains closed against the heat — then out onto the verandah. She had put on her sun-glasses — you remember those black things people used to wear? So dark you couldn't see a person's eyes?

'Eugenie was on her knees, kneeling by the gate like a native woman, surrounded by her bags. Eugenie was hugging the boy, and the boy was hugging the dog.

'June shrieked for Joseph. She stayed on the verandah. Not once did she put her feet out on to the dust. She stayed on the verandah and shrieked for Joseph to close the gate, to close-that-gate-NOW!

'And there was Joseph coming from the long grass with a panga in his hand, towards the gate. That was almost his undoing. They could have hanged him for that. Why was the houseboy carrying a panga? — they wanted to know. For an extra five bob. It was Harry who confirmed it. Probably saved his life — they'd rather have hanged a servant. But Harry confirmed his story. He'd offered him five shillings extra to help cut the grass in the afternoons. It was his time off then, you see, between washing up after lunch and bringing in the dhobi to iron at four o'clock.

'He came up from the bottom lawn, still with the panga, stopping short of the gate where Eugenie was kneeling in the dust and the boy with her and the dog turning to look because it was black shapes he was trained to go for.

'Another shout from the verandah. 'Shut that gate!' Joseph looked back at June, holding out his hand, as if to say, this memsahib is here, as if June could not see the white woman kneeling there in the dust with her packages.

'June stayed on the verandah, shaking. Joseph could see her there in the shadow, with the murram drive, hot as new-baked pastry, lying between them; he could see the shivering cloth of her dress, her arms waving, her throat hoarse from shrieking.

'David wriggled out of his mother's embrace. He called to June, 'It's alright, Mummy. She's going now.'

'Joseph went forward to help gather the bags.

'Now it was Eugenie who screamed. Not at the houseboy, not at Joseph who had put the panga against the fence to free his hands for the bags. She screamed at David — whether for calling June 'Mummy', or for his dismissive words, 'She is going now,' like a servant woman — no-one can say. But the bags fell sideways, parcels spilled into the dust.

'Eugenie's scream brought the dog to life. It went for Joseph's leg and then his chest. Joseph curled on the ground, kicking, trying to protect himself. His shirt was red with blood. David pulled on the dog's collar, pulled with both arms, his shoes slipping in the dirt until the ayah and the gardener came, drawn by the barking and screaming, out from wherever they had been watching to drag the dog away.

'Only then, when the gardener had the dog on its chain and the ayah, moaning, was wiping Joseph's wounds with her apron, only then did they look for the memsahib, for June, who should be in charge now.

'June was on the verandah. Face down on the red tiles. Eugenie against a pillar, embracing herself, rocking; the panga, part of the blade still shining, lying where she dropped it.'

Jessie touched her face, her cheeks were glossy with tears.

'I wasn't there, of course. But I know that story by heart. I heard it a hundred times in that court room, told from every angle, but the first time was that very day. The priest called me — though God knows how he knew the number, Eugenie hadn't been to church for years. Perhaps it was Harry who told him — anyway the priest called me, came to fetch me from the bungalow. We went straight to the school to get Olivia. Regina wasn't there. We couldn't find her and I didn't much care. Olivia looked so little, so pale in the hard blue colour of the uniform they wore. No-one asked why she cried. We assumed, the priest and I, that she was weeping for her mother, for the dreadful events in Lavington Green. But it was not. It was her period. Nature had chosen that day, of all the days in her life, to make Olivia a woman. She had to press for my attention, 'Auntie Jess, Auntie Jess, I'm bleeding. I don't know what to do.'

'Eugenie hadn't prepared her, hadn't warned her.' Jessie coughed. 'I shouldn't speak of it to you, it's no talk for a man's ears, but the poor child asked me if she would bleed to death? Imagine it? She'd had no mother at all.'

Joseph came in to pour another cup of coffee. 'Would you like a biscuit? Joseph, bring the biscuit tin. That bungalow was filthy. Dennis had been dead three months but his room hadn't been touched. Posters all over the walls — motorbikes — even on the ceiling! For another woman than Eugenie you might have thought it sentiment. You might have said the room was a shrine to her dead son. But you couldn't say it of Dennis's room. The dust was so thick in there. The place was simply forgotten.

'I spent all that I could spare. Lawyers, barristers. Crowds of people took my money. Taxis up to Mathari — that's the asylum — for the half hour they would let us see her. If it wasn't for Harry Crane sending a car every day I'd never have been in that court-room. I'd never have heard the lies, the abominations. Africans wearing wigs and gowns — can you imagine it? No air conditioning, their faces dripped with sweat. One took off his wig, right there in the court-room, and mopped himself with it. The sons of cattlemen — it was a mockery!

'The trial lasted two weeks but when the jury went out they were back within the hour, Manslaughter. It was a relief. Insanity was somehow better than evil. It was easier to think of — to say it was not my beloved Eugenie, but a woman deprived of her senses, who went up that drive with the panga.

'I stayed there in that bungalow all through the long rains. Regina smoked. It is one of the things that has stuck to me. I can't abide an ashtray, the sight of filters smeared with lipstick. Regina was shameless — going out to the reporters, swapping lies for cigarettes. They slept on the lawn — and in a bus at the end of the road. Harry paid for us to have a guard but one man was nothing against those greedy photographers.

'Poor Harry. He was like a balloon gone down, punctured. When he came into the court I hardly recognised him. The man had shrivelled up like a grape in the sun. He had eyes only for David. When the boy came in I thought he might weep. And that child.' Jessie's finger waved towards Michael, vaguely, for she was pointing not at her listener, but at the child in court, David, all those years ago. 'And that child never cried once: not even when his father appeared.'

'Who? Which father?'

'Jones, of course. The flesh and blood. The Father Unknown. Pointing in the court: he is my son.

'The reporters went wild. The Judge banged his hammer . . . '

'Gavel.'

'What?'

'It's called a gavel — the Judge's hammer.'

'Oh.' Jessie lost her stride. 'What did I say?'

'You called it a hammer. It doesn't matter, tell me the story.'

The moment had gone. Jessie sighed, laid her gnarled fingers flat in her lap. 'Well that was the end of it, bar the shouting. Harry didn't want the boy. June was dead. All the reasons had gone with her. The boy was sent to the priests. They said he was cruel, Harry Crane, but I don't think he meant to be. They say he put money into a trust fund for the boy. And the school had a swimming pool built and a gymnasium. They named it after him: Crane Hall. The boy boarded then, even during the holidays. The priests were glad of the money. It was the time when all the whites were pulling out. The optimism had gone. People realised that things would never be the same. Even the good schools were filling up with black children. The priests were glad to have young David. They were glad of Harry's money.'

'Has Harry replied to your letter?'

'I've not heard from him. Perhaps he's dead. Who knows, after all these years?'

'And David?'

'I didn't see him again until he was eighteen.'

'He came to you?'

'He did. You should have seen Joseph's face. They knew one another again; even after all those years and David grown so tall, his hair flowing down his back — the wild, curly hair of Gareth Jones. He'd even grown a beard but Joseph knew him. He stood in the doorway, David was taking his case out of the car. 'Bwanakidogo.' All in one word, out of Joseph's mouth.'

Jessie shrugged. 'Bwana kidogo — little master, but all one word, and then the fist. You know how they do, these blacks? — like children, stuffing his fist into his mouth while David walked over, holding out his hand.

'Later they sat on the verandah, drinking beer. I didn't like it, of course, a servant on the verandah, but Joseph never took advantage. David said he'd always wanted to know. It was one of the great questions of his life — not Eugenie, not his mother or his sisters — but what became of Joseph, the servant.

'And he was here, all the time. He'd been stitched up at the City Hospital. I guess Harry paid the bill, I never asked. He was healed by the time of the trial. Turned up on the back step of Eugenie's bungalow, asking for work. Harry had paid him off — generously, I don't doubt. Harry was a man who paid his debts. But Joseph wanted work and no-one would give it. He'd been with June since boyhood and only had the one reference — only one reference and scars to frighten the life out of you. So he came back with me and he's had steady work and an easy life — but the loneliest that could be. Not being local, you see, there's no-one of his tribe down here. No wives, no sons. I sent him back once, drove him down to Mombasa and paid the train fare. He was back within a week. Said he'd never go again. I didn't ask.'

★ ★ ★

Almost as she had predicted, Jackson arrived a minute or two before noon. They heard the wheels on the drive, the slam of a car door. Jessie remained in her chair. After a pause Joseph appeared, followed by a short man, about twenty-five years old, sturdily built, with bright eyes and a big smile.

Jessie's greeting was dismissive. 'I expected you earlier.'

'But I have made many arrangements. Jackson has hired the best vehicle in Mombasa.' As he spoke, the African's eyes lingered on the room, taking in Jessie's furniture, the ornaments and

194

pictures. It occurred to Michael that all this was new to him, that never before had Jackson been let into the house.

He shook Michael's hand as Joseph had done, clasping palm and thumb and palm again. 'I will show you this vehicle.' Michael followed him out of the room and through the hall to the front of the house. Parked by the mango tree was an old Landrover.

'You see? It is excellent!' Jackson opened the driver's door and patted the wheel. 'This car will go very far.'

Jessie interrupted. 'You're only going to Nairobi. After that it will be up to Mr Ballantyne. Come, there is no time to be wasted.'

Joseph appeared with Michael's bag and while Jackson opened the back, Michael turned to Jessie. She was frowning. 'You're not to let that boy take advantage, Michael. He's a good driver but he needs to be kept in place.'

Michael reached to shake her hand but found himself patted away.

'Go on, now. You don't want to be driving in the dark.'

'Thank you for — '

'Go on, go on.'

He saw that she wanted no sort of goodbye. All her farewell was in the frown on her forehead and the agitated hand, waving him away.

He shook Joseph's hand, pressing money into his palm. Jackson revved the engine and they raised a small cloud of dust as he circled the cacti.

'Michael. Let me know,' cried Jessie, wiping her cheeks.

'Of course I will.'

As they hurtled out onto the road, Jackson tapped the steering wheel with satisfaction. 'Is a good car. The miles will pass away.'

'Did Mrs Bell tell you why we are going?'

'Sure! To find your girl.' Jackson grinned across the cab. 'Hakuna matata. We will find her.'

'What does that mean?'

'Hakuna matata? It means No Problem. We will have No Problem!'

With a deft movement the African flicked away the corner of a blanket covering what appeared to be a square box on the seat behind to reveal a crate of bottled beer. 'You see? We will be happy as we drive.'

Michael could think of little to say in return. He felt acutely aware of the proximity of the African. He had thought himself cosmopolitan, that all his travelling for the bank had cured him of fear, but there was a smell of fresh sweat on Jackson's clothes, of youth and confidence beside which Michael felt pale and weak, as if his white skin were a sign of inner feebleness.

'You work in England?'

'Yes,' said Michael. 'In London.'

'You like it? You got a big job?'

Michael smiled. 'I guess so. I'm a banker.'

'You are a bank?'

'No, I work for a bank.'

'Lots of money every day, eh?'

For a moment Michael thought of trying to

explain, but abandoned the idea. For the first time in his life it didn't matter about the bank. It was of no concern to Jackson what he did or who he was. For Jackson he was just a white man.

21

On the bleached ashlands of the mission, the First Sunday of Advent had signalled preparations for Christmas.

David unpacked a plastic crib — a white Mary and Joseph, gaudily painted. Rachel, the young Samburu girl who taught the infant class, helped him set up a trestle table in the chapel. Using sand and stones from the desert, they built a setting for the crib — a nativity scene. Around it, crowding the medieval-costumed figures, were donkeys and camels, goats and Wise men, crudely carved, the legacies of generations of children.

Rachel taught the little ones Christmas carols: 'Hark the Herald Angels Sing', 'While Shepherds Watched Their Flocks By Night'. The latter appealed especially, for all the children knew their family herds, and the little boys longed for the day when they would follow their older brothers on the long treks in search of grazing and water.

And this year, as if to mark the coming of Christmas, there had been a Visitation. Not a flight of angels or glory shining on the ground (Is it like rain, Mr Jones? Is the glory on the ground like rain?), but a plane, two planes, a Beach Baron and Cessna 420, as the older boys were quick to point out, to show David how they knew one from another of these rare visitors from the sky. All day the planes had droned, riding low, mostly far away, towards the lake. On the third day the Cessna landed, scattering goats and children from the dusty playground of the mission airstrip. The men who climbed out wore uniform. They sat on David's verandah and were offered tea and goat meat from the women's store, pounded and fried and preserved in a thick layer of grease. The visitors were relaxed. David had the impression of a holiday — as if the purpose of the visit was the enamel mugs of tea, dosed with condensed milk, the quiet sitting in the shade.

There was talk of a white woman, some foolish girl lost.

'What was she doing up here?' asked David.

The older officer shrugged. 'This we do not know.'

'Was she an aid worker? A researcher?'

The policemen mopped their faces. 'Unfortunately the file is in Nairobi. We were not given these details.'

There was no reason to ask her name. David had no cause to think he should know her name.

The goat meat was left uneaten, a quiver of distaste on the faces of these men from the South. Late in the afternoon they eased the belts of their uniforms and went away in their aeroplane.

'The Angel of the Lord came down,' sang the older boys, giggling in the classroom. One took to wearing a strap crosswise from his shoulder, like the visitors' uniforms, and strutted about the compound. The little ones, practising their nativity play, pushing and shoving in the aisle of the chapel, wore their beads likewise, imitating their brothers.

And there was a rumour. Whispers in the classroom. Laughter and hand signals when David turned his back to write on the blackboard. The rumour was of a woman on a manyatta, a white woman.

Should he be concerned? It would be another aid worker, some misguided female from the Peace Corps or the VSO, or one of the plethora of agencies who came and went, leaving nothing but their condoms and empty film canisters . . .

There was quarrelling in the compound, a twisted shape unmistakable among the lean running bodies in the playground. The mission children herded round.

'I want to be a Wise Man.'

'You cannot be.'

The crippled newcomer was pinched — on his good side, his undamaged side — and mocked: 'You can be a snake.'

'I want to be a Wise Man!'

'You can only be a snake that slithers on the ground!'

Rachel shouted, clapped her hands. The children dispersed as she approached, their victim left to scuttle away to the chapel.

At the end of the day David found him by the altar, his twisted body curled on the concrete floor.

'Well, Mosa? So you have come to see us again.'

David took the little fellow's hand. He knew the child, had known him since the day his parents had carried him to the mission, still smelling of his burns, the cloth from his mother's wrap stuck fast in his wounds. They had brought him to be blessed before dying. There was no priest, no-one but David to dip his finger in the holy water, drizzle a silent, godless blessing on the child. The parents went before sundown, the father tetching at the tears on his wife's cheeks.

Weeks later, when David drove him home to the manyatta, disfigured but healed, he was greeted with silence. There was no place for a cripple in the life of the tribe. He could neither tend goats nor carry water.

'What is it, Mosa?'

The child began to weep, pitifully, sustaining his sobs long enough to be gathered into the white man's arms, to have the close knit curls of his head — avoiding the scarred, bald side — softly patted.

'I think Mosa is feeling very sorry for himself,' said David.

Mosa looked up at him. One of the miracles — even David would use the word, unthinkingly, a miracle as a kind of godless fortune — one of the miracles was that Mosa's eyes were sound. That, in the moment of falling, as the upset stove scattered its bed of burning coals in his path, some ancient instinct had turned the child's head, the scalp and neck taking all his head's share of the burning. His eyes, thus saved, looked at David out of the scarred face, as clear and sorrowful as a puppy's.

'I am a good boy. I try to help my brothers but I am not allowed. Even today I tried to milk the goat to help with the nursing — '

'Who are you nursing?'

'I spilt the milk — '

'Is somebody sick?'

'The pot went from my hand.' The child held out his good hand. 'When I walk, it goes sideways and Grandmother hisses.'

'Is it one of the children who is sick?'

Mosa looked sly. 'I have come far this day.'

'I know you have, Mosa. It is very far from your house to the mission. The last time you came I had to drive you home in the Landrover. Do you remember? All that precious fuel just for Mosa to go home.'

'I have walked all the way!'

'And you will have to walk back again. I can't use all the fuel playing taxi for Mosa.'

'But I will walk! I can walk!'

'Yes, you can.' Once more David patted the soft springy hair. 'Everyone knows Mosa can walk now. And because he can walk, he can find his way home.'

He shifted the weight of the child on his knee. The daylight had gone. Through the open door of the chapel came the sounds of darkness: cicadas, laughter from the huts outside the compound. Someone had lit David's lamp and left it on the step outside.

'Everyone knows that Mosa can walk. What nobody knows is why Mosa walked to the mission today.'

Silence. David could almost hear the child's thoughts, calculating how much the truth might be worth.

'Did he come to be in the Nativity Play? Is that why Mosa came?'

'Hmm . . . ' The child squirmed a little. 'They say I have to be a snake.'

'Who says so?'

'The children! That I can only be a snake.'

'What does Rachel say?'

'She says I have come too late.'

'And what part would you like to play?'

'I want to be a Wise Man — with donkeys. My uncle has a donkey.'

'And can you ride a donkey?'

'Hmm . . . ' The little boy clutched David's shoulder. 'If someone will tie my legs — if someone will help me, I will ride this donkey.'

Mosa spent the night with David: it was not the first time the child curled contentedly on the mat between the metal bedstead and the wall, beneath the picture of Harry Crane and June with the child in their arms and the dog at their feet.

In the morning there was maize-meal and milk, the voices of the mission women, smoke from the cooking fires. Mosa was anxious, squirming his crooked limbs.

'What is it now, Mosa?'

This from David, smoking a cigarette and drinking black tea, laced with whisky.

'Will I be a Wise Man?'

'You'll have to be a good man first.'

'I am good.'

'And you'll have to be a truthful man. You'll have to tell me all the truth.'

And so it came out. A donkey for the Wise

Man — Mosa's legs tied around its belly — and a length of cloth wrapped Arab style about the scarred head. So David received the story of the white woman found crawling in the desert: the chance of money, talk that a search was on; Mosa's grandmother promising a return on the investment — coins and notes if they could put out enough to make their guest well again. And no small investment: milk and meat; a gift for the loiboni — who would take no payment, for such payment would dirty his hands, but would accept a gift, the best and healthiest of the home herd.

But the guest was not thriving. Even expensive packet medicine, from the mzungu who had come with the clinic two seasons past. Even this medicine did not cure. The guest lay in a hut. She smelled foul — foul with sickness and not the ordinary stink of the fields — she grew thinner and whiter.

'Grandmother says her skin is like the clouds — in places you can see through to her blue veins and small hungry bones.'

'Do you know who she is, Mosa? Is she the girl they are looking for?'

'Maybe — '

Maybe.

22

The band started up. Two fiddles, an accordion and drums. Encouraged by much whooping and whistling, Darren led his bride onto the dance floor. Coloured lights swirled overhead, gleaming back from his glossy, oiled hair. The bride lifted her skirts and began to jig.

Regina felt pale. She pinched her cheeks to bring back the colour; her skin felt rubbery and slightly numb. There had been a tray of sherry by the door, a line of Irishmen and women, nodding hats. The bride was no more than a girl, pearly skin with two pink flushes on her cheeks where all the guests had kissed her. Women in short black frocks with aprons like frilled hankies filled their glasses with champagne. Harry said it wasn't champagne but 'fizzy German'. She drank from his glass as well as her own and when the time came for the toast a little hiccup escaped into the silence.

The wedding service had gone on forever, and was followed by a nuptial mass, inaudible whispering from a distant altar. She had started out feeling warm and radiant from a hot bath, but the heat was soon lost in the greeny-grey light of the church. Her dress was too thin. She could feel the gooseflesh on her shoulders. Harry had put his coat around her; she shrank inside it, cuddling herself in the warm, woolly smell of him.

Without a pause between tunes, the dancers

skidded around the floor. The waitresses took off their frilly aprons and joined the dance. The bride's veil was thrown aside, her plump face glowed with joy and perspiration. All around them, the guests clapped and whooped.

Harry shouted over the din. 'Did you ever learn country dancing?'

Regina cupped her hand over his ear. 'It was ballet that I learned.'

Harry smiled, a little crooked smile.

Regina lifted her chin. It was important to lift the chin, otherwise the little fold of slack skin, that all her exercising had not removed, would settle in a rim around her face. 'Do you think they'll serve coffee?'

'I don't know, do you want some?'

Regina cupped her hand again. 'I drank too much wine.' She patted her cheeks. 'I feel a bit numb.'

'Do you want to go home?'

'I just want some coffee.'

Harry looked around for a waitress. There seemed to be none on duty. In the corner of the hall a bar had opened. He could see guests with money in their hands. There was no sign of any coffee.

'It looks as though the hospitality's over.' He loosened his tie. 'Shall we see if we can get coffee somewhere else?'

'Isn't it too soon? We mustn't offend.' She heard herself picking out the words.

'They won't miss us now.' Once more, Harry put his coat about her shoulders. She thrust her feet into her shoes but as she stood up the world slipped sideways. She felt the hard polished floor under her hands. Harry groaned.

'Did I hurt you, Harry? I didn't mean to hurt you.'

'I wasn't expecting the weight.'

'I didn't mean to . . . ' Regina forgot what she was saying. Laughing Irishmen crowded round her, a circle of faces like bright lollipops.

'Is she all right?'

'Sure, she's had a few.'

'Can happen to anyone.'

'Is it you that's with her, sir?'

'It's Harry Crane she's with.'

She was brought upright and there was the face of the groom, shiny and smiling. 'Harry's just here in the chair, Mrs Crane. He's just winded.'

'Was it the floor, made you slip?'

'It's just my shoes,' said Regina. 'I'll be all right if I take off my shoes.'

Someone shouted to the groom. 'You'd better watch your bride, Darren. It wouldn't do for her to go slipping in her condition.'

The pavement felt cool and firm. Harry was beside her and behind them in the hall, the band had begun again.

'I'm very sorry, Harry? I'm sorry I made such a fool of myself.'

He said nothing. Regina held out her shoes.

'They've got slippy soles, look . . . '

He didn't look. His arm was up, hailing a taxi. She watched the numbers on the meter, almost four pounds before they turned into her road.

The cab stopped and there was a click as he released the door.

'Won't you come in, Harry? I'm sober now, really I am.'

He climbed awkwardly out of the cab and paid the driver.

'Are you hurt, Harry?'

'It's nothing. It's my back — it gives me trouble, sometimes.'

'Was it when I fell? I didn't mean to fall, it was the shoes and the wine.'

He leaned heavily upon her as they mounted the steps to the front door. She took his coat and went straight to the kitchen to put the kettle on. When she returned he was stretched out on the sofa.

'Shall I get you a pillow?'

She brought the best one, frilled satin. A present from Thanos — for a long-ago birthday when the name Regina had still meant good fortune for him.

'Look, it has my name on it. Even his bastard brothers wouldn't take that.' Harry let her tuck the pillow behind his head. 'I should have put my name on the cooker, shouldn't I?'

He closed his eyes and immediately his face relaxed, slackened.

'You look so old, Harry.' The words were out before she had thought of them but he didn't seem to hear. She hurried to the bathroom and studied her reflection in the draughty yellow light.

You look old too, Regina Jones. Old and used.

Harry was sleeping, he'd let the coffee go cold. She made a fresh cup and put it on the hearth by the gas fire. His eyes were still closed. For a while she sat by his feet. He didn't stir. She put on the television, an ancient veneered box, rented in her name. The first channel was showing a film about Australia. Flat baked plains and squashed suburbs. The animals were exotic, the people ordinary and dull. With all the sun and the space, it should have looked like Africa, but it was unlike, utterly unlike the world she remembered.

When the film ended she was hungry. The wine had left a sour taste in her mouth. Behind her on the sofa, Harry snored.

'Harry — ' She shook his hand. 'Harry — do you want something to eat?'

He stirred. 'What time is it?'

'It's only eight o'clock. I'm hungry — we've had nothing since the wedding breakfast. Shall I make a sandwich? Do you like pickle? I can do corned beef and pickle.'

She watched him moisten his lips and swallow.

'Have you anything else?'

'Sardines, nice ones in tomato sauce. I can do sardines on toast.'

Harry shook his head. With stiff movements he eased himself off the sofa. 'I shouldn't be here, Regina.'

'Is it better? Do you feel better?'

'Yes, yes. It was only a twinge.'

'I'm sorry I fell. Did I say that already? I am sorry though, I meant you to be proud of me.'

Harry looked up at her. 'You look so like Eugenie sometimes.'

'You think so?'

'Sometimes you do.'

'Crazy like her, you mean?'

'Not at all. She wasn't always crazy.'

Regina switched off the television. 'I'm going to see her on Saturday.' She reached for a bundle of letters that rested on the mantelshelf. 'Most of the letters are for Thanos. I haven't answered them. How do you write that letter? Dear someone, I am sorry to tell you he is dead?'

She handed him an envelope. 'But this one was addressed to me, so I opened it.'

She kept talking while Harry read the letter.

'Why would they say that, Harry? What does it mean?'

The letter was short. Doctor Morris would like a word with Mrs Paros. Could she ring and make an appointment?

'I'm going anyway. It'll soon be Christmas. I always go at Christmas.' She looked at Harry. He said nothing, waiting. She turned away, fiddling with the letters on the mantel-shelf. 'I used to go — I used to go a lot. Every month, at least.' She turned back to him. There were tears in her eyes. 'She never knew me. Not once. After a while, the weeks and months go by. It gets harder to make the effort, to start again — '

Harry nodded. 'Are you the only one who goes? Does Olivia ever go?'

Regina pulled a face. 'Once they told me she did. I don't know when. I never saw her there. But this,' she raised the letter, 'why does this Doctor want to see me?'

'Perhaps they want to move her,' said Harry. 'Maybe the hospital is being closed — so many seem to be closing down these days.'

Regina sat on the arm of the sofa. 'She doesn't want to move.'

'If she no longer requires treatment they may want to give her bed to someone else.'

'And then who will look after her? I can't take care of her! I don't even have a home for myself!'

'There'll be some sort of community care, I'm sure.'

'Community care — have you seen what happens? They're out on the streets; cardboard cities. Is that what they plan for my mother? Is that what we have come to?'

'It won't be as bad as that.'

Suddenly, unexpectedly, Harry reached for her hand. It surprised Harry because he had not thought of it in advance, and it was years since he'd held anyone's hand. Hers felt warm. Harry held it lightly in case she wanted him to let go.

Regina was surprised too. His hand was firmer and stronger than she might have imagined. At first she kept still, it felt so strange to be holding his hand. And then, when the strangeness subsided and their skins settled against each other, she felt herself moving towards him, his hand pulling hers, just as she was pulling his, bringing them together. Suddenly they kissed and she felt him come to life, fully of urgency, like a young man.

23

Voices. Low, guttural murmuring from the other side of the enclosure. She shifted herself. Her eyes blurred. Slowly she pulled them back into focus. The ant that she had been watching, bearing its load in and out of the thatch, was gone.

Something had changed. Not the going of the ant, for that was not change but the passage of time. The change now was something she could feel, an alteration in the air, the difference between darkness and shadow. It was the change that comes when a sleeper stirs in the night, the muscles of the body tingle in response to a new pressure. Such was the change, a change of pace, in the whistles of the goatherds, in the flat muscular feet of the headman, heavy on the beaten earth, the quick dark and light of his passing across the entrance to the hut.

And voices. Not loud, no more than a murmur, but heard. That was the difference, the change. Clear across the enclosure, as if the children had been hushed, babies put to the breast, goats distracted by feed or water, there had come a silence sufficient to carry the murmuring of men, sounds spilling and shelling to every corner of the enclosure; like an overspill of water, seeping and creeping, so that even there in her hut, against the rustle of thatch, the buzzing of flies, she could hear the voices of men. And specifically, quite distinctly and unarguably, the voice of a white man; a

212

different timbre, a sound less hollow, more of a whine than the tribesmen made. And without laughter, without the shouts and claps, the quick 'Hahs' that were the everyday exchange of these people.

The voices came nearer. Olivia tried to lift herself. The lightness she felt was illusion. Her body was a dead weight, too heavy to move. With an effort she turned her head, peered through, towards the opening where the flap of hide that served as a door was hooked back for the day-time. The women were nowhere to be seen; goat boys sat on the ground chewing stalks of grass.

The headman touching his forehead as he talked, feeling the contours of his face with long, broken-nailed fingers. The white man walked behind him, an unbuttoned shirt showing the last traces of a chequered pattern, hair glistening on his chest. Something about him, something in his stride, in the height of him, in the way he stood, not twelve feet from the hut, looking away from her, talking to the headman as if they had moved only for exercise and the proximity of the hut no more than coincidence, nothing that could influence the pattern of their talk; there was something familiar. She wanted to call out, she wanted to step out into the light, into the long low rays of the sun, to stand there bare foot on the beaten earth and call out to him, 'Have you come for me, David Jones?'

He had not looked at her directly. She had not seen all of his face, but she knew it to be his name. Her own name. The name of the man who stood so easily with the headman, shaking his head; who,

213

as she watched, reached into a pocket of the faded shirt and extracted three cigarettes and put them in the headman's hand, and then extracted two more, one for his own mouth, one for the headman. And then the slow, silent business of the headman producing a match from a deep buried pocket in the layers of khaki and the drapes of cloth that he wore against the day, the two men bending together, hands cupped to shield the flame from the wind.

They walked away, leaving behind the smell of the match, a whiff of sulphur and two puffs of smoke that scattered in the wind as fast as she saw them, the lighted splinter rolled against a wet fingertip and placed back in the box that went back into the pocket between the layers of cloth.

'Hey there!'

It was her voice that had shouted 'Hey there!' A shout no more than a puff of breath in her throat.

Olivia closed her eyes. The noises of the manyatta had begun again; the clatter of pots and women, laughing.

Long, long, later, or so it seemed, although the light was still there, as if it had waited, the sun suspended while she slept, she gathered herself once more to consciousness. Huge black feet stood beside her face. Beside them were the smaller feet of Marie-Therese. The weight of her head was an anchor, holding her lightened, empty body on the ground. 'Tsk, tusk,' she heard them say.

'Eh . . . '

'Tsk, tsk.'

24

The van swerved, so violently that Michael banged his head on the side window. The wheel juddered in his hand, dragging the vehicle sideways, crunching into the dirt at the side of the tarmac.

Jackson was on the back seat, fast asleep. He had not moved.

Michael squeezed his arm, pinched his cheek. 'Jackson, wake up! We've had a blow out.'

The African did no more than stir, as if a fly had irritated him. Michael touched the place on his head that had hit the side window. It felt tender and bruised. He opened the door and climbed down. The front left tyre was split, a drape of black rubber lying in the dust. He knelt down. The dust was warm under his knees. After the noise of the engine, the constant rattle and crash, hot wind screaming through the ventilators, the silence of the roadside was almost tangible, his ears rang with it.

The tool kit was in the back; a rusty box containing an ancient jack and a collection of spanners. 'Made in China', stamped in crooked letters on the shanks. Extracting the spare wheel entailed the removal of a rusted metal panel in the floor. None of the spanners in the tool box fitted the nuts that secured the panel. He improvised with a combination of an over-sized spanner and a screwdriver. The spare, when at last he pulled it free, was even older than the one that had burst, unevenly worn, strips of tread between bald patches.

Sweat prickled on his forehead. Rings of dust marked his arms as he pumped the jack handle.

Jackson's face appeared in the window.

'What are you doing?'

'Changing a wheel.'

'Am I on a jack?'

Michael nodded. 'You'd better keep still.'

'You know what to do?'

Michael wiped the sweat from his face with a handkerchief. 'I know how to change a wheel.' He paused. Almost to himself he added, 'but I've never done it like this. I'd never have imagined myself doing it like this and in a place like this.'

They were roughly half way along the road from the coast to Nairobi. In front and behind, the tarmac strip stretched to the shimmering horizon. On either side was seemingly endless bush, red murram and scrubby grass dotted with the occasional thorn tree. The wheel-nuts were thick with a crust of grease and dust the colour of dried blood. He lifted the wheel from the hub and leaned it against the side of the van. He rolled the spare to the front of the car, lifted it onto the studs and threaded the nuts on.

With the jack down he tightened the wheel-nuts and banged the cover back into place.

'We'll need to get two new tyres in Nairobi.'

'New?'

'Have you seen the state of these? And while we're at it we'll get a second spare. One isn't enough.'

Jackson sank back out of sight. Michael climbed back into the driver's seat. The cab smelt of sweat, of Jackson's breath, of stale beer and sweet smoke.

They arrived in Nairobi just before sundown. People were going home, streaming along the roadsides, clinging to the rails of overcrowded buses, sweating in private cars. The last of the jacaranda blossom drifted brown and dry in the gutters.

Michael booked them into the same hotel as before. The receptionist looked long at Jackson and then stared at the register. As she placed the room-key on the counter she smiled, a spread of white teeth, one with a smear of lipstick.

'We hope you enjoy your stay.'

As Michael reached for his bag, she produced a fistful of faxes. 'We did not know you would return, Mr Ballantyne. We sent a message to London that you were no longer here.'

Most of the faxes carried the bank's insignia. David Elliot had written personally. 'We sympathise with your problems, Michael, but you must get in touch. We must know your movements.' Another was from Gillian. 'What the hell are you doing, Michael? Everyone is asking. Please phone at once.' The last was from his father, handwritten and signed 'your old Pops'. The words above were brief. 'Don't weaken, Michael. You have gone so far, there must be an outcome. You know your own reasons for this adventure.'

The room was exactly like the first. Twin beds, a bible on the bedside locker.

'We can't stay here!' Jackson cried as Michael tipped the bellboy. 'This place is for Nothankyous!'

'For what?'

'Nothankyous.'

'What are they?'

'No-Thank-Yous — it is what we call tourists. Because they say it all the time. You walk up to a tourist on the beach and before you say hello, even before you open your mouth, they say 'Nothankyou'.'

Michael lifted the telephone receiver and dialled.

Jackson sat in the armchair and pulled open the door of the mini-bar. 'Is there supposed to be beer in here?'

A voice on the telephone distracted Michael's attention. He asked for Inspector Ojekwo and was surprised to be put straight through.

'It is good to hear from you, Mr Ballantyne.'

'I'm in Nairobi.'

'Where in Nairobi?'

Michael told him the name of the hotel.

'How splendid.'

'Do you have any news for me?'

'We have news for you, Mr Ballantyne. We have located the brother.'

'I thought — ' Michael stopped his tongue. There was no point in scoring, in reminding the Inspector of the report he had been shown of the interview with David, weeks before.

'Where is he?'

'We found him through the school. The fathers have a mission out in Dida Galgalu. Do you know this place, Mr Ballantyne?'

'No.'

'Not many know it.'

'Does David know where she is?'

'We had a report of a white woman up there.'

'I know, Mrs Bell gave me your message. I thought she might be here already, that she might be here in hospital, safe — '

'No Mr Ballantyne, she is not here.'

'Where then?'

'We are still waiting for details.'

Michael sighed.

'Mr Ballantyne?' The Inspector's voice came on again. 'Why don't we meet? I could explain the situation more clearly than over the phone.'

'I'll come to your office.'

'Oh . . . ' Ojekwo let the sound linger. 'Some things are better discussed in less formal surroundings. What about your hotel?'

'Here?'

'Yes. It's a long time since I had a meal there.'

'A meal? D . . . do you mean come to dinner?'

'Thank you Mr Ballantyne, you are very generous. I'll see you at eight.' The line went dead.

Michael replaced the receiver and went into the bathroom. Reflected in the mirror, his face looked thinner, sharper featured. There were lines in the corner of his eyes that had not been there before.

* * *

The terrace restaurant was lit with dim anti-mosquito lighting. A softly hushing fountain filtered the noise of the city. Parties of men and women sat at tables clustered with beer bottles and glasses, their features lost in the semi-darkness, he could see only the gleam of yellow light on black skin, or a flash of teeth when someone laughed.

Michael felt displaced. He had chosen a table out on the terrace to be away from the tourists in the bar, from the hoot and shriek of their laughter; but still he was the only one alone, a solitary man in a sea of talk and gaiety, of confidence, comfortable waves, summoning another bottle of beer, or papaya juice, more of what would make more of their laughter.

At ten o'clock, when the tables round him had emptied and filled again, two hours later than he had promised, Inspector Ojekwo appeared. Michael stood to greet him.

'Don't get up. Did you have a beer already?' Without waiting for an answer Ojekwo summoned a waiter.

'Two Premiums.'

The Inspector shook his hand, holding it in both of his own.

'What news is there?' Michael demanded, unable to contain his impatience.

'You are angry because I am late?'

'No — well — '

'After you phoned we had further news. I am late because of paperwork.' He paused. 'Do you know of this, Mr Ballantyne? Do you know of our flying doctor service?'

Michael nodded. The Inspector filled his glass.

'Well?' demanded Michael. 'Is she here? Have they brought her down?'

'I will tell you, Mr Ballantyne.' He took a swig of beer. 'It need not be me, you understand. I could have left this job to my subordinate, or some foolish young man from your High Commission, someone who does not know the story and has never met you. But I am telling you myself, Mr Ballantyne, because when it is bad news it is best heard from the horse's mouth.'

There was a rushing noise in Michael's ears, his vision narrowed, as if he was looking through a tunnel, as if all there was to see was the face of Ojekwo. 'What bad news?'

'It was her brother, it was David Jones who called for the doctor. There was a delay.'

'What is wrong with her?' Michael shouted his question, but in his own ears his voice was faint, heard as if through the wall of interference.

The African drank deeply from his glass. There was a fine rim of froth on his upper lip as he reached across the table and took hold of Michael's hands.

'I am sorry, my friend. She has been days in the desert. Then the village people — ' He shrugged as if to apologise. 'They know nothing of the European weakness. Dehydration, sunburn, dysentery . . . '

Michael's hands were held in a vice.

'She will not be a pretty sight, Mr Ballantyne. I am afraid it is true.'

'But she is alive?' Michael shouted, trying to release his hands. 'She is alive?'

Across the terrace people turned their heads. A woman who had her spectacles on her head, like an aviator's goggles, pulled them down to look at him. A waiter hovered. Ojekwo ordered brandy. His handkerchief smelled of cologne.

25

Late in the night he heard Jackson stir in the twin bed beside him. A match was struck.

'Are you awake?'

Michael grunted.

There was a stink of smoke. He heard the low whistle of Jackson's breath.

'You should try some of this. It will make you feel better.' The glow moved towards him across the space between the beds. A moistened roll of paper and sweet tobacco was thrust between his fingers.

Michael breathed in, coughed.

'Not so fast,' Jackson whispered. 'That's it. Take it in, slowly, *pole-pole*.'

Michael lay back against the pillows. The smoke filled his head with sweetness.

'What did you give the policeman to eat?'

'Steak.' Michael coughed a little, then took another puff. 'And fried potatoes.'

'I had the same!' Jackson cried. 'I rang the telephone and it was brought to me. A tray with a cloth, and ketchup, *maridadi sana!*'

'Good,' said Michael.

Jackson's voice changed key. 'I'm sorry for your trouble.'

Michael murmured something.

'She is cured now, in the hospital?'

'Not cured. They do not yet know if she will survive.'

Jackson blew a mouthful of smoke. 'But we can pray for her.'

Michael sighed. They had said the same in the hospital. 'We must pray to God.'

With shame he remembered the thought he had had at the time. The God you pray to cannot be the same as mine. His God was English, present in the fabric of the village church at Highhurst, in the hymns he sang at school, in the words of the vicar who buried his grandmother. A tradition more than a personage, an idea as English as muffins; utterly remote from the crowded circus of the hospital.

'They have not br . . . brought her here!' The words exploded from his mouth as he was led along a warren of corridors lined with beds, camp-beds, mattresses on the floor, black, hopeless eyes staring from coverless pillows.

Ojekwo, who had finished his dinner with great relish and then eaten from Michael's plate too before offering to drive him to the hospital, put his tubby fist against Michael's chest. 'Be grateful, my friend, this is the best.'

The corridors seemed endless. They were led by an auxiliary in a faded blue overall. Michael was aware of the privilege, the difficulty he would have had if the policeman had not, beyond all call of duty, escorted him.

A pair of orderlies thundered past, bearing a stretcher on which lay a man with an open wound on his chest.

'A fight in a beer hall,' said Ojekwo. 'It will have been a broken bottle.'

Michael found himself staring at the ragged,

bloody skin, remembering Joseph's scar. Joseph had survived.

At last there was a staircase; across the door of a single lift there was a sign, 'Out of Order'.

They walked up two flights. Ojekwo panted beside him. 'This part is still for private patients. If we did not have their fees there might be no hospital at all.'

The contrast was startling. Gone was the clamour and stink of the corridors. Here there was unfilled space, a smell of disinfectant, a nurse in uniform sitting at a desk between two large low-lit wards. She led them to a door at the side, a room separated from the ward by glazed walls.

'The doctor is examining her now, you may only look.'

There was little to see; a row of white-coated backs bent over, a woman wearing a plastic apron bustling about with trays and swabs. Momentarily she looked up and Michael recognised the Dutch nurse he had talked to in the hotel.

She opened the door but did not let him through and did not smile. 'So they found your girl.'

'Is . . . is . . . ?'

'She is alive. The consultant will tell you more when he has finished.'

Ojekwo went home. Michael sat beside the nurse's desk and sipped sweet tea. After an hour or so the side room emptied and he saw the Dutch nurse point him out to a small man who was wiping his hands on a towel.

The consultant had a strong accent. It was hard to concentrate on what was said, hard to stop a flood-tide of questions.

'There are no broken bones. She is very weak but the response to rehydration is good. There is some infection of the wounds on her feet and the burns but, provided she survives, this can be treated.'

'What are her chances?'

'We will know better tomorrow. She was fit before this happened?'

'Yes.'

'Good. She will need to be strong. Strong in her mind as well as her body.'

There was a moment, when at last he sat beside Olivia's bed, appalled by her peeling shrivelled face, swollen lips, cratered like crackling on a pot roast, her body, naked but for a kind of diaper, shapeless as a plucked, skinny chicken, bones and veins almost visible through skin that was a patchwork of puffy blisters, shiny with ointment, a moment when he wanted no more of it. There was nothing here to love. He felt utterly tired, tired of being bewildered, tired of this woman for whom he had broken every rule, who did not understand his achievements, for whom everything he owned and was and would become was useless.

He sat in silence, thinking of all his dreams, the way she had looked curled on the sofa in front of his fire, the sleeves of his sweater dangling down beyond her hands, of the abacus on his desk, of the breasts that had nestled in his hands, unrecognisable now.

For a long time he sat in silence and then the words came out in a rush. 'Olivia! Olivia! You've got to get better. Do you hear me? Please get better.

Please be yourself again. I can't stand it here. I want to take you home. I want you to be well. I want everything to be normal . . .'

'Michael?' A whisper.

He jumped. Her eyes were open, blue and clear and familiar.

'For God's sake, how long have you been awake?'

'I don't know. Things seem to come and go.'

'Have you been listening to me babbling on?'

'I didn't have a choice.' A blistered hand hovered near his face. 'Poor Michael, have you been having a terrible time?'

'I can't tell you. This country is a nightmare. Everywhere is so bloody crowded and dirty. You can't rely on anyone, no-one speaks English, nothing makes any sense — and the smell — '

He stopped. Her fingers had moved towards her lips. He realised she was smiling.

'Oh God, listen to me. You've just been through hell on earth and here I am complaining about the smell.'

'You mustn't make me giggle. It hurts my face.'

He restrained himself from lunging at her, gathering her into his arms and squeezing with delight that she should want to giggle, even at his own expense; she could not be dying if she wanted to giggle. He leaned very close. 'I love you, Olivia. I'm going to take you home. I am going to take you to Highhurst.'

'I didn't talk to him. I didn't speak to David.'

'That can wait now. You have to concentrate on getting better.'

'But I must do it.'

'You can't possibly, look at the state of you.'

'I want him to know.'

Michael sighed. 'You are a stubborn woman, Olivia Jones.'

'If I wasn't stubborn I'd be dead.'

By the time he'd thought of a response she had fallen asleep.

'She is better than I expected. I can't believe she will die.'

Jackson passed the joint back across the space between the beds and Michael took a long drag, resisting the urge to cough as the smoke filled his lungs. He breathed it out through his nostrils, pacing its flow.

'Still you must pray to God.'

'No. There is something more pressing than prayer.'

'More pressing? What is pressing?'

'I must do what she came for. I must go and see this god-damned brother of hers and get him to come to England.'

'And this man, her brother, he is at the place where she is found?'

'It's some distance away, but the same area, yes.'

Michael took another drag and coughed. 'Do you want to go home, Jackson? There's no point in you coming with me.'

'I promised Mrs Bell that I would keep you safe and sound.'

'But you haven't helped.' Michael heard himself belch and, to his surprise, chuckle. 'I had to do half the driving, you've been drinking beer and sleeping in the back.'

Jackson clicked his tongue. 'After tonight you will need me. The places you are going, white men do not travel alone.'

Michael passed the joint back and saw the butt glow again.

'Where did the policeman say this lady was found?'

'He showed me on the map. A place called Dida Galgalu. A black desert, he says, a hundred miles from the lake — from anywhere.'

'And this is where we are going?'

'That's where the brother is.'

'It is safari mkubwa. A long way.'

'You don't have to come.'

'Of course I come. Jackson is your friend.'

'You're no good to me if you're drunk.'

He heard the African move. The bedsprings creaked and then a light came on. He was propped up on the pillows. 'After tonight, we make serious safari. After tonight, no more beers.'

'How soon can we get there?'

Jackson climbed out of bed and crossed the room. He was naked. Without the slightest embarrassment or self consciousness he brought the map and laid it out on the sheets over Michael's legs.

'Here?' Jackson's finger, a rim of dirt under the pink nail, pointed to where, with a pencil held between two unbending fingers, Olivia had marked a cross.

'Yes. There seems to be no road at all,' said Michael.

'Tomorrow we will get a bigger map,' said Jackson. 'It will show us the tracks that lead there.' He paused to run his teeth behind a dirty fingernail. 'We can drive each other and you will see Africa uncooked.'

'Uncooked?'

'What is the word?'

'Do you mean raw?'

'Yes, I mean Africa, raw.'

26

Two days later they departed at sunrise, leaving the city on a fast broad highway, markings newly painted, white on black. Jackson was driving. Michael sat beside him, gazing out at miles of suburbs, patches of prosperity, estates of white painted houses with tinted glass and security guards in uniform, divided by shanty towns, children and chickens running in the dirt, a barber shop by the road, a sliver of mirror hanging from a tree.

They had called at the hospital on the way out. Olivia was awake, propped on a mound of pillows. Her skin, shiny with cream, was already beginning to heal. A nurse had washed her hair, trimmed her nails.

'They've been feeding me with baby food and porridge and the most disgustingly runny scrambled egg.'

'Good, eat lots.'

'The porridge reminds me of England. I keep thinking of the autumn, of rainy pavements and snowfalls. I never thought I could miss them.'

Michael hovered by her bed, frustrated that there was still no part of her that was safe to touch. He wanted just to gather her up and make her well, to give her a long warm hug.

'And crumpets and honey.'

'You shall have them. You shall have everything you want.'

They did not speak of his impending journey but as he bent to plant a feather kiss of farewell on her lips, she stared long and hard into his face. 'Don't be too brave, Michael. I don't want you to be anything other than you are.'

* * *

After the suburbs there was grassland, bridges over streams the colour of strong-brewed tea. An hour passed before they reached the emptiness that he expected, looked for: green turning to brown. A cowman in a tattered shirt lifted his stick as they passed. The gesture was for his herd, waiting to cross from the other side. The road deteriorated to pitted tarmac, cracked and narrow, but Jackson made no allowance for the change. He drove as if they were pursued. The air was filled with the whistle of wind and the clatter of stones thrown up against the reinforced base of the cab. Michael watched Jackson's hands. The gear-stick rested in the strong web of yellow-pink flesh between his finger and thumb. He mused on the strangeness of the colour. Never having thought of it, he'd assumed a black man was black. Jackson's colour was as varied as his own.

After miles of dry grass, yellow and brittle, and low thorn trees squatting over sparse pools of shade, like umbrellas in a dun-coloured carnival, the road started to climb, winding back and forth along the side of an escarpment. Michael realised, with a surge of enthusiasm, that they were on the edge of the Rift Valley.

Jackson pulled into a lay-by. 'Here we can stretch our legs.'

The African went behind a bush to pee. Michael stood at the edge of the road, his clothes fluttering in the warm draughts of air rising, and heard the long, uninhibited stream as Jackson relieved himself.

Humming, Jackson returned to the cab and extracted a cardboard box containing a picnic from the hotel. He opened bottles of warm Coke and ate a cheese sandwich between puffs from his cigarette. Michael shook his head as the box was offered to him. His stomach felt full and tight as a closed clam shell.

They left the Rift behind, weaving north through an area of stony hillside, the road a raw surface of rock and loose stones that followed a twisting route around the hills. There was nothing to be seen but scrub and parched grass and occasionally, a glimpse of a dry river bed, snaking by the road. Late in the afternoon they reached an area of highland that was cool and green. There were herds of humped cows and skinny goats in the charge of small boys, and sometimes clumps of conifers, long branches hanging to the ground, like the wings of ragged birds. A series of small roads began to converge on theirs and before the daylight was quite gone they could see, lying in a flat-bottomed valley, the lights of Maralal.

'There is a lodge here where you can stay,' said Jackson, as they weaved through the main street. Camels and barrows slowed their progress. Michael noticed the women, their features unlike those he had seen further south. These faces were fine, slender, liquid eyes picked out by the light of kerosene lamps hanging in the doorways of shops and stalls.

The lodge was little more than a large house with wide verandahs and echoing wooden floors. Rich smells wafted in from the town, of spiced meat roasting on open braziers, the sharp, sour smell of camel and goat dung, and overlaying it all, a hint of green, of the cool stands of conifers that draped the hills around them.

He washed in a leaky basin in one corner of his room and exchanged his dusty shorts for a pair of jeans. Jackson led him to a cafe in the town. They sat on metal chairs and ate a roasted chicken with fried rice.

'Now we have some beer.'

Amused by the ease with which his promise not to drink was abandoned, and too thirsty himself to protest, he followed the African into a ramshackle bar where the beer was as warm as the damp air, and the froth from the bottle coated his lips and the unlicked places of his mouth.

Jackson left him alone at the bar, loping off to talk to a man whose tight blue jeans were tucked into fringed cowboy boots. A few words were exchanged and the man turned to look at Michael. Michael nodded to him but there was no response.

There was no evidence of wine or spirits for sale. Jackson had advised him to drink bottled beer — 'Beer is safer than water . . . ' Some customers drank from the familiar brown glass bottles but most were served by means of a soup ladle from a tub behind the bar.

The barman saw him looking at it and grinned. 'Brewed for a good stomach, my friend. Some men go blind.'

'Blind?'

The man shrugged. 'Or dead.'

Michael surveyed his surroundings, above the heads of the drinkers the cracked ceiling was decorated by a faded paper chain with a fold-out Christmas tree at the centre.

'Is it Christmas already?'

The barman smiled. 'Very soon.'

Michael took his beer and sat down at a rickety table. There was no sign of Jackson. Across the room, a woman was folding her vast, painted lips around the head of a bottle. Her thighs bulged under a short orange skirt. Her eyes were closed. He watched the swell and fall of her throat as she drew the liquid in. When the bottle was empty, she licked her tongue around the top, stood it carefully on the table and opened her eyes.

Too late, he looked away. From the corner of his eye, he saw her push back her stool and move towards him. He looked at the bar. Sweat seemed to hang in the air like a fog, a waterlogged mist, dampening the bodies of the drinkers. Urgently he looked around, but there was no sign of Jackson.

'Hello, baby.'

Michael nodded.

'You buy me a drink?'

It was easier to say yes than no. He raised his hand to a youngster who was struggling through the crowd with a tray of bottles.

'Two beers, please.'

'Four.' It was the woman.

'I only want one. It isn't chilled.'

The woman shrugged. 'Four — ' she repeated.

Four bottles were put on the table. Michael put a note on the tray and a trail of change slipped into his palm.

The woman was already drinking, eyes closed, drawing the beer into herself, like a suckling child. When the first bottle was empty she picked up the second. One eye opened, above the line of the up-raised bottle. After a moment she put it down, empty.

'You want fuck, baby?'

Michael swallowed. 'I'm just waiting for a friend.'

'One hundred shillings.'

Michael shook his head.

She shrugged, causing her massive breasts to heave beneath the nylon sweater.

'Fifty — no games.'

She placed a warm hand on his crotch.

He shook his head once more, tried to pull back his chair, and found himself against the wall. The woman laughed. She tugged at the zip of his fly.

'No. That's not why I'm here.' He leaned back as far as the trapped space of his chair permitted. To his horror, he realised his body was responding to her hand. 'Please — '

'You like?'

She grinned. Her face loomed close to his. He could see pearls of sweat above the line of lipstick.

Someone appeared behind her, looking at Michael over her head. It was Jackson's friend. 'You want this girl?'

Michael shook his head. The man said something to the woman. She gave one last squeeze, withdrew her fingers and heaved herself out of her chair. With slow movements she gathered all four beer bottles, including the one that Michael had started, against her breasts. Michael looked up to see Jackson laughing down at him.

'Come on, Mr Michael. Do up your zip. Jackson has come to save you.'

Meekly Michael followed him out of the bar.

★ ★ ★

They left the hills behind, following the road across a bleak, dry plain. The surface was hard, with corrugations that shook the vehicle and its occupants in ceaseless head-aching unison. Almost a whole day had passed, interrupted by a single township, a cluster of shops and little boys running after the van. Jackson pointed ahead. In the distance, where the road disappeared into greyness, rose a wide, scar-sided mountain. 'Mount Kulal. The people up here believe it is where God lives.'

'Aren't they Christians?'

'They mix it up. Many are baptised but Kulal is where God lives. It is where the wind comes from. You will see, further on, how the wind could make you think of God.'

They spent the last night on the road. Jackson produced two old and somewhat smelly blankets.

He gave one to Michael and took the other outside where he settled himself on the ground beside the van.

'It is more comfortable,' he said, answering Michael's unspoken question. 'In the morning Mr Michael will be stiff and sore. Jackson will be full of life.'

Doubled up on the back seat, Michael could see Jackson's point but nothing would persuade him to sleep on the ground, at the mercy of whatever crawled there. With this thought came his worst and most vivid image of Olivia. Dear God, what had she endured? What nightmare had she lived through? Anguished and sleepless, he shivered under the dirty blanket and stared out at the stars.

27

The mission was unfenced. On one side was a length of levelled ground marked by white painted stones. On the other a clump of green vegetation, starkly bright against the grey desert, marking the site of a fresh water spring.

Jackson had parked the van a way back.

'Won't you come in with me?' Michael had asked. 'Don't you want some water or something?'

'Later I'll come.' Gently Jackson had pushed him through the door. 'I will sleep now, while you do this business.'

Michael wondered what 'this business' was. He wondered, now that he had come all this way, whether there was really a purpose in this journey. Was it possible that he could persuade David Jones to do what she wanted?

A butterfly fluttered ahead of him, yellow and blue, like a small coloured phantom. He looked back at the van. All that could be seen of Jackson was a pair of feet sticking through the open window of the cab.

A row of shrubs had been planted by small heaps of rock that marked the entrance to the mission. The shrubs were in flower, a single bloom on the head of each stem. A show of ragged daisies. The main building was a long low structure of mud and stick with a corrugated roof on which a wooden cross turned and twisted in the wind. He could see small children, scarcely dressed, sitting in the shade. As he approached they started jumping up, shouting at him. There was a stampede of small, bare feet, tiny hands reaching up, cries of 'Jambo! Hello!' He felt himself smiling, greeting them in return as they clutched his hands and his legs, and even the hem of his shorts.

'I am looking for Mr Jones, Mr David Jones.'

'David! David!' they shouted, pulling him to the side, towards another building with windows down each side, glassless squares of mesh lined up to catch the breeze. As he came close he could see heads popping up, brief darting glances, against the light. A voice called out. The children stopped, letting Michael go so suddenly that he staggered.

The man on the step wore a faded tee-shirt. His hair was dark and curly, eyes like Olivia's.

'David?' Michael held out his hand. It was shaken in a limp, casual way. 'I'm a friend of your sister, Olivia.'

'You drove here alone?'

'No — there's someone in the van.'

The white man remained on the step, leaning against a post and looking down at Michael.

Michael felt awkward, suddenly embarrassed. This wasn't what he'd expected. Not that he could have described what he'd expected, or hoped for.

'You'll want to wash.' David stepped down onto the dust. He was tall, with a lean wiry strength that revealed itself in the way he walked, loping effortlessly with a minimum of wasted effort; the same loose-limbed walk Michael had seen among the Africans. He remembered Jessie's story of

Gareth Jones, the run on lipstick in the white settlement north of Mombasa. Was it this look that had fluttered their hearts all those years ago; this calm, lash-heavy stare?

David led him across the mission compound. There was no tarmac, no grass, nothing but the loose, stony sand of the desert and the dust rippling over his shoes in the breeze. David wore no shoes. His feet were flat and wide. Like his legs and arms, the upper parts were covered in dark hair.

His feet would be hard, Michael thought, a native's feet.

David opened an unpainted door beside the classroom. The room was narrow and dark; a shower-head stuck straight out of the wall. Beside it was a hole with concrete footholds on either side. The smell was strong and brown, the smell of quarters, of unwatered Africa.

'We're short of water,' said David. 'If you could keep it brief.'

Michael used the lavatory and then turned on the shower. There was only one tap. It was unmarked but the water was warm, fed by a pipe that snaked across the baked earth of the compound outside. He stood under the head and let the thin, warm trickle wet his hair and his clothes.

He emerged dripping, for there was no towel. The children had gathered once more beside the chapel. A lesson was in progress; a young girl in a European dress pointed to a blackboard propped against the chapel wall. From the classroom alongside came the sound of chanting and once more, heads appeared, popping up and down against the light. David was

241

waiting in the shade, watching the class of infants by the chapel. He stirred as Michael approached.

'What should we teach these children?'

'What?'

'History? Geography? English?' David's expression was absorbed, full of concern, as if the question had troubled him for years. 'What about Art? Most of these children have never seen a colouring book. They'll trade two litres of goat's milk for a biro.' Briefly David laughed, a sharp ironic sound. 'Why should we teach them Art? That's what the Inspector of Schools said — the one time that he came — all dressed up in his suit and his briefcase. He counted the names on the register and wrote in his report that we should teach more History.'

Michael remained silent.

'Why not Art? How is Art less useful than History or Mathematics? There could be a Gaugin here, a Matisse who has yet to see a paintbrush.'

'Don't they have their . . . ' Michael faltered, he couldn't think of a better word. 'Don't they have their native art? Don't they carve?'

'Carve? Only rubbish. The traditional stuff has been squeezed out. Now they make nothing but stools and spears. The tourists take them as far as the airport and throw them away. The spears are too big for hand-luggage, too awkward for suitcases.'

'What kind of art would you teach them?' Michael asked, drawn into the debate, in spite of himself.

'Colour,' said David. 'Colour and light. There is so much colour up here.'

Michael raised his eyebrows. 'It all looks grey to me.'

'You haven't looked properly. The grey is actually a composite of yellow, red and brown.'

Michael ran his hands through his hair, drying awkwardly in the hot sun. Was this what he had come for? To discuss the colour of the desert?

'I've been staying with your aunt, Jessie Bell.'

'She must be upset — about all this.'

David spoke abruptly but Michael had the impression of something being set aside rather than dismissed. From the door of what appeared to be an office, he said, 'It's the priest's room really, but I use it in his absence.' He sat behind a desk and took a bottle of whisky from the drawer. 'I've been saving this.' He offered Michael the open neck of the bottle.

The whisky was unlike any he had ever tasted.

'They make it down-country,' said David. He turned the bottle round to show Michael the label. 'Highland Mist.' He took a long swallow and patted the pockets of his shirt. 'Do you have any smokes?'

'I don't — but my driver . . . '

'Where is he?'

'He's waiting in the van.'

David found a cigarette in the drawer of the desk and lit it, letting the smoke out with a sigh. 'Poor old Jessie. Did she tell you about us all?'

Michael nodded.

'White mischief gone sour, eh?'

Michael said nothing. He could think of nothing to say. Whatever he had expected, it was not this, sitting in this small, stifling room, drinking whisky.

David offered the bottle again. The second mouthful was less shocking than the first. He put the bottle on the desk. 'The flying doctor — couldn't he have come sooner?'

David waved his hand. 'It's a she. The flying doctor is a woman. She had another call. By the time she came back — ' He made a little flicking sound with his fingers.

Michael looked away. Could that be how it was, here in this desolate place? Life and death in the flicking of a finger. He put the bottle to his lips and once more the whisky burned his throat. David puffed at his cigarette, blowing the smoke through the window. Michael searched for something to say.

'Was there a charge? Did you have to pay for the doctor?'

'There is no charge. They like you to make a donation if you can.'

'I should like to make a donation.'

David waved his hand. 'It's been dealt with.'

'Surely the mission cannot afford — '

'The mission? The mission has nothing to give. It was I, or rather Harry Crane who paid!'

'Harry Crane paid?'

'It was his money — his conscience money — that sits down in Nairobi, festering. This was as good a use for it as any.'

In spite of himself, his preoccupations, Michael felt a curiosity. 'What do you mean, his conscience money?'

'The money he put in trust — half the proceeds of his fine house in trust for the child he no longer wanted. It kept my old school in chalk for a decade.'

David was offering the bottle again. 'Do you want some more?'

Michael shook his head. 'No, thank you. But tell me, wha . . . what is it that you do here?'

David took a drag of smoke from his cigarette and exhaled through his nose. 'I teach. Geography, History, English.'

'I thought perhaps you were up here training to be a priest.'

'Up here? You don't come up here to train for anything.'

'I just thought — Jessie thought — '

David waved his hand towards the open door and Michael had a sudden sense of the dry, unlit space of the compound outside.

'The people here are already Christians,' said David. 'They'll tell you their names — Matthew, Mark, Luke and John — there's even a Judas — someone made a mistake. You should see them all on Sundays; all the singing and clapping. God, to them, is chang'aa.'

'Chang'aa?'

'The spirit they drink.'

Michael was perplexed, then he saw what David meant, God in oblivion, in the bar where Jackson had taken him, in a brown scummy liquid served from a bucket.

David was stubbing out his cigarette. 'That driver of yours must be thirsty.'

'He has some water in the car.'

'Are you going to leave him out there all day?' David rose and opened the door. 'Let's go and find him.'

They walked back across the compound. The older class had finished. Girls and boys, teenagers, spilled out into the sunshine. More restrained than the little ones, they eyed him from afar.

Jackson was sitting in the van, the doors wide, his feet up on the dashboard. He grinned at Michael.

'This is David Jones.'

Jackson shook David's hand. 'We came a long way to see you, Mr David Jones.'

'Would you like something to eat?'

Michael caught the stale smell of Jackson's clothes as he stepped out of the vehicle. I must have smelled as bad, he thought. We must be a ripe pair.

They ate on the verandah outside David's office: into metal bowls a young woman ladled a kind of salty porridge with fried sweet potatoes. Jackson ate a huge amount and at the end, smacked his lips with satisfaction.

David gave him a cigarette and swept spilt grains of salt out onto the dust. He turned to Michael. 'I'll take you there if you like.'

'Where?'

'To where she was. The manyatta. They'll let you in. I'll tell them you're the husband.'

There was no road, only a path, wide in places as a river widens to bend, carrying the prints of goats and unshod feet.

'You should understand what it means for these

people,' said David. 'The goats are their livelihood. All their wealth is on the hoof. The boys who found her made a huge decision — that one of them, the biggest one, should leave the others with the herd and carry her back. It was two days walk. He carried her all the way.'

'Did he bring her to the mission?' asked Jackson.

David shook his head. 'He took her to his family. We only knew because of Mosa.'

'Mosa?'

'You'll see him later. A little while ago there was an accident in the manyatta. Mosa fell into a fire. You know they keep them by the door of the huts, great braziers of charcoal, white hot — and the totoes running in and out. You'd think there'd be more accidents than there are.'

'What happened?'

'He upset the whole thing. I think his mother was scolding him. He ran straight into the hut, kicked over the brazier and fell onto the coals. They thought he was dead, 'gone back', as they say. So many children die young it is the custom that the clan does not 'see' a child until it reaches puberty. If a younger child dies it is mourned only by his parents, in private. For the rest of the clan he has simply 'gone back'. They believed he had 'gone back' but he survived. They brought him to the mission. It was a kind of miracle, but still they were ashamed; they did not want a mutilated child.' He smiled. 'Now he comes and goes. Stays here for a while, then returns to the manyatta. No-one really wants him but he is very bright. Already he has Swahili and will learn English with no trouble.'

He turned to Michael. 'Who knows, Mosa could be my Gaugin, my crippled Matisse-in-waiting.'

'What has he to do with Olivia?'

'He came all the way here. It's thirty kilometres and he can hardly get off the ground, but somehow he came — all the way from his village. It was he who told us she was there. That they had a white woman up there, holding her for a reward.'

'A reward?'

'Yes. I think that was the idea — a way to make a bit.'

Michael looked up. 'They weren't the kidnappers?'

'Not at all. I told you, the goatherds found her. They found the tracks.'

'What tracks?'

'Hers. They were curious and followed them — and found her.'

'But they didn't bring her to you?'

'When the boy carried her home his family were perplexed. She had sunstroke, her skin was burned raw, her feet were infected. They were going to bring her in and then they heard of the search, that it was a white woman for whom the aeroplanes had come. If they kept her for a while, maybe a reward would be offered.' David stopped. He looked into Michael's eyes. 'You must understand there was no malice in it. People have been lost before and rewards offered. It means wealth beyond their wildest dreams. They meant no harm. She wasn't fit to travel anyway. They thought they could nurse her back to health.'

'She had dysentery.'

'Dysentery, sunstroke, dehydration, fear, infected

sores.' David shrugged. 'All those things. They did their best, paid the loiboni for medicines. She cost them a goat.'

'The loiboni?'

'The local witch-doctor.'

'You c . . . c . . . can't be serious?'

'Of course I'm serious.'

28

The manyatta stood on a rise of ground, a half moon of huts behind a kind of thatched, thorny fence.

'The fence is for the household herd,' said David. 'They'll keep a few goats here for milk. The rest are out grazing, two or three days walk away. They have to go that far to find the grass.'

'But why stay here at all? Why not at least find some shade?'

David shrugged. 'There's always a reason. The village is on higher ground, you notice — it rains here about twice a year. All the lowland is flooded. The place blooms with flowers and mosquitoes.'

'It doesn't look as if it has rained for years.'

'It rained while she was here. It's one of the reasons why they kept her. There was a little rain, not enough for grass but perhaps a sign of more to come. They decided she had brought it to them, that if she stayed there would be more.'

Trying to ignore his feelings, the hammering in his head as they stepped down into the glare of the sun, Michael forced himself to look around.

David was pointing to where the rise of land was steeper, almost a shallow cliff. 'The flood water runs along there. There's a temporary river that brings sand down from the hills; it's a soft powdery sand that they use for cleaning.'

David stopped a few yards short of the stockade.

'Wait here. I'll tell them who you are.'

Jackson positioned himself behind Michael. His face was composed into an expression of intractable sorrow, his wide, smiling mouth turned down at the corners. David talked to an old man by the fence. Cigarettes were passed. At last he came back.

'You can go in.'

Walking in line, they entered the enclosure. Chickens scuffed the dirt round their feet. The ground was littered with the small droppings of goats.

An old woman advanced towards them; teeth protruded from her mouth like bent piano keys. She was gabbling, holding something out to him. It was an empty packet of Arret.

'This is the one who nursed her. She wants you to know that they gave her this medicine. It was very expensive.'

'I will pay her,' said Michael. His voice sounded far away. 'I will pay for everything.'

The old woman, still chattering, led them to a hut that was slightly smaller than the others.

'This hut was built for a new wife,' David translated. 'But now it will be used only for storage.'

They stepped inside. The hut, that had seemed so mean and low from outside, was bigger than it looked; unexpectedly cool. The woman pointed to a space on the floor. There were signs of much sweeping but the hut was entirely empty.

Jackson gave a little whistle. 'You know I never saw inside one of these before?'

Absently, Michael turned. 'Never?'

251

'My father had a concrete house. With a tin roof. He was a very important man.' Jackson swelled himself up. 'Now I live over the garage.'

Michael nodded — but only part of his mind had engaged in the exchange. The rest of his being was gathering into itself, his stomach tying into a knot, the swell of his chest like the bag of a pipe filling with air; a noise came out of his throat. Jackson's arms were about him, and the thin crabby fingers of the old woman, catching him as he dropped to his knees.

Aware that the others had left him alone, he allowed himself to shed a tear. That she should have been here, lying in such a place with diarrhoea and burns. He turned to the old woman, intending to shout, but found her leaning towards him, offering a corner of the cloth that was draped about her to wipe the dust and tears from his cheeks.

Michael reached for his wallet. 'I h . . . hope this won't offend you. I want to pay you something because you were kind to her.' Without counting, he pressed a bundle of notes into her hand. She said something incomprehensible, nodded and grinned. As he turned to go she reached out.

'Marie-Therese.' She tapped her breast. 'Marie-Therese.'

'That's your name?' He pointed to himself. 'I am Michael, Michael Ballantyne.'

She repeated it after him, her twisted teeth making it an entirely different name.

They drove back in silence, David and Jackson together in the front, Michael alone in the back. From time to time Jackson would turn his head to give Michael a wide grin of encouragement.

'You can sleep here,' said David when they reached the mission. 'It will be dark in an hour or two.' He opened out a pair of canvas beds and put them side by side on the verandah. 'You'll be cooler out here than inside. Are you taking something against malaria?'

Michael nodded and turned to Jackson. 'What about you?'

The African shrugged. 'I don't need all those pills.'

'Do you take them, David?'

David shook his head. 'I'm like Jackson, I've been here too long to take pills against the place.'

When the beds were set up Michael touched David's arm. 'Can we talk now, about why I have come?'

David shrugged. 'I'm going over to the chapel. You can come with me if you like. I think there's someone waiting for me over there.'

The sun was slipping down, sending long, narrow shadows across the mission compound.

Michael kept pace with David's long, confident stride.

'Olivia wanted to ask you something.'

'I guessed she did.'

'It's about your mother — '

They had reached the steps of the church. Above the door, a wooden cross turned in the wind. 'Here he is.'

'Who?' Michael followed David's eyes. At first he could see nothing but was then aware of a movement in the shadows. A child appeared,

253

crouching against the step.

'Mosa.'

David leaned down to speak but the child scuttled away, crab-like into the darkness.

'If he could have surgery now, while he is still little, he might walk upright again. Before long it will be too late. He will have grown too crooked.' David opened the chapel door and Michael followed him inside.

The building was about thirty feet long and twenty feet wide, with wooden benches nailed to the floor. In one corner, set out upon a trestle table, was a nativity scene, a plastic crib, surrounded by small crudely carved animals. 'The noise in here, when we have a mass, is astonishing. The children sing out their hearts — you can hear them right out on the plain.'

The altar was a wooden table supported on one side by a stone column. Segments of coloured glass had been stuck to it in the shape of a cross. Beside it was a statue of the Virgin Mother, bearing remnants of luminous paint.

'When Mosa told me there was a white woman in the manyatta I had no idea who it was. I went over there to see if it was true.' David cleared his throat. 'You never know with a child. Sometimes they imagine things.'

'But you knew the police had been searching for a woman.'

'Yes, but that was far away. They were looking around the lake, nothing to do with this district.'

'But you knew who she was. That it was Olivia. They interviewed you. I saw the report!'

Michael's voice bounced back off the bare walls of the chapel.

'No-one told me who she was. There was just this woman lying in a hut, vomit and shit all over the place. We had to go via another mission to get enough petrol to make it back. I radioed from there for the flying doctor. We had two flats. It always happens, you only get flat tyres when you're in a hurry. And all the time she was shouting out my name. David Jones. David Jones. I couldn't understand it.'

'It was you she wanted to see.'

'I know that now.'

'That was why she . . . she came here in the first place. She wanted to find you.'

'I know, I heard all that. But at the time I didn't know who she was. I thought she'd just learned my name from Mosa. It was eerie, hearing my name shouted like that, her voice getting weaker and weaker. When we got back I thought the doctor would be waiting but there was no-one. They had come and gone while we were away. They couldn't wait, we were too long getting back and there was another call. Rachel, she's the teacher you saw earlier,' he indicated the empty compound, 'she took the message. They said they'd deal with the other call and come back to us. I sent another message saying this was an emergency. It was getting dark. We lit fires. Do you know what that means in this place, to burn wood? It is so scarce it feels like burning food. But we built fires on each side of the airstrip. They came very late. We could hear them circling. The fires had burned low. I radioed again, I told them she was dying, that they were wasting their time, but they landed anyway. Risked their lives.'

'That was pretty cool. To tell them to go home when there was a girl dying.'

David was silent.

The cross on the roof creaked overhead.

At last his voice came out of the darkness. 'It is how things are up here. It is real life, you have to make the decisions. There's no bloody cocoon up here, no nannies, none of the things that you pen-pushers are so sure of.'

Michael coughed. 'I don't exactly think — '

'I must ask you a question, I wasn't going to but I need the answer, I need to know the score here. Why the hell didn't you come before this? Why weren't you up here, when she was missing? Why weren't you looking for her yourself?'

'I . . . I . . . tr . . . tried, I . . . ' The words wouldn't come. 'Th . . . the p . . . pol . . . police . . . '

David thumped his heel against the wall. 'Spit it out. You were too scared, too damned chicken.'

He turned away, walking towards the altar.

'Mosa?'

Michael went outside. A dry wind shuffled the night air. Across the compound the light from David's room fell in bright yellow squares on the ground.

'Come on.' David was coming through the door, the child in his arms. 'I didn't need to say those things. Sorry.'

As they approached the light, Michael saw that

the child was watching him. He said something to David who laughed.

'Mosa says you are the whitest man he has ever seen.'

★ ★ ★

They sat up late, drinking the whisky, watching insects flit and cluster round a single kerosene lamp. Michael had been speaking for some time, describing his visit to Eugenie, the kind of place it was, the suggestion that her health would improve if she saw her son. While he spoke Mosa crept in and folded himself onto David's knee.

'Look,' said David. 'Look, I'm out of all that shit. The woman I knew as my mother is long dead.'

Michael felt suddenly exhausted. For a second he found himself wishing for a telephone to ring, for his desk at the bank, for a mug of instant coffee, for the whining voice of his secretary, for normality, for certainty.

'It's really not my business,' he said, conscious of his voice, of the absent stammer, the rich pompous accent bouncing off the concrete walls, 'but if you would come, it might do some good. At least for Olivia, if not Eugenie. At least all this will not have been such a waste.'

David lit another cigarette, carefully blowing the smoke above Mosa's head.

29

Olivia sat up. A pale afternoon sun washed the bedroom walls. Through the window she could see the lawn, a dark wintry green rising gently upward towards an ornamental stone wall. Beyond it was a field where two horses grazed, their dark coats draped in faded grey blankets. From time to time their tails flicked at imaginary winter flies.

She pulled herself higher on the pillows, careful of her tender, healing skin. On the bedside table a mug of tea cooled on a tray beside an untouched bottle of orange squash and a jug of water under a beaded cloth. In a while she would take the tray downstairs, finding her way along the passage, the narrow staircase that led directly down to the kitchen. Faintly, through the gently creaking silence of the house, came the sound of a radio, the exaggerated voices of an afternoon play. The housekeeper would be listening in the kitchen while she ironed and John Ballantyne would be in his sitting-room, hearing the same play from separate radios, part of the ritual of the old, faded house.

Of her arrival at Highhurst she had only a hazy memory. There was Michael holding her hand as a private ambulance conveyed her from the airport, ignoring her protests, that she could walk a little, she could have managed in his car. Then the long drive, leafless trees in the moonlight and his father waiting in the porch in his dressing gown, sucking an empty pipe as Michael carried her into the house.

The days developed a pattern. Slow mornings when she stayed in bed, rising gently before lunch, slipping on loose tee-shirts and huge flapping sweaters from Michael's wardrobe. Lunch was eaten in the morning room with John Ballantyne. She grew to look forward to the warm soups, the old man's commentary on the news of the day, and talk of the neighbouring farm that had once been part of the Highhurst estate and long since sold to a man 'whose stairs don't make it all the way to the attic, my dear. There is nothing so dangerous as a madman who owns land.' There were tales of the village, battles over plans for development on the ridge, Olivia delighting in the old man's sardonic humour.

References to her convalescence, to the causes of it, were rare but at the end of the first week he paused on his way off to the afternoon play. 'My dear, you really do look better.'

She smiled. 'I feel better.'

'You know, I got caught like that in the war — in Egypt. Spent three weeks in a tent hospital, thought I'd never walk again.' He rolled up his sleeve, exposing white wrinkled flesh that was soft and papery but unscarred. 'Nothing to show for it now, eh?'

Michael came home late in the evenings, his suit creased from the commuter train, utterly tired. His bag bulged with reports and papers but the real work could only be done face to face, making amends with his clients and colleagues, attempting to undo the damage of his unscheduled absence, to lift the question mark that hung now over his previously unblemished career.

His father retired early, leaving them alone in the kitchen to eat the housekeeper's slow-cooked hotpots and casseroles, foil baked chops or sausages under a layer of light batter.

Dimly through the sleep-lost days of her convalescence, Olivia grew to understand the enormity of the step Michael had taken in bringing her to Highhurst. She understood that for the first time there had been no family debate, no unspoken permission sought or granted. The easy rhythm of the days was broken at the weekends, when Michael's sisters and their husbands and children congregated, as if Highhurst were a magnet, a place where the Ballantyne traditions were upheld, reinforced.

Too weak at first, to join the gathering, Olivia was visited. Shy children hovered in the doorway; slowly she learned their names, persuaded them to come close, to be unafraid of her appearance. Their behaviour, in its different way, reminded her of her little visitor at the manyatta. Michael had spoken of him, of David's affection for him.

The older sister, Gillian, came upstairs to shoo the children away. In her hand was a large canvas bag from which she extracted a piece of needlework before pulling an armchair close to the bedside light. She was as tall as Michael and looked so like him it was difficult to feel uncomfortable with her. Her sweater and corduroy jeans were baggy and flecked with hairs from the dog. Her hair was cut short, as sensible as her shoes and her face. When she spoke there was an echo of Michael, of her father. She had inherited John Ballantyne's directness, but lacked his humour, his gentle sense of irony. Gillian spoke to Olivia as if there could be no danger of causing offence, as if, whoever she was, and ill as she was, she could take what had to be said on the chin.

'You know, this is utterly out of character. Michael's always been reliable. He's never done anything remotely like this before.'

Olivia wanted to know what it was that Michael had never done, what, of all that he had ventured and endured in the preceding weeks, had his sister found so surprising, but there was no need for the question. The answer was soon as clear as could be. It was she, Olivia, the manner of her appearance — her presence in the house — that caused the consternation.

'It's not that there's anything to object to,' Gillian went on, threading her needle as she spoke. 'Now that you're here, I can see exactly what has happened. It's just that until now he's always brought girls home early on. He's always wanted to know what we thought. With you, well — '

The needle was raised and put down again. 'It means he's deadly serious, of course. You know that?'

Olivia found herself smiling. 'I think I do.'

'Preposterous behaviour. Running out there,

261

abandoning his responsibilities. We heard he'd gone off searching for you by himself. Alone in the desert, for God's sake. We've been out of our minds with worry.'

Olivia wondered where this story had come from. Surely not Michael?

Gillian chattered on. 'Of course it wasn't true, thank God. He was sensible enough to wait. But he might have told us. He might have let us know he was all right.'

'I'm sorry I've been the cause of it all,' said Olivia. 'I was rather foolish. There've been endless warnings of banditry. I suppose I just thought I knew better. I even wore his earrings. When they were stolen I didn't care, it was too trivial. But later, when there was nowhere to go, when I was literally cooking in the sun, I wanted those sapphires, I wanted all the certainty, all the things I have never really wanted before.'

Gillian put down her sewing.

'You know that those sapphires belonged to my mother?'

Olivia shook her head, regretting the rush of words. Had she made things even more difficult for Michael?

Gillian changed the subject. 'I gather that he did succeed in persuading your brother to come over here.'

'Yes.' Olivia eased herself against the pillows, settled her hands where the softness of the duvet would support her arms without pressing on tender new skin. 'David will be arriving in a few days.'

'Why didn't he come straight away? He could

have come back with Michael. It seems rather single-minded — '

'He is bringing a child with him. The child needs some remedial surgery — they have been waiting for a bed.'

Gillian sliced a thread with her teeth and leaned towards the light to thread her needle.

'When will he visit your mother?'

'The day after Boxing Day. Michael has offered to take him down there.'

Gillian shook her head. 'To the asylum?'

'It's actually called Castleton Hospital.'

'I hardly know what to say. It's so hard to think of one's little brother being mixed up with such a thing.'

Olivia closed her eyes. 'I haven't asked him to go with David — it's something he wants to do — but it means so much to me, more than I can say. I feel so grateful to him.'

'Michael can't build his life on your gratitude.' The cotton reel made a small slapping noise as it hit the bedroom table. 'The boy is besotted. You mustn't string him along. If you are no more than grateful, you should leave him alone.'

Later in the evening Michael brought her supper on a tray. He had opened a bottle of wine.

'Gillian's been up, I gather.'

His eye-brows rose but Olivia didn't answer.

'She's not as fierce as she seems.'

'She wasn't fierce at all. But she's very protective of you. She obviously thinks I'm just stringing you along.'

'How so?'

'She said you were besotted. You must be, or you couldn't have broken so many Ballantyne regulations.'

Michael poured a second glass of wine, hers was hardly touched.

'She said you've changed out of all recognition.'

'Well that's hardly true — '

'No, I think she's right. What I want to know is what you got up to when I wasn't there.'

She lay back while he talked, listening not only to the words, the tale of his journey north, the catch of delight in his voice as he described the Rift, but to the change of tone, the complete absence of the stammer, a confidence that was not the confidence of a banker, of the heir to Highhurst, but of someone at ease with himself.

'I was a coward, you know.'

He put up his hand to stop her answer, poured himself another glass of wine. 'I could have gone up there sooner. I should have done.'

'It doesn't matter, now, Michael.'

'But I need you to understand it. I was just out of my depth. I wouldn't do it again.'

'How do you know?'

'Because I've been up there. I don't just mean to the desert. I've been out of my life. The mould is broken.'

'So carry on, tell me the rest of it.'

He poured the rest of the wine into his glass and told her the story of Jackson, of the beer hall in Maralal, the girl's hand on his fly. Olivia laughed aloud. 'You? You were fondled by a whore in a beer-hall?'

264

Michael shared her laughter. 'Incredible isn't it?'

'And you smoked pot with a naked African?'

'I did! The pot was wonderful.'

Olivia found herself leaning forward, the sore straining of her skin ignored, pulling him towards her, the last of the wine slopping onto the sheets, searching for his lips.

'I love you, Michael Ballantyne.'

30

Silver strands of tinsel decorated the departures board, beside it a tree with blinking lights, 'Away in a Manger' coming over the loudspeakers. The carol was distorted by the high glass ceilings of the railway terminal, crowded with hurrying people and bright kiosks selling croissants and coloured scarves.

'How come you only paid half for your ticket?'

Harry smiled. 'You don't miss anything, do you, Regina?'

She hurried beside him as he left the ticket office. 'I have to know — especially about money. A woman in my position, abandoned — '

Laughing, Harry held up his hand. 'Don't tell me again, Regina.'

'But it's true. You saw my house, how they have emptied it. Now I have two months' grace. That is all Mr Cyril Haig can manage. After eighteen years, eighteen years of cooking, cleaning, modelling. I was the one who made Thanos Paros famous. But now, because he's dead, I must get out — like a stray cat.'

'Who is Mr Haig?'

'My solicitor,' Regina said with a faint air of grandeur.

'Your solicitor?'

The grandeur faded. 'I went to him for Legal Aid. But I don't qualify — I won't fill in their stupid forms.'

'So you'll have to pay his bill?'

'One hundred and ten pounds — and for what? A few letters to those lousy brothers. It was no more than a friend would have done for me — if I had a friend. Instead I have to pay Cyril Haig one hundred and ten pounds.'

'But he got you two months' grace? You can stay in the house for that long?'

Regina nodded. 'It's cheaper than rent, I suppose. I would have paid more than one hundred and ten pounds for two months in a bedsit.'

'Have you started looking?'

'For a bedsit? No.' She paused. 'First I have to think about things. I'm no spring chicken. What job could I get? A waitress perhaps? Running about on my feet all day? Other people's dirty plates? What kind of life would that be?'

She was not complaining. Harry had learned already that Regina did not complain — she merely stated facts, as she saw them. She was trying to explain something to him, and in doing so, explain to herself. As if it was she who must first understand what had happened, that her life with Thanos had been a kind of cul-de-sac; that with his death she had reached the end of it.

As they walked she took his arm. Through the layers of her red quilted coat and his heavy, tweed overcoat, he felt her comfortable plumpness.

'You still haven't told me.'

'What?'

'Why did you only pay half the fare?'

'Because I am an old man. I am what is called a senior citizen.'

She looked at him, sly eyes behind the fringe of blackened lashes. 'Not so old as all that!'

Harry felt himself smile, and then blush. Her eyes carried the memory of Darren's wedding night, their slow, shy coupling. He had fumbled like a boy and when it was over, she wept.

He had been filled with remorse. 'I'm sorry, Regina. I didn't intend that this should happen . . .'

They had rolled together, in the course of their passion, onto the space between the sofa and the fire. The gas hissed at them. Harry looked at his body laid out beside hers, white and lined. Hastily he started to dress. 'You must forgive me, I've never done anything like this before. It was the champagne.'

Regina giggled. 'It wasn't champagne, Harry Crane, it was fizzy German.' She was pulling at his shirt, unbuttoning it as fast as he buttoned it up. 'Anyway, we cured the pain in your back.'

On the train she took off her coat.

'Shall we have some coffee?'

She was wearing a blouse of some silky material; a gold chain dangled into the soft hollow below the top button. She wore lipstick the colour of apricots and in her hair was a wide gold slide. She reached for her handbag. 'I will buy.'

'Please, let me.' Hampered by the table, Harry struggled to his feet. She was already in the aisle.

'With two sugars, yes?'

Harry subsided. 'Thank you, Regina.'

When she returned she sat in the empty seat beside him.

'It's nice of you to come with me.'

He raised his cup to hers. There was nothing to say. No way to explain the little wish he harboured, that she might ask him to escort her; his pleasure when she suggested it.

'I used to go every month,' she said. 'The first Saturday. Thanos used to tell me it was my woman's time, sending me back to her womb.'

'Did Eugenie recognise you?'

Regina touched the slide in her hair. 'She pretended not to, but sometimes she did. To be honest, I don't know. It was all part of her performance.'

'Do you think that's what it is, a performance?'

'Not completely, but partly. She knows enough to keep herself safe from the world.'

And the world safe from her, thought Harry, safe from flying blades, from blood on a red-tiled floor. He stirred his coffee with a tiny plastic spoon.

'You're too thin, Harry Crane. For a man who takes so much sugar. I must drink mine with nothing and still I have this.' She put her hand where her stomach swelled against her skirt.

'There's no harm in a little fat,' said Harry. 'Women worry too much about it.'

'Your wife was very thin, was she not?'

Harry turned. Until now, there had been no mention of June, no reference to her at all.

'You remember her?'

'Of course. I knew her face. She was thin, like our mother, and always frowning. We had to watch out for her, keep a look-out. Eugenie posted us about, like detectives.'

'Where was this?'

269

'The library. Olivia outside on the lions, me in General Fiction, pretending to read. You must have known, she must have told you how Eugenie prowled around the children's shelves, as though she would find David there, like a book to be taken away.'

Harry stared at her in disbelief. 'I thought I knew about everything. June used to tell me such stories. I didn't believe there was anything I didn't know.'

'She must have told you about the library. You've just forgotten it.'

'I have forgotten nothing, I cannot.'

'But it's all so long ago. We're different people now. Three times seven, there is nothing of them left.'

'Three times seven?'

'Three times seven years. That's how long it is. I have this theory, you see, that we have seven-year lives. That's the time it takes to change. Over seven years the cells of our bodies are completely renewed, and that must mean that every seven years we're different people.'

'And these lives, do they start and end abruptly?'

'There's nothing sudden. The change is day by day. Today I still have a shred of the person I was seven years ago. By next year it will be gone. That person will have vanished. You could see it in Eugenie. The day he was born she was still herself. By the time of the library, when he was seven, she was crazy. It was the same with me. When David was born I was still a nice little girl. You remember, on the boat with Dennis? Nice children. But by the time of the library I was bad, completely bad.'

'These occasions in the library. Was it after Dennis went to sea?'

'It was, but his going didn't matter. She couldn't have cared less. They had a little ceremony at the railway station — all the cadets' parents on the platform. They had a band and the mothers cried. Not our mother. No-one cried for Dennis.'

'Were you there — at the ceremony?'

'Yes. I went with the teacher, the one who put him up to it. We stood at the back and afterwards the teacher took me to the ice-cream parlour. It was such a treat. I ate so much I felt sick. I think he meant well, that teacher. I think he knew how things were at home. Maybe he thought the Navy would give Dennis a chance.'

She sipped her coffee and both of them looked out of the window. 'It wasn't his going that mattered. It was his death. Dennis's death was the end of something for her. She had no men left, no-one like Gareth to look at. Olivia and I — ' she shrugged, 'we were useless to her.'

'And you?'

'Oh! I was probably crazy too. It was the beginning of another cycle, you see? I had to fend for myself. Why should I stay? Why should I see my mother hanged?'

'She wasn't hanged, Regina!'

'But I didn't know. Those reporters said she might. They liked to see if they could crack the carelessness of my face.'

'What did you do?'

'I came to England. I had bad luck. I mean — '

she came close to Harry, he could see that there was glitter in the pink powder on her cheekbones, ' — I mean really bad luck. The kind no girl should have. I worked with my body. Anybody who would pay. I am not proud of it. And then there was Thanos. He used to smell, you know, disgusting. He put this greasy stuff on his hair, on his beard. But his house was warm, and he liked me; he was kind to me — just like you are kind to me.' She smiled. Her face was very close to his. 'Though you were not always the kind one, Harry Crane.'

'I never meant to be anything else.'

'It doesn't matter now.' Regina squeezed his hand. 'You are kind now.'

How could he tell her that he had done everything he could: all he had strength for? And it hadn't been entirely bad, some good had come of it. There was a letter in his pocket, an airmail envelope, neatly typed. The logo had changed again, Patel & Patel (Incorporating Karanja & Co):

Dear Mr Crane,

As you are aware, Mr Jones is entitled to receive income from this trust. You are also aware that, because of his lack of demands, a large sum has accumulated. Mr Jones has informed us how he wishes the money to be spent. We propose, unless we hear from you to the contrary, to carry out the wishes expressed by Mr Jones.

Yours etc.

Patel & Patel

Enclosed was a glossy copy, made on an old fashioned copier, of a letter from David to the solicitor. His handwriting was round and clear. He had sent an invoice of some sort. There was the name of a boy, Mosa Lehabora who needed surgery. It was to be done privately in London. David asked that the bills be settled promptly, so that neither the boy nor his parents should suffer any embarrassment.

Harry had replied to Patel & Patel at once. Darren was away on his honeymoon, the temporary girl took down the message with slow indifference. 'Do exactly as Mr Jones directs. Do not seek further instructions from me. All monies are to be put at the disposal of Mr Jones.'

There was no reply. Harry had expected none, but the copy of David's letter remained in his pocket, like a guidebook, or a map, essential information for the time that lay ahead.

Regina interrupted his thoughts. 'Look, we're here.' She stood up, zipping herself into the red coat.

Harry opened the carriage door and offered his hand as she stepped down to the platform.

'I wonder if she will know me this time. Or will she play the usual trick?'

'She didn't recognise me when I came here,' said Harry. 'She didn't even know my name.'

They hired a taxi from the station. 'This is the bit I always hate.' Regina moved closer to him as they drove down into the valley, through the birch wood that screened the asylum from the road. 'I hate these trees, hiding her away.'

*   *   *

A game of rounders was being played. The coloured clothes of the inmates flowing uneasily together behind the fence.

'Do you want me to wait?' the taxi driver asked.

'I don't know how long we'll be.'

'I've got another pick-up in the next village. I'll come back in an hour, if you like?'

'That'll be fine.'

'I don't want to be here as long as that,' Regina whispered to Harry. 'Sometimes ten minutes is too long.'

She walked ahead of him. Behind the fence a woman in blue trousers made a full round. She clapped her hands. No-one else applauded.

The receptionist was not the kindly nurse who had greeted him the first time. 'We have come to see Doctor Morris,' said Harry. 'Doctor Morris has asked to see Miss Jones.'

She consulted a diary.

'Will you wait, please?' Her shoes clicked importantly.

'What is it about?' Regina called after her but the woman had gone, out of earshot behind a white-painted door.

They sat on a seat under the window. Beside them stood a small Christmas tree, bedecked with tinsel and silver baubles. At intervals lights winked at them, alternating pink and green. At the foot of the tree was a collection box for the mentally ill. Harry leaned forward and dropped in a coin.

Regina fingered the gold chain round her neck. 'This has never happened before. They used to be nice to me, no formalities.'

In the light from the window Harry could see that her hair changed colour at the roots. The hair that grew from her scalp was streaked with grey.

A man approached. He wore a pale suit and a paisley bow tie. He held out his hand to Harry.

'I am Doctor Morris.'

'I am her daughter,' said Regina, sharply. 'It is I who have come.'

Hastily the doctor shook Regina's hand too. 'Your mother has had an eventful day, Miss Jones.'

'Eventful?'

'Someone has come whom she has not seen for many years.'

'Who?'

Harry held his breath.

'Two people have arrived.' Morris's voice was smooth. 'One is a friend of your sister, Olivia. His name is Michael Ballantyne.'

'And who else?'

'Mr Ballantyne has brought your brother David with him.'

'Uh!' Regina's hand covered her mouth. She subsided back into the seat. After a moment she looked up. Her eyes were fierce. 'You mustn't let her see him!'

'She has already seen him. They are together now, in the ward.'

'You've let him in? Just like that!' Her voice rose, filling the empty hall like a voice raised in church.

'Do you know what he caused?'

Harry took hold of Regina's arm. 'Caused? David caused nothing.'

Regina pulled away. Her expression was savage. 'You keep out of this, Harry Crane.' A tremor had taken hold of her. She pointed a shaking finger. 'You keep away from my mother.'

The doctor stepped forward. 'We do know, Miss Jones. We do know the history. But he has come so far to see her — after such a long time. We took a calculated risk.'

'And me? I am not consulted? Though I am next of kin, and came every month even though she never said a kind word, never knew me. Her own daughter. Her only real daughter — the only one who did not betray her . . . I . . . '

Regina broke off. Her eyes were brimming with tears, her mouth working soundlessly. Harry took her hand. 'I'll wait out here, Regina. I'll wait out here for you.'

He saw the whites of her knuckles as she took a tissue from her handbag and with shaking fingers wiped streaks of mascara from her cheeks, renewed the apricot lipstick. After a moment she snapped her handbag shut. 'There. I'm ready.'

Doctor Morris led her away. Harry watched until the white painted door swung closed behind them. Regina walked stiff-backed, like a smart, brisk soldier, but below the hem of her skirt a thin line of black petticoat hung down, betraying her.

★ ★ ★

276

Two men, their backs to the door, jackets off against the heat of the ward, were sitting on either side of Eugenie's bed. She was sitting on it, fully dressed, clutching the metal edge, as if she was afraid of falling off. Her eyes followed Regina as she walked towards them.

'Hello Mama.' Regina kissed Eugenie on the cheek.

The taller of the two men was very tanned, very handsome. His sheepskin coat lay on a chair beside the bed. It was stiff and new; the coat of a stranger, arming himself for winter. Regina sat on the opposite side of the bed.

'You look like him!' her voice cracked out.

'He does, doesn't he?' Eugenie's tone was conversational. 'Just like Dennis. Even the hair, the way it curls behind his ear.'

'Not Dennis! I'm not talking about Dennis. He looks like my father!'

'Your father, dear?'

'Gareth Jones.'

Eugenie shook her head. 'No. Gareth was David's father.' She turned, smiling. 'It is the same face. They all had it, all my darlings.'

Regina jumped off the bed.

'I am Regina! I am one of your darlings!' Her voice boomed around the ward. 'Why do you pretend?'

The nurse came forward, waving to Regina to hush.

'Did she cry for Olivia?' For the first time Regina addressed the two men, turning in error to Michael. 'Did you tell her my sister was set on by bandits,

277

left to die, burned half to death in the desert? Did she? Did she shed one tear?'

Michael reached out across the bed. 'I'm not your brother. My name is Michael Ballantyne. I'm a friend of Olivia.'

She slapped him away. 'Olivia is alright! She had Jessie. She didn't need a mother. This boy didn't need a mother either. He had two! But Regina had nothing! Not then, not now! This one, who pretends she can't see me, that's all the mother Regina has!'

The nurse hustled Regina away. They could hear her shouting in the corridor. Michael turned back. Eugenie's expression was still calm, smiling a little.

'It is my Gareth all over again. Just the boy he was.' She held her hands out to David. 'Here, I can't manage my gloves. You take them off for me, will you, David?'

With the utmost care, David pulled the cotton gloves from her fingers. Michael felt his stomach contract at the sight of her misshapen knuckles, sticking plasters had come off with the gloves, exposing fresh oozing scabs.

'I've been trying so hard, David.'

Casually, as if he could not see, or was trying to reduce, the significance of the moment, David asked, 'What were you trying to do?'

'I was cleaning the tiles, David. I was trying to get them clean again.'

'Which tiles?'

'On the verandah. Don't you remember?'

'They're all clean now, mother. You don't need

to worry about them any more.' David smiled at her and gently put her hands against his cheeks.

★ ★ ★

At the sound of Regina's voice, loud and hoarse with distress, Harry stood up. He could hear someone hushing her. He stared helplessly at the white painted door. The shouting faded away. After a moment he sat down again, watching the winking Christmas tree.

The hall was growing dark, with the thin quietness of a room temporarily empty. In the garden beyond the window, patients were gathering around a woman in a tracksuit. No sound came through the glass.

At last an internal door opened and a tall youngish man came through. He carried a waxed jacket over his arm, around his neck a soft cashmere scarf. Harry searched his face. His skin had a mottled look, as though he had recently been over-exposed to the sun. Harry moved along and the young man sat at the other end of the window seat, looking out through the window.

'I think it's going to rain.'

Harry proceeded cautiously. 'I see you've been somewhere warm.'

The young man nodded. Suddenly he turned to Harry full on. 'Was it you who brought Regina here?'

'Why, yes. I came with her — I heard her shouting just now.'

'Yes. It's not an easy time for them all.'

'I understand,' Harry hesitated, 'I understand that her brother is in there.'

'That's right.'

Harry let out a little sigh, partly disappointment, partly relief — that this wasn't David, then. His David had not become so unrecognisable.

He stood up. 'I think I'll take a turn around the car-park.'

Outside, rain had started to fall, a fine sea spray on the darkening afternoon. He passed through the gate in the high white fence. There was no sign of the taxi. But for a sports-car in a bright shade of yellow, the car-park was quite empty. He turned up his collar and went to stand under some trees. The game of rounders had all but ceased; there was just the one woman, her blue trousers lightened by the mesh, solemnly clapping as she completed round after round.

Harry felt very calm; it was as if, in this place, separated from the world by its fence and its trees, the two halves of his life, that had seemed so irrevocably severed, might be rejoined. David was with his mother. Eugenie with her David.

The young man must have been the friend, the one who went to find Olivia. Harry tried, without success, to remember the name. Jessie had mentioned it in her letter, but it would not come to him.

At last, the main doors swung open. Regina came down the steps and through the gate. This time she had made no effort with her tissue; mascara was smeared like a panda's markings round her eyes. Without a word she put her head on his shoulder and cried, adding the wetness of her tears to the rain on his coat, a smear of apricot on his handkerchief.

They were still there, sheltering under the trees, when the gate opened again. Two men came through. One was the man he had spoken to in the hall, the other was taller still, with long dark hair and suntanned skin. Harry watched as they got into the yellow car. They did not notice the couple standing under the trees. The tall one got out again to take off his coat. As the car pulled away, Harry raised his arm to wave.

* * *

In David's kingdom, the school room was crowded. The children were learning a new song. Rachel clapped her hands and the small bodies swayed together, arms upraised, one little girl's voice ringing out high above the others. They were practising for Pentecost. There was much to celebrate: the mzungu had returned, not as the Saviour, a ghost with tongues of fire, but fatter and smiling and bearing gifts that made the mission rich.

In the compound, beside the old Landrover, a second vehicle stood, shiny with newness. The older boys rolled its name on their tongues and argued with one another, which is the finest, this vehicle or the one Leiguchu drives now, as he hurries about the plain, baptising.

As well as the new car, David had brought books and writing materials from the south. And there was news of Mosa; Rachel had told how soon the cripple

281

would return, not the fire-bent creature that he was, but almost upright, mended, healed by the mzungu loiboni.

As the children sang they could see David in the compound, loading the new vehicle with provisions for his journey across the plain. He would take basic medicines, second-hand clothes and shoes; he would talk to the elders, promising to feed their children if they were sent to his school. Sometimes he would be welcome and sometimes not, and always beside him would be one of the old askaris with his rifle and his spear, and his rungu tucked safe beneath the seat.

THE END